D0812291

SAVING FACE
and Other Stories

SAVING FACE AND OTHER STORIES

NORAH LOFTS

Doubleday & Company, Inc., Garden City, New York
1984

Library of Congress Cataloging in Publication Data

Lofts, Norah, 1904–
   Saving face & other stories.

   Contents: Now you have me—Lord, who is my neighbour?—Saving face—[etc.]
   I. Title. II. Title: Saving face and other stories.
PR6023.O35S2 1984   823'.912
ISBN 0-385-18717-3

   FEB 2 1 '84

Library of Congress Catalog Card Number 82-45872
Copyright © 1983 by Norah Lofts
All Rights Reserved
Printed in the United States of America

CONTENTS

1. Now you have me   *1*

2. Lord, who is my neighbour?   *29*

3. Saving face   *57*

4. God's own elect   *74*

5. Gateway to happiness?   *100*

6. The natives are friendly   *123*

7. The horse-leech hath two daughters   *156*

8. Debt of gratitude   *194*

9. A late flowering   *208*

SAVING FACE
and Other Stories

1

Now you have me

The voice on the phone was pleasant.

"I'm ringing about that advertisement for somebody to walk a dog."

Mrs. Bracey said, "Oh, yes. Will you do it?"

"If the times fit."

"Oh, almost any time would do." She sounded very eager. "You see, I'm quite alone now, and I cannot walk Fritz myself. He's getting quite fat." She reminded herself that people who lived alone tended to become terribly garrulous. She had noticed it in other people ages ago when she still had friends.

"I could do it at eight in the morning and then again some time in the evening. Say about six."

"That would do admirably. When could you start?"

"Tomorrow morning."

"That will be wonderful."

"And how do I find you?" In the advertisement, which had that morning appeared for the third time in the local weekly paper, Mrs. Bracey had given merely the telephone number. She was cautious and rather nervous, and feared that some ill intentioned person might see in such an advertisement an admission of loneliness and weakness. She now gave her address: 4 St. Mary's Square.

"Oh, easy," said the voice. "Be seeing you."

Nothing had been said about remuneration, but Mrs. Bracey was in the happy position of not having to count pence too closely. The price of everything was rocketing, and she had never really become accustomed to decimalization but she had enough. She had a Home Help who received £2.50 an hour, and it was by that measure that she was prepared to pay the dog walker. She would, of course, time the walks. She was old, hideously lame, but nobody's fool.

Having arranged as well as she could for Fritz's well-being, she could look at him without that feeling of self-reproach which had occasionally troubled her. Maybe it had been a bit selfish of her to acquire, at the age of eighty, a young puppy. But even then—three years ago—she had been lonely, and a dog was company. Also she'd always had one, all alike to look at, sleek, tan coloured dachshunds. In nature they varied, and Fritz was definitely lazy. Admittedly the garden was small, but a more lively animal could have run around its perimeter or run to and fro across its lawn. Fritz scorned such do-it-yourself measures. He simply ambled to the nearest bush, lifted his leg, and returned to the house. Refused admission for however brief a time, he howled and barked so that the immediate neighbours complained.

Before her accident, Mrs. Bracey, remarkably spry for her age, had taken Fritz into the Abbey Gardens and, in the area from which dogs were not banned, let him loose, and if children were playing there, he'd joined in their games with a quite ruinous enthusiasm. The children played nowadays with plastic footballs, easily punctured, but so long as Fritz enjoyed himself and the children would accept monetary compensation, all was well. "Buy a real ball," she had once said.

Then she'd had her fall, inexplicable—just something that happened to old people—and then the dear old man who kept the garden in order had made it his business to see that Fritz had exercise—twice round the square or even as far as the shops. But death had robbed her again, and there were no replacements for faithful old retainers. Still, she had obtained—or appeared to have obtained—somebody to walk Fritz.

And there was another thing about keeping a dog—you could talk to it. To talk to oneself sounded a bit crazy, but to talk to a dog was entirely natural. She now said, "Tomorrow, darling, somebody is coming to take you for a walk. I do hope he's nice."

The boy roared up next morning on one of those very loud motor cycles. It was just eight o'clock, and Mrs. Bracey was in her dressing gown, looking out of the window of the hall. He *looked* nice. His fair hair was properly cut, and he was clean-shaven—that is, if he was old enough to shave. He wore brown jeans, a thick, high necked sweater of a pleasant blue colour, and over it a waistcoat of what looked like brown suede.

Mrs. Bracey had the door open before he could ring the bell. And then a most tiresome thing happened. She had been holding Fritz's leash, slackly, in her left hand—her right as ever clutching the four legged stick which was her strength and stay. And just as she opened the door and said, "Good morning. How good of you to . . ." the wretched dog pulled free, scampered across the hall, leash trailing, and back into the bed-sitting-room which was now Mrs. Bracey's world—if one excepted the kitchen and the downstairs cloakroom.

She had meant to hand the dog over at the door, but now she was defeated. She said, "Oh, what a nuisance! You see, if he's gone under my chair, I can't possibly haul him out. I cannot stoop."

"I'll get him," the boy said. "I suppose he's shy."

A nice way of putting it. But now the boy was not only into the house but into her very room—and the bed unmade! The boy seemed to notice nothing. Mrs. Bracey, much as she loved dogs, admitted that she would have hesitated to reach in under an armchair where a strange dog lurked, but the boy seemed to have no fear at all. He bent over, found the leash, and hauled. He said, "Come on, old chap. Nice walkee." He glanced at Mrs. Bracey and said, "What's his name?"

"Fritz. You are accustomed to dogs?"

"Brought up with them." That sounded reassuring.

She watched from the window again. The boy took long strides, and Fritz, after hanging back for a bit, gave in and began to trot. Much relieved, Mrs. Bracey hobbled to her kitchen and proceeded to make her breakfast.

When she had been told and was finally convinced that she would never walk freely again, she had determined to stay as independent as possible and had spent money on making the kitchen manageable. Everything just above waist level and plenty of sockets: kettle, toaster, grill, boiling ring, and small oven. All so well arranged that she could cook, dish up, and eat a meal with the minimum of effort.

Her bed-sitter, as the Home Help would call it, was equally geared to her needs. A bed high enough to be got into and out of without pain and her chair. Between them the big table holding the telephone, the neat book containing telephone numbers important to her, a jotting pad, a handsome old tea caddy which held all her medicaments, a big cigarette box, lighter, and ashtray, and a bowl of pot-pourri. When the old gardener lived, she had almost always had at least one flower, too, but those days were gone for ever. Facts must be faced. Live to her age, and you'd outlived everybody. Marooned on the island of longevity.

The front door opened; the young cheerful voice called, "We're back. Returned empty!" What a nice way of putting it, Mrs. Bracey thought as the dog scampered in and stood up on his hind legs so that she could unsnap the leash.

The whole exercise, she reckoned, had taken exactly half an hour; £1.25 by Home Help standards.

On the phone the boy had said "about six," but he came soon after five and caught her unready. And Fritz behaved just as disgracefully, so that, with one thing and another, she had no chance of asking the boy his name or what he thought she owed him.

On the Sunday morning she was prepared. When she opened the door this time, she had firm hold on Fritz's leash, and she said, "When you bring him back, would you like a cup of coffee?"

"That'd be very nice. Come on, lazybones."

They sat side by side on stools at the kitchen counter. She had added toast and marmalade to her offering, and he ate with obvious appreciation. It was a brisk late September morning, unfriendly to the old, but the boy was all aglow, his face coloured by youth and health and exercise.

He told her a little about himself; his name was Tony Felsham, and he was a student at the College of Further Education, the big modern building on the Clevely Road.

"And where do you live?" she asked, showing a friendly interest. She meant where was his home. She was curious about his background, because he was so different from the young she had heard described or read about.

"Just at the moment I've got bed and breakfast at a house on the Horton estate." "Estate" was a word that had changed its meaning in the last fifty years.

"What do you do for other meals?"

"It varies. There's a canteen at the college and another at the Leisure Centre. If we're in funds, there's Wimpy's and that Chinese takeaway place."

The mention of funds reminded her that he had now devoted at least three half hours to Fritz's service and that she now owed him £3.75. But he said, "Lord, no! You can't call it work! And a breakfast like this—real coffee—would set me back a pound anywhere. Say one-fifty. And don't pay till the end of the week. I tend to get spent out."

He then, unlike anyone else she knew, switched the conversation from himself to her. It was indeed a remarkable thing as Mrs. Bracey had once remarked bitterly: meet with an accident and break your hip, and everybody with whom you subsequently came in contact had a relative, if only a son-in-law's great aunt, who'd had a fall and broken not only a hip but both arms as well. And most of them had made quite dramatic recoveries! Such tales seemed to hint that Mrs. Bracey's misfortune was far from uncommon and that she was a malingerer, deliberately clinging to her stick, insisting upon remaining lame.

The boy did not take that attitude at all.

She said, "My accident was quite unaccountable. I did not slip or stumble. I was actually just there, about to give Fritz his luncheon biscuit. And down I went. I'm probably the only person to be taken to hospital with a Spillers Shape in each hand."

"Who found you?"

"The dear old man who used to do my garden. He happened to be here that day, and he managed everything very well. I was in hospital for a month."

"But you're still lame?"

"I am indeed. Expertly pinned together, but old bones don't hold as they should. I'm really extremely fortunate to be mobile at all."

This was not what she thought or what she sometimes said, but she liked the boy and was showing him her best face. And he responded in the right way.

"How do you manage about shopping and such like?"

"That, I admit, is not always easy. I have a Home Help. She comes on Tuesdays and brings in what I have listed the previous week. If I think of something omitted from the list, I can telephone her. But almost invariably I get her husband, who is extremely deaf." Or exceptionally stupid or worse, deliberately unhelpful.

"And then I have a very nice District Nurse, Sister Turnbull. She comes on Thursdays and brings anything I need in the way of medicines. She also most kindly changes my library books and takes bed linen and heavy bath towels to the launderette." (Sister Turnbull had no inkling of it, but she was one day to be well rewarded for such exertions. Mrs. Bracey gave a convincing impression of a lady living on a limited income, suffering from inflation. But interest rates galloped alongside mounting prices.) "Smaller articles I deal with myself," Mrs. Bracey said. And the pride in her voice was pardonable, for, all things considered—especially the difficulty of wringing things out with only one hand—the effort was almost as great as that needed to climb the Matterhorn.

"I come past shops," Tony said. "Maybe I'd be too early in the morning, but I could shop at midday and bring things along in the evening. Is there anything you want tomorrow?"

"Indeed there is. As you may imagine, I depend largely upon cheese. And Mrs. Lomax—that is my Home Help—seems not to understand. She always brings hard cheese, what I call mousetrap —and wrapped in such very resilient plastic that I often think, when wrestling with it, One could starve with this in one's hand. Oh, I know the French behaved very badly over a cargo of lamb, but I still have a weakness for Brie and . . . The name eludes me for the moment. It is not that my memory is failing; it just stages a wildcat strike now and then."

"I'll see what I can find tomorrow," Tony said.

He would never have admitted to anyone, but he was fascinated

by her. He'd never met anybody remotely like her. Such a way
with words and so brave and, odd as it might seem, nice to look at,
despite her age—which he judged to be about ninety. And he was
sorry for her. Even her taste in cheese was pitiable. In an old
fashioned shop which he had never entered before, he found
French cheeses, Brie and Camembert, full ripe, oozing, and to him
stinking. They reminded him of something he'd heard or read
about deprived people—Chinese? Japanese?—anyway long ago,
letting their fish go rotten because rotten fish did more to flavour
their rice. Did she, dainty as she looked, prefer rotten cheese to
vary the monotony?

With this in mind on the evening of Tuesday, he brought a treat.
A proper fish and chip supper.

He gave the warm parcel into her hands as he took Fritz's leash.
He said, "Keep it warm . . . and perhaps . . . two hot plates."
For he was willing to admit that she was on the fussy side—but that
was part of her charm.

Mrs. Bracey said, "Tony, I probably sound like a dinosaur, but I
have never before tasted real fish and chips. When I was still active
and my husband . . ." Oh, don't be idiotic! Poor James dead and
gone twenty years. "I think restaurants were calling potatoes prepared like this french fries. But they were nothing like as good as
this. I now understand why fish and chip shops have invaded the
Costa Brava. . . . But now . . . tomorrow, or some evening convenient to you, you must allow *me* to stand treat."

That was not entirely successful; on her behalf Tony brought in a
meal from the Chinese takeaway place, and Mrs. Bracey said,
"Don't think me ungrateful, dear. Maybe taste goes along with all
else. I always imagined bamboo shoots as rather like asparagus, but
to me they taste of nothing at all."

He took that move in the supper tit for tat game in the right
spirit, and Mrs. Bracey asked Mrs. Lomax to bring in half a pound
of best back bacon sliced very thin and two good fillet steaks.

"Expecting company?" Mrs. Lomax asked, meaning well. Meaning must she go up and make a bed in one of the rooms now never
used.

"Oh, no," Mrs. Bracey said. What company? she thought. So she showed her nastier face and said, "Surely, Mrs. Lomax, I am not asking for something so extraordinary."

Mrs. Lomax was never quite sure where she stood with old Mrs. Bracey who could, as now, turn a bit cantankerous for no reason at all. The one advantage of the St. Mary's Square job was that it was so clean. The old girl was as neat and clean as a cat. All Mrs. Lomax really had to do was to run the Hoover over the bed-sitting-room carpet and a mop over the kitchen and hall. Anything that Mrs. Bracey could do, she did do. Home Helps went into some pretty grotty places in the course of a week and not everyone was grateful, but . . . But Mrs. Lomax felt more at home with people she could bully.

Mrs. Bracey thought it very odd that both Mrs. Lomax and Sister Turnbull, such very different people, should react in the same way when she said she had found somebody to walk Fritz. They both seemed suspicious and, could it be, a trifle resentful? But why? In no way did the boy impinge upon their well defined duties. Mrs. Lomax said darkly, "You wanta be careful. . . . Students these days are a rough lot." And she knew what she was talking about because she had a cousin up on the Horton estate who'd once let a room to one, so-called . . .

Mrs. Bracey had heard this story before, and she suffered from a low level of boredom. Dull and empty as life was, must the persecution of tedium be added? She'd learned the trick of switching off her attention. Of this audience withdrawal, Mrs. Lomax took a charitable view. "Deaf" she would not think—there was her own dear husband, growing more deaf every day. So she chose the next word, which was "daft."

Sister Turnbull, hearing about Tony, said, "Do you think it altogether wise to let in a complete stranger? I think I'd better ring up this college and check up on him."

"Whatever they said—even if they said they'd never heard of him—would make little difference to me. One must speak as one finds."

And she found him delightful. Fritz was getting slimmer already. And she herself was getting fatter because of the shared suppers. She could not afford to put on weight, that much more to heave about, so she cut down on lunch.

After supper he always washed up, and he was so neat and handy that one day she asked, "Can you by any chance cook?"

"After a fashion. Nothing fancy. Why?"

"I was thinking that, if you could spare a little time on Saturday or Sunday, we might have a proper joint. In that oven." She indicated the one she could no longer manage.

"Make it Sunday. Shall I buy it? What would you like?"

"What would *you?*"

"Oh, I like anything. How about beef? And Yorkshire pud?"

"And sprouts and roast potatoes. How greedy I sound. But it seems such a long time. . . . Even before I became a Fallen Woman, a joint for one didn't seem worthwhile."

"Have you been alone long?"

"I've been widowed longer than you've been alive. But I had a resident cook-housekeeper and a daily woman. They both retired, it must be six years ago."

"Ah, well," he said, "now you have me."

Then one morning he arrived in a glum mood, a mood much in tune with the morning. Typical November, overcast, cold, and raw. Mrs. Bracey was aware of the change in him, and worried as she grilled the bacon and made toast and brewed coffee. She suspected girl trouble, for though he had never mentioned any girl specifically, she was aware that he led a busy social life, centred about the Leisure Centre.

This morning the exercise with Fritz had not made Tony glow; he looked pinched and miserable, and although he ate, it was with less than his usual obvious enjoyment.

Presently she asked, with a most uncharacteristic diffidence, "Tony, are you feeling quite well?" In their delicately balanced yet perfect relationship, such a query was permissible. She would never have dared ask, "Why are you unhappy this morning?"

"I'm all right, thanks. I've had a bit of a shock."

"I'm sorry. I hope nothing serious."

She poured his second cup of coffee and wondered. A shock implied bad news. From home?

The rather curious thing was that never once had he made any mention of his family or background. He never referred to the past at all; he might have been born, so far as she was concerned, when they met in her doorway.

"For me it is. But I don't want to bother you about it. Something'll turn up."

"I should not regard any problem of yours as a bother, Tony. Is it . . . money?"

"No. I always paid my rent on the nail. But the people where I lived are moving out, and the people moving in have three or four children. They don't want a lodger, so I'm out."

"You have tried to find—other accommodation?"

"There just isn't any. I know. I've been hunting for ages. I hated the place I was in, and I hated the people. But at least it was a bed."

She was definitely not rash or impulsive. This was something that needed to be thought about. She said, "Try not to worry too much, Tony. I'll think about your problem—and we'll talk it over this evening."

That day she was very careful with the whisky.

Both her old doctor, now unfortunately dead, and her new one —probably cleverer, but less attentive—had thought that whisky, in moderate quantities, was a good thing. It had anaesthetic qualities and was a better soporific than drugs, and it provided some warmth, some feeding value. Mrs. Bracey didn't really like the taste of it, but she liked the effect it had on aching joints and low states of mind. Today, because she must think very clearly, she took only one very modest drink with her bread and cheese lunch. She therefore regarded the problem clearly and bleakly.

Most arguments seemed to be against offering Tony one of those unused bedrooms. If he lived here, he would have to have a key, and she would be unable to put the chain on the door. He might, for all she knew, keep late hours. Again, if he made his home here, he would expect to ask his friends in, and they might not be likeable. On the other hand, she had space, and if she failed to offer it, it might ruin their happy relationship.

Did he drink? She'd never seen him later than about seven in the evening, and in describing the Leisure Centre he had mentioned the bar there.

Back to the key again.

Sister Turnbull and Mrs. Lomax would, she was sure, disapprove and use phrases like "being taken advantage of." But, dependent as she was upon their good services, she could not be ruled by them, could she?

She hated this indecisiveness, regarding it as a sign of old age. In the past she had always known exactly what she wanted to do and gone ahead. Now she either did not know what she wanted or was afraid. "Suppled by Time and tamed." That was an abominable thought. Really, such dithering was disgraceful! She'd make up her mind immediately and take her early evening drink. There! she thought, once again defiant.

Tony came quite early; he gave her a warm parcel and said, "Kentucky Fried Chicken. It's a new place. They say it's good." He hauled the reluctant Fritz away. She had, until that moment, attached little importance to the dog's attitude towards the boy. He was just a lazy dog who associated Tony with the unwelcome exercise.

What about canine instinct? Really, what nonsense!

She switched on her small oven to mere retention heat, opened the parcel, and put the four good hunks of chicken in a fireproof dish. She went back to her room, had another drink, and felt much better.

"Tony, I have been thinking. I have plenty of room. Would you care to live here?"

He seemed almost to choke. "Do you mean that?"

"Of course."

"That'd be simply wonderful. Honestly, I was beginning to think I'd have to join the squatters."

Mrs. Bracey had heard of them and strongly disapproved. "Tony, you would never . . ."

"You can't sleep in the street," he said.

She gave instructions. The bed, indeed the whole room, would need airing. And the linen cupboard was just opposite the head of the stairs.

"Can I come in tonight?"

She had not visualized anything so sudden; she had not realized how the young lived from day to day. But he explained. His old landlady had warned him in good time, but then he and a friend had an eye on another place, and that had only fallen through last night, and that was why he'd been so miserable this morning.

"Then you must go up at once and turn on the electric blanket and the fire. The room to the right at the head of the stairs." It had always been a guest room, wardrobe and chest of drawers empty.

Tony said, "I'll go and fetch my stuff."

And in the morning Mrs. Bracey knew that she had been wise, for the little luxury which she had missed more than anything—early morning tea—was brought to her bedside. Not since the retirement of the cook-housekeeper . . . Well in hospital, admittedly, one did get an early drink of something which, since it could be given no other name, must be called tea—a harsh dark brew served in a cardboard beaker. This was very different, her own pretty things and hot water.

"How very kind of you," she said.

And not only kind, cunning, for he had brought in Fritz's leash and had snapped it on before the dog could take evasive action.

Mrs. Bracey propped herself up and luxuriated—there was no other word for it. Then, much fortified, she heaved herself up, hobbled to the downstairs cloakroom, washed her face, arranged her hair, and prepared a good breakfast.

And after that the quality of loneliness changed. However late the boy might be, he was coming back. She could not put the chain on, but she must leave a light burning. And empty space upstairs, a thing of which she had always been conscious, bore down on her no more. She slept much better. And when, some time—it was mid-November and terribly cold—he asked could he have a bit of a party, she was all enthusiasm.

"Oh, do. Open the drawing room. Make a huge fire. Poor room, once so merry. I sometimes just peep in, and it looks so desolate." The word "party" was very evocative, and she said, "Oh, and flowers. That shall be *my* contribution. November. Carnations, I think, for the stand between the alcoves, and something fragrant. Freesias or hyacinths."

He tried to conceal his dismay.

"That's awfully kind, but . . . I think they'd feel more at home up in my room."

"With only two chairs?"

"That'll do. We all like sitting on the floor."

"Well, of course, you know best."

She was not one of those old idiots who talked about being

young in heart, and she had had no intention of joining his party; but she had visualized seeing the room gay with flowers and fire-light once more, and herself in one of the wing chairs and saying a few words of welcome. Also she was rather curious about his friends, not one of whom she had ever seen. He was so very different from her mental picture of the young. Could they all be as nice?

Between then and the party, which took place on a Saturday, she tried to show interest without being inquisitive, but Tony's answers were curiously offhand. How many people would be com-ing? He couldn't be sure; he'd asked a lot, but they wouldn't all turn up. On the day itself she mentioned provisions for the party. "Oh, most people bring something. I've laid on some beer."

He must have told all his friends to come in very quietly, for though Mrs. Bracey sat in her room positively listening, she heard very little, just the ghost of a sound now and again: a laugh quickly hushed, a step in the hall. Then from Tony's room came the blare of music—if indeed such a noise could be so called. Fritz proved anew his absolute worthlessness as a guard dog; he'd had his run— a very brief one—and his dinner, and now snoozed by the gas fire, ignoring the invasion.

Mrs. Bracey felt vaguely resentful. After all, this was her house. Surely in common courtesy Tony could have brought two or three friends just to say good evening. And presently it was evident that she had been quite forgotten. Presently she'd be obliged to go and forage for something to eat.

Somebody at least had the good sense to mute the noise, which at its worst had a kind of sonic boom which made Mrs. Bracey's glass shudder against the decanter. She poured herself another drink, thinking with self-scorn, Taking to the bottle for comfort, like a baby!

Then the door opened, and Tony came in carrying a tray.

"A bit of everything," he said. There were four half rolls, split lengthwise and buttered and topped up with various things. Prawns curling side by side, a sardine, a slice of ham, rolled, some sort of grey paste. On another plate were two squashy looking confections, one oozing jam, the other cream. Also on the tray was an ordinary tumbler containing two inches of a thick looking golden fluid.

She was unbelievably touched.

"How very good of you! But, dear boy, far too much. You must take some back."

"Just take what you fancy," he said agreeably. "The patty's good. Real duck."

"Now duck is one thing I never cared for. I'll have this and this. They look delicious." She selected the ham and the prawns. Tony took up what she had rejected and ate them.

"This you must try," he said, indicating the glass. "It's a drink everybody's crazy about at the moment. *Not* very alcoholic, lots of real cream in it. Do you good. Well, I must get back. I'll try to keep the noise down."

"Oh, I hardly hear anything. Have a good time. Good night."

Fritz roused himself sufficiently to deal with the two cakes, and presently Mrs. Bracey, feeling much better, sampled the liquid offering. Far too sweet and cloying for her taste. On her next trip to the cloakroom she must empty it away. Not for anything would she hurt the boy's feelings.

And now, with the house full of people, she could indulge in something she had for a long time been forced to forgo—the Horror Film on late TV. She had always liked being mildly frightened, but it didn't do when you were alone in the house.

On Monday afternoon she was alone in the house when the front doorbell rang. She still kept the chain on during the day. She was expecting no callers. Her wine merchant still delivered, but this was not his day. She was occasionally bothered by people doing what they called market research and other people seeking to interest her in some very curious forms of religion.

Through the limited space that the door would open, she peered out and was horrified. She could see only a section of the creature there on the step, but that was enough. Far too much hair and painted in stripes all over, bright ochre, shocking pink, and vivid green. And its clothes suggested nothing but a refugee from a chain-gang: a kind of boiler suit, patched and fringed and with *chains* in the most curious places.

Before she could speak the apparition said, "Tony live here?" A male voice and rough.

"What Tony?"

"Felsham. Somethink about an 'edge."

She had mentioned the sorry state of the hedge at the bottom of the garden and the lawn, and Tony had said he'd see if he could find somebody.

She knew a moment of agonizing uncertainty. Was she about to do what one was constantly warned about, admit a stranger? With very shaky credentials?

"Look," the creature said even more roughly. "Are these your shears, or ain't they?"

Into the space he pushed the handle part of the shears. The tie-on label read "Bracey. £1.50." She then remembered that Tony had said something about getting the shears sharpened.

"Well," she said dubiously, "I suppose it's all right. You'd better come in."

"I should think so! Can't do much about an 'edge standing 'ere, can I?" He sounded really hateful.

Then a ludicrous yet alarming thing happened. The catch on the chain would not unfasten, and she must deal with it one-handed. As she struggled, the boy said, even more impatiently, "Whass smatter now?"

"The chain has stuck. I can't move it."

What he did, what he used, she couldn't see, just his hand round the edge of the door and a flash of metal. The chain fell away.

So of what use were safety chains?

He came in, and she had a clear view of him. The hair really was fantastic, the centre piece cut shorter and brushed up on end and coloured scarlet, exactly like a cock's comb. Both Mrs. Lomax and Sister Turnbull had described this latest freak of fashion, but frankly she had not believed them. Both women were given to exaggeration. Now here she was, alone in the house with what she sensed was a potentially dangerous young man. And armed.

"Where is it?"

She was quite surprised to hear her own voice say with cool authority, "Follow me."

She made her unwieldy way across the hall, into her own room and pointed through the french window. The boy pushed past her quite roughly. Fritz got up, tail awag, even making welcoming noises. Wretched dog! He'd known Tony now for several weeks, Tony took him for walks, occasionally fed him and had never been given any kind of welcome at all. And when the boy tugged the window open so roughly that it hit a nearby table and walked out, Fritz followed.

And for a simple reason, Mrs. Bracey thought angrily. Even the most devoted dog lover must admit that dogs liked unsavoury smells—and this boy stank! Dirty clothes, sweaty feet. The ill odour tainted the air even after he had launched his attack on the hedge. Quite insupportable. She was obliged to go to the cloakroom and find a spray called Fresh and use it liberally.

Then she thought about paying the terrible fellow. She kept rather a lot of ready money handy these days; she needed it for Mrs. Lomax's wages and for the shopping and for the milkman. She invariably tipped the man who brought whisky and arranged it within easy reach in the cupboard under the stairs, and took away the empties which, strictly speaking, he was not required to do. She now went to her money drawer, third one down on the right of her writing table, and took out six pound notes. Enough? It was, she supposed, just possible, though highly improbable, that he had paid for the sharpening of the shears. Add another pound, just to be on the safe side and then lock . . . But where was the point in locking drawers when such terrible types had tools that made nonsense of safety chains.

And, oh, dear, oh, dear, what was he doing to the hedge? The old gardener had kept it flat as a billiard table, but it had grown since his death. But at least it had grown with something approaching evenness. The terrible boy was just slashing at it, leaving a jagged outline, infinitely more unsightly than the overgrowth had been. Most distressing!

And now loomed up the worst part of the day. She'd always hated twilight, even when she was not old, lonely, and lame, even when the evenings held promise of pleasure. It was the death of the day.

Ordinarily at this time, she went and made a cup of tea and brought it into the room. Sister Turnbull had found a wonderfully ingenious arrangement by which a person with only one hand to spare could transport certain things. It was a round basket of cane with its area divided into compartments. Nothing could slip. It had a high, firm handle.

But today she would not use this treasure. The awful person

might come in and expect a cup. And, really, she felt that if he once drank from one of her cups, she would feel compelled to smash it.

She switched on some lights, and as though that had been a signal, he came in.

"And now, what do I owe you?"

"Three pound."

By today's measure not too extortionate; but a lot to pay for having a hedge made to look like a jagged range of teeth. . . . She would not make that mistake again!

"Where's Tony's room?"

"Why do you ask?"

"Because he said go and wait in 'is room."

The funny thing was that she had never thought of it as Tony's room. It was one of her rooms, and Tony was really a guest.

"Don't bother. I can find it." He pushed past her again, and she heard him go loping up the stairs.

She could now go and make that cup of tea. And while she was waiting for the kettle to boil, she heard, in the bathroom immediately above the kitchen, unmistakable sounds of a bath being drawn. All the plumbing in this house was ageing, but it had been installed when both material and workmanship were sound; pipes hiccuped a bit, and some taps made queer noises, but everything worked and would serve her time.

What did strike her as quite extraordinary was that somebody should come in and make so free with what was her bathroom—and her hot water.

Tony arrived. He said, "It's beginning to sleet. I'll give him a short run."

"It's hardly necessary. He pranced about all afternoon with a terrible . . . Tony, I do not wish to offend you, but somebody who said he knew you—and had my shears . . . And slaughtered the hedge and took a bath. And is now up in your room."

"Oh, good!"

"What is good about it?"

"Well . . . He did come. And he brought the shears back."

He spoke as though both actions were slightly out of character.

"And he has taken a bath."

Tony laughed. "He could do with it. Poor chap, he's been squatting in a house with no water."

She had heard about squatters and had no sympathy at all. She now associated the practice with the tool the boy had used that afternoon.

"Looking as he does," she said coldly, "he could hardly expect more orthodox accommodation."

"You don't like him?" Tony sounded genuinely surprised and hurt.

"Like him? I detested and distrusted him on sight. You can't possibly like him."

"But I do. There's no harm in Joss. And it isn't like you to be so . . . censorious. And I'm very sorry you took against him, because, you see, I . . ." He suddenly looked away and shuffled his feet. "I hoped you'd let him share my room for a bit. Just till he finds somewhere."

"I shouldn't dream of it."

"Because of the hair?"

"Partly. Not entirely. His manner. Everything."

"He never had a chance. That hair and silly gear is a sort of protest. Just to be noticed. And now the place where they were squatting has been bulldozed. . . . Mrs. Bracey, I more or less promised . . ."

"You had no right to do so."

And something flashed, swift and deadly. She saw the whole delicate fabric of their good relationship threatened. Unless she gave way now, things would never be the same again. Her hold on the boy was almost non-existent. His on her was double: she was dependent—and she was fond.

"Just for tonight, then."

"I knew you wouldn't let me down. I've been telling everybody you had a heart of gold! And, you see, he did take a bath as soon as he had a chance. I'll go and find him some clothes."

The rate at which her mind was working made her slightly dizzy. She was neither ignorant nor innocent, she read voraciously and could face facts.

This was a very peculiar friendship, look at it how you would. And never once, even under the prod of playful teasing, had Tony admitted to having a girl friend.

"You must also prepare another room," she said. "Yours is only a single bed."

The thing might exist, but nobody should say that she had encouraged it.

"I'll do my best to find him some place. And I'll keep him out of your way."

Life made a slight kaleidoscopic shift. Tony as usual brought the tea, and Mrs. Bracey said, "If I feel like breakfast later, I'll get it myself."

Tony understood. "I could feed him upstairs," he said, rather as though he had installed an unhouse-trained dog. Then, within minutes, the door opened a little, and Joss said, "Come on, you!" The unreliable Fritz jumped down from her bed and went willingly. No fussing with leashes and coaxings.

She had no intention of paying the usurper—that would be to acknowledge his status here—but she wished to be fair, so when it was her turn to provide supper, she insisted that Tony should buy enough for three. But there was no more companionable sitting side by side in the kitchen. She stayed aloof, her supper on a tray. Fritz ate most of it.

Yet, in a way, she was less lonely because both boys were there in the evenings.

So it came to Friday evening, and the door opened just as she had poured her first after-tea drink. She imagined it was Joss coming for Fritz; the dog suffered a similar illusion and rose, ready and waiting.

"You wait. Mind, outa the way," Joss said.

In his hand he held some very dirty pound notes. (Sister Turnbull, at fairly regular intervals went to the bank for Mrs. Bracey, and invariably brought virgin notes.)

"Come to pay you," Joss said ungraciously.

"You owe me nothing."

"I been here since Monday."

"But I do not take lodgers! On that point I wish to make myself absolutely clear. Purely to oblige Tony I allowed you, much against my better judgement . . ."

But he had the congenital thickhead's advantge of not listening.

"Take it for my food, then."

And before she could speak and say that she did not take board-
ers either, he put the money down on her table and turned, saying,
"Come on, you," and went out with Fritz leaping up at him,
excited, ecstatic.

The money still lay there when Tony came in carrying with care
a few sprays of freesia in one of the slender vases unused since the
old gardener's day.

"You mentioned them once, didn't you?"

"Yes. But I didn't intend . . . You really must not waste your
money on me." She sniffed them delightedly. "They are sweet. So
many flowers now seem to have no fragrance. Thank you *very*
much. But you mustn't do it again." She turned slightly in her
chair to set the vase on the table, and there were the dirty notes.

"Oh, look," she said, "your friend put that money there. I don't
want it. I told him so, but he just took no notice. Please return it to
him."

"He can afford it, you know. He got his Unemployment today."

"That is quite beside the point, Tony. You know how I feel. I
don't want him or his money."

"But I can't say that. He was trying to do the right thing."

The flowers were responding to the warmth of the room, and
their fragrance increased, softening her.

"Let us compromise. Ask him to cut the lawn. I know it is far too
late, but it should be done. Give him three pounds and then . . .
Wait a minute." She rose and hobbled to her money drawer and
took out two notes. "Buy a joint of beef."

That appeared to be a happy arrangement. Joss—Mrs. Bracey
could never bring herself to speak his name aloud but she could
use it in her mind—cut the lawn on Saturday afternoon, spending
about a quarter of an hour on a job which had taken the dear old
gardener three times as long, and Tony was obviously a very good
shopper; the beef was excellent.

On Monday, about half-way through the morning, Mrs. Bracey
became aware of an odd feeling. That she was not alone in the
house. She'd always been very much aware of the empty space
upstairs, something that it would be silly to think about and quite
despicable to be scared of. Empty space was just that and no more.

Now it was as though she had suffered, for some time, from a slight nagging pain which had suddenly ceased.

She felt, in fact, on Monday morning the same relief from that particular little bother as she had during the visits of Mrs. Lomax or Sister Turnbull, and since Tony's coming to sleep, during the night.

She heard no sound. There was absolutely nothing to account for the feeling, but once it came upon her so strongly that she limped to the foot of the stairs and called:

"Is there anybody there?"

And that was quite shocking. Giving way to fantasy. Tony and his horrid friend had left as usual on the motor bike; she was alone in the house and giving way. Shouting upstairs, like a lunatic! Really she must be more careful.

Then, later on that same day, something else happened, equally idiotic, equally disturbing.

Her room looked out on to the garden, her kitchen on to the side entry where the dustbin stood and where Tony now kept his motor cycle; but from the hall window she had a good view of St. Mary's Square, and she could stand there for a limited time, one hand on her stick, the other on the window sill. Not an easy exercise and not very rewarding, for the square was very quiet except when there was a funeral—from which she turned away—or a wedding which she watched with interest.

There was no such activity this afternoon. In fact the only moving thing was—well, was it a girl? A tangle of dark hair, slim legs in tight dark jeans, and a short brilliantly red jacket. Walking across to the opposite side and nothing extraordinary except Mrs. Bracey's absolute certainty that the boy/girl had just emerged from her own side entry. A completely unjustifiable assumption.

The figure gained the opposite pavement and turned. And the unisex concept was shattered. No fashion in the history of time was less kind to a heavily pregnant female. In fact the pseudo-masculinity made mock.

Mrs. Bracey had herself never been pregnant—once a grief, but long outgrown—but watching the girl stroll out of sight around the corner, she thought, They may have gained something, but they have lost more, poor things. She was herself far too young ever to have worn a crinoline, but she had heard firsthand stories of how,

by the careful hitching up of hoops, women had managed. Subse-
quent fashions had been a little less merciful until the arrival of
specially designed maternity wear; but nothing had been so stark
and cruel as this.

Tuesday was the day for Mrs. Lomax, who had withdrawn her
disapproval of Tony when she realized how much sheer weight of
the shopping he had shouldered. Also, since his coming, the old
girl seemed to have sweetened up. And the telephone calls which
had so greatly annoyed Mr. Lomax had ceased entirely.

Thursday was Sister Turnbull's day, and for that Mrs. Bracey
must make preparation, getting the downstairs cloakroom
warmer than usual, laying out her clean underwear, inspecting
her money drawer, and if necessary writing a cheque to Self.

Sister Turnbull possessed an extraordinarily acute sense of smell,
which was both an advantage and a drawback. She claimed to
have smelt diabetes before the sufferer had a clue to what ailed
him; in a seemingly clean house she could scent dirt, and incontinence could not be concealed from her.

On this Thursday morning she gave Mrs. Bracey her usual
cheerful greeting and then immediately said, "Have you taken up
smoking again?"

"No. Dr. Edwards is so against it. And in hospital it was not
allowed. I quite broke the habit."

"Does that boy smoke?"

"Occasionally."

"Where is he now?"

"At the college, of course."

"Then something is smouldering. Upstairs."

Mrs. Bracey wished most urgently that Sister Turnbull should
not know that she had taken in yet another stray, so she said, "His
room is first on the right." Then supported by her stick and the
newel post, she waited. A door opened and closed. Another
opened and slammed; a third and the unmistakable sound of female voices raised in altercation. Mrs. Bracey began to tremble so
violently that but for the support of the newel post she would have
fallen.

Sister Turnbull came round the curve of the stairs, her cheeks
flaming, her breath coming short. But she was a professional and,

before she said anything, had her strong arms around Mrs.
Bracey's slight figure and practically carried her into her room.
She poured a small, strictly medicinal, measure of whisky. Yet
despite this considerate behaviour, her manner became positively
accusing and reproachful.

"You knew," she said, and it was not quite a question.

"No. At least, I had suspicions." Her hand or perhaps her head
shook so much that a little whisky spilled. Awaiting Sister
Turnbull's ministrations, she had donned her better dressing
gown, and she regarded the dark blotch on the pale blue velvet
with disgust. She did not want to become an old sloven with
stained, spotted garments.

Scrubbing the spot with a tremulous hand she said, "A woman?"

"A foul mouthed little slut. Lolling in bed and smoking. She was
most abusive. I don't think I could repeat, even to my husband,
some of the names she called me."

"Oh, dear. I am indeed most sorry to have put you in such a
horrible situation."

One thing about the old girl, she could be trying, fussy, and
headstrong, but she had manners. Sister Turnbull was slightly mol-
lified.

"I expect I shall survive." Then her eyes narrowed, and she
asked, "Exactly how many of them are you harbouring?"

"I agreed to accommodate a friend of Tony's—purely on a temporary basis. I did not know about a girl."

"You suspected something of the kind?"

"Perhaps suspect is too strong a word. I did have a feeling of not
being alone in the house. And once I saw a girl in the square and
felt that she had just emerged from my side entry. Is the one
upstairs pregnant?"

"Seven months if a day. And verminous! You know I can scent a
louse at ten yards. They've been squatting, you know, in a condemned house in Fargate Street. No water or electricity. It is
demolished now. The thing is, what are we to do? The police
might help . . ." Her tone was dubious.

"I don't think they could. No crime has been committed. And I
should dislike the fuss. No, I shall simply ask them to go. It is my
house."

"The house in Fargate belonged to Mr. Briggs, and there they had broken in. But he couldn't get them out. Of course you made a mistake taking in the first boy. I said so at the time."

"Yes, I remember that you did." Mrs. Bracey spoke rather crisply. The whisky, small as it was, had steadied her considerably.

Sister Turnbull looked at her watch. On Thursdays she ran to a tight schedule. Mrs. Bracey should by now be washed down, sprinkled with talcum powder, ready to don her clean clothes. The next case was more urgent—badly ulcerated legs to be dressed.

"I'm afraid I must go. I'll come tomorrow, early. About half-past eight. Oh, and don't worry about what I said about vermin. There's some very good powder; I'll bring some along."

"That would be most kind."

Sister Turnbull rather regretted having mentioned vermin to such a painfully fastidious old lady. And she felt bad about leaving her to face what was to be faced, even though she had brought it on herself.

"Whatever you do, don't try to talk to that slut. What's the other boy like?"

"Awful. Quite awful."

"Well, if you run into trouble, call the police. They might at least come and show the flag as it were. And—you have my number." Though it was really no part of her duty to organize people's private lives. Still, she felt responsible, especially knowing as she did the state of Mrs. Bracey's heart.

"I hope they leave without trouble."

Mrs. Bracey did not anticipate trouble from her two unwanted guests. She felt that she was in the right and had only to be firm. Her fears centred around Tony. That challenge had flashed once and unmanned her. If he adopted that love-me-love-my-dog attitude again, she meant to be very firm. If he came into the open and said that if they went, he'd go too, well, then, go he must. Tony had many admirable qualities but absolutely no discrimination. Nor, in foisting such people upon her, had he showed much consideration.

And after all, if he left, she'd be no worse off than she had been when she had drafted that advertisement. Except, of course, that she was some weeks older, and towards the end of life, as at its beginning, every week counted.

She dressed with especial care, choosing a dress of black silk, very old but dignified still.

All day she remained optimistic and resolute, doing the little routine things, letting Fritz out and in again, giving him his small midday meal and preparing his larger one for the evening. Poor Fritz, he would miss the horrible boy. Like Tony, he chose his friends badly.

She boiled an egg for her lunch, for today she could not count upon supper; the confrontation must come first. She dusted her room.

Twilight, the dread hour, came early with great dark snow threatening clouds piling up in the west. Despite the tea, her spirits declined, and a horrible phrase, an echo of her poetry reading days, lodged in her mind: "Naked shingles of the world." Matthew Arnold? Yes. It said it all.

Oh, well, it would soon be time for a drink.

She heard Tony and his horrible friend arrive. They came into the hall, laughing and talking. Not a care in the world. Tony went into the kitchen, and Joss came on, as was usual now, to her door. He opened it a few inches and said, "Come on, you," and but for Mrs. Bracey's grip on his collar, the demented dog would have gone.

She called, "Fritz is not going out this evening. Will you tell Tony I wish to speak to him?"

Tony came, and his first words were disarming—they would be! "Anything wrong with Fritz?"

"He is quite well. I am not. I am extremely upset. Tony, I know about that young woman!"

If that took him aback, it was only for a second.

"Oh, well . . . I suppose sooner or later . . . Though we told her to lay low."

"Tony, how could you do it? You've placed me in a most unpleasant situation. I understand she is pregnant. Are you responsible?"

"God, no! Nor is Joss. We never set eyes on her till about three weeks ago. She just drifted in to the place where he was. Then that was knocked down. . . . She was sleeping in the Abbey Gardens. In this weather. And her state . . . It made us feel uncomfortable about being comfortable. And beds not used."

It was her first glimpse of the freemasonry of the young, the acceptance, by two such divergent characters, of a pregnant stranger and a concern for her. Admirable perhaps. But this was no time for such weakening thought!

"That sounds very fine. But what about *me?* This is my home. I cannot have it turned into a common dosshouse. You brought them in, Tony; you should tell them to leave. But if you shrink from doing so, I must do it myself."

"Do you mean—*now?*"

As though to underline the poignancy of that question, the wind, with a moaning shriek, flung a handful of sleet at the window.

"That would be my wish. But I have no desire to be harsh. First thing tomorrow morning. Is that understood?"

Now was the moment she dreaded. But he did not mention himself at all. He gave one of his small shrugs and said, "You'd better talk to Joss. I'll fetch him."

He hurried away with the air of somebody escaping. She drew a deep breath of relief. The terrible thing had not been said. And of course she had been foolish to fear it. Tony had sense enough to see that his adding himself to the homeless would serve no purpose. And, she thought with complacency, he had argued very little; he recognized firmness when he saw it.

She heard him shout, and almost immediately the horrible boy was there.

There'd been no time for even the hasty conference. Yet Joss knew.

He came in, kicked the door shut, and once again Mrs. Bracey had to restrain the perfidious dog.

"You can't do it. You can't turn us out."

"I fail to see what is to prevent me. This is my house—a fact that seems to have been overlooked."

"You're doing the overlooking. You took me money."

"I beg your pardon?"

"You 'eard. You took me money. Five pounds. A week's rent."

"I did no such thing. In fact I never touched your money. I asked Tony to give you three pounds to cut the lawn. Which you did. The other two pounds, with some added, bought Sunday's joint."

"It don't matter 'ow you spent it. You took it. A week's rent. Paid on the nail. As agreed."

"Agreed? By whom? Certainly not by me. I should never have dreamed. Purely to oblige Tony, and *greatly* against my own inclination—and better judgement—I said you could sleep here. Just for a few nights. Then you smuggle in a female, of low morals, verminous and foul tongued." Venom swelled in her. Never mind the weather. It would do him good to sleep out in the snow. "I'm asking you to leave my house immediately."

"And I'm telling you can't do it. You took a week's rent. Granted, I ain't 'ad a rent book, as required by law, but we'll sort that out later. Fact remains, I'm a tenant, and you can't evict me. Not without a court order. Cost you fifteen pounds and take about six months. That's the law."

"That I simply cannot believe."

"There it is. And the girl's covered too. As me wife."

"But Tony said . . ."

He cut in rudely.

"Never mind Tony. If I say she's my common law wife, then she is and entitled to the same treatment as a legal one."

"What arrant nonsense!" She could not believe that such an iniquitous state of things could possibly exist. But he sounded so confident, so well versed in this one aspect of the law. Speaking perhaps from experience. Well, however many women he might have bamboozled in the past, he should not fool her!

"I shall consult my solicitor first thing in the morning."

He said, "You do that." And his face underwent a change, quite horrible. Not a smile or a grin. A mocking leer, an expression worn in old portrayals of Satan—and infinitely more frightening than the horns, the hooves, and the tail. " 'E'll tell you the same. And charge you." He turned the leer upon her table.

"And you oughta ask yourself 'ow you'd look. Memry so bad you make a bargain and then say you didn't. And 'alf sozzled most of the time."

The cruel words, deliberately spoken, cut like a whip, but the last drop of adrenalin upheld her.

"It would be your word against mine. I have lived in this town for forty years, and my word has never been questioned. You . . . Why if you told somebody the time, he'd check on the nearest clock." He actually laughed. Of course it was impossible to insult such a person. "What is more, Tony knows the truth. He'd confirm what I said."

"Ah! Would 'e? Tony ain't no fool 'owever soft 'e may act. 'E'd know better than get acrorst *me.*"

A chill crept into the cosy room and into her vitals.

She should have realized. Poor Tony was being intimidated.

Upon that thought she broke. Her heart jolted to a stop, and blackness closed in. Had she been standing she would undoubtedly have suffered another fall; as it was she merely sagged sideways against the wing of the chair.

She did not hear his last snarled words, "So now you know!"

Consciousness flickered back, and with it despair. In that killing climate the human spirit cannot survive; it must seek comfort or die.

There were sounds of activity from the kitchen, radio music from upstairs. A cistern flushed, and the girl, no longer a stowaway, laughed. Mrs. Bracey thought; It is all too awful, but at least I am not alone. No, I am not alone . . .

2

Lord, who is my neighbour?

One glimpse of her new neighbour confirmed Mrs. Armitage's fear that dear Alice's place in her life and at her bridge table would remain unfilled. Yet the niceties of proper behaviour must be observed; old residents should call upon newcomers, and tea should be offered to those whose crockery was still in crates. So just before four she set her tray, switched on her kettle, took a few steps, and tapped on the door of Number 2.

"Good afternoon. I live next door. My name is Mrs. Armitage. I wondered if you would like to come in and have a cup of tea."

"That I should. My name's Corder. Down, Jumbo, *down.*"

Discreet little peeps from her kitchen window had informed Mrs. Armitage that the incoming furniture was all big and heavy, quite unsuited to its new environment. She had not seen the arrival of the dog, but she now saw that he matched the furniture exactly. Mrs. Armitage was rather tall, but when Jumbo stood on his hind legs to greet her, his muzzle reached her shoulder. He had recently eaten something greasy, and nuzzling against her, he left a dark patch. She had never been a good washer of woollies, so that would mean the cleaners'. Perhaps her face betrayed her, for Mrs.

Corder said, "You don't like dogs?" an accusation of heresy rather than a question.

"Oh, I do. Indeed I am very fond of all animals."

"He ain't very obedient. And he's too big. But he's bin a stray once, poor chap. What could I do?"

Conversations about pets tended to be lengthy, as Mrs. Armitage knew, so murmuring about the kettle, she turned and led the way into her own flat.

These flats had been specially planned for old people and had no hallways. What did old people want with halls—waste space and in winter cold. The architect, an imaginative man, had visualized an Elderly Person, boiling, say, an egg, and just reaching out to answer a tap on the door.

Mrs. Armitage's kitchen was so painfully neat and clean, it could have come straight out of an exhibition.

Jumbo started to howl.

"Oh, God!" Mrs. Corder exclaimed. "Well, if we can hear him, he can hear me. Jumbo, shut up! Lay down!" To emphasize her orders, or perhaps to assure the dog that she was not far away, she reached out and rapped on the dividing wall. One of the matching tins on the top shelf attached to that wall jumped and would have fallen, had not Mrs. Corder fielded it neatly with her left hand and restored it to its place, saying, "Jerry-built!"

They went into the sitting-room.

The architect had not planned separate bedrooms. The Elderly Person of his imagination might well appreciate the saving in heat which a curtained archway afforded. An Elderly Person could open the curtains and warm up its sleeping space before retiring. Also, if the EP had a television set and placed it strategically, it would be visible from the bed if the EP retired early or suffered some mild indisposition.

The curtains at Mrs. Armitage's front window, which overlooked Elmwood Avenue, matched the ones which hid her bed, dark blue velvet, faded in streaks but velvet, now obtainable only at great cost. Her carpet was also blue, retrieved from what at the rectory had been called the blue bedroom. It did not match the curtains, but it toned in. For some reason varying shades of blue never clashed as greens and pinks so easily did.

It was, Mrs. Corder conceded, a pretty room but cold.

The thoughtful council had provided an easy, efficient system of heating, hot air through vents in the floors and controlled by a touch on a switch. Tenants were, of course, supposed to pay their own gas bills.

It was March, a sunny day but chilly, and Mrs. Corder decided that her hostess was either impoverished or mean. That she was a lady was proved by the tea. The beverage so weak that it could barely crawl out of the pot and poured into the cups first, the milk to be added according to taste. Not the best milk, either; silvertop not gold. Accompanying this unsatisfactory brew were some biscuits which managed to avoid being either sweet or savoury. Still, it was well meant. And one day in the not too distant future, Mrs. Corder would offer some return hospitality. Meanwhile, here was her opportunity to find out something about this place in which she had so unaccountably landed.

"Hev you lived her long?"

"Almost three and a half years."

"D'you like it?"

"On the whole, yes. There are certain disadvantages. I have a rather bothersome knee. On bad days I find the stairs trying." (But dear Alice had always done the necessary shopping on such bad days.)

"I read all about the argy-bargy that went on about them stairs. It was all in the *Baildon Free Press*. When these places was being planned, somebody with a bit of sense in his head said old people should be downstairs and young ones up. Then somebody mentioned prams, and that was a clincher. Little did I think then that I'd end here myself. And I don't reckon I shall be here long."

"Oh?" Mrs. Armitage said on that rising, enquiring note and with that little inclination of the head that invited further egotistic monologue without showing vulgar curiosity.

"No," Mrs. Corder said. "What happened to me was all wrong. Mr. Wyckham said so hisself. It was like this—yes, thanks, I will— my husband was Mr. Wyckham's gamekeeper, and we'd lived right there in the cottage in Layer Wood, and Mr. Wyckham would never of dreamed of turning me out when Jake died. He said so hisself. But he had to sell that bit of his estate, and the Forestry Commission bought it. Anybody else, I reckon, couldn't have chucked me out. But with government departments thass all different. They had to have a forester, and he had to hev a home. And Mr. Wyckham hadn't got a spare cottage just then. But he did promise me. The minnit old Job Borley give up the ghost . . ." She drank her second slightly stronger cup of tea with audible appreciation and crunched the perfectly ordinary biscuit with the noise of breaking twigs.

"Oh, Layer Wood," Mrs. Armitage said with more animation than she had previously shown. "Where exactly were you, Mrs. Corder?"

"Nettleton. Not in but near. Two miles about."

"Then we were almost neighbours. My husband was rector at Talbot St. Mary and Talbot St. Agnes. He worked so hard and organized so well, that then he was given Stratton Strawless. I think—and I shall continue to think—that overwork killed him."

"A pity. Myself, so far as I'm anything, I'm Methodist."

Well, Methodists were very worthy people, and more than one historian held that the Methodist movement had saved England from the revolutions which had engulfed less fortunate countries.

"Ah, yes," Mrs. Armitage said with her small, deliberately sweet smile. "We seem to have suffered very similar fates. Naturally the new incumbent needed the rectory. I could not possibly afford to buy a house, and nowadays there is nothing to rent. So here I am. And quite thankful really."

Mrs. Corder took and crunched another biscuit.

"Maybe I should be. It was neighbours I dreaded . . ."

She realized that she was speaking to one, and her colour deepened.

"I mean," she said, a note of apology in her voice, "never having had one. Thirty-seven years, all my married life, I'd lived there at Layer. Not that we was lonely. Jake had a sort of jeep, and often we'd go down to the pub, or if there was anything on . . . But I had a niece lived on an estate once, and neighbours were a pest, she said. Popping in and out. And always on the borrow."

"I don't think that should be a problem here," Mrs. Armitage said in the light, almost playful voice which was the product of years of parochial visiting. "I promise you, I am not a borrower. Nor most certainly is Mr. Goodchild in flat four. A most determinedly independent character. And at the far end there is a Mrs. Finchley whom I hardly know by sight. She is a nurse—retired now I understand, but she takes private cases and is away most of the time."

"What about downstairs?"

"There we are truly fortunate. Both the Wrights and the Arbons are very nice couples, with very young children. I believe that in some of the other blocks, bigger children use the balconies as playgrounds and are rather noisy at times."

"I can't see the point in them balconies. To my mind they'd have done better to have put a bit more space into the flats." She looked around again. "Of course you've got all little nice things. Mine are big. Silly, like, I hung on to my Welsh dresser. It was my granny's and made by my granddad. I didn't feel I could ditch it. And if Mr. Wyckham is as good as his word—I mean even Job Borley can't live forever, can he?"

"If he does, he will establish a record."

Not a remarkably witty statement but the kind of thing which, said the right way, would have brought a smile to the bridge table. But wrong in this context. To Mrs. Corder, Job Borley's life expectation was no matter for flippancy. She gave Mrs. Armitage a blank look and then got down to reality again.

"And what about shops?"

"There's a little shopping centre in Briarwood Avenue, the first turning on the left from here. Of course, there is little choice, and I have noticed that prices are rather higher than in the town. The bus service is very bad. None at all on Mondays, Thursdays, or Fridays, and nothing comes nearer than the school at the edge of the estate. And that is a long walk with a load of shopping."

"I call that bad," Mrs. Corder agreed. "Oh, blast that dog. I must go or the Cruelty man'll be here."

Jumbo, fearing that he had again been abandoned, was not only howling, but hurling his weight against the kitchen door. Mrs. Armitage's door shuddered in sympathy.

"Well, thanks for the tea. Soon's I'm straight, you must come and see me."

"And I hope you will be very happy here."

To this Mrs. Corder responded with a kind of grunt.

Left alone, Mrs. Armitage washed up, reset the teatray, put out more biscuits, and began to prepare some dainty sandwiches, it being her turn to act as bridge hostess. In the happy days when dear Alice was alive, they'd always shared these preparations in this flat or that. For some reason they never played in Mr. Goodchild's flat, but when it was his turn to be host, he always brought a bottle of sherry and a selection of what were called Danish pastries. He gallantly claimed that this extravagance must be allowed him. "As I am the only male chauvinistic pig," he said. Apart from this there was no competition in that standard of hospitality, for everybody knew that shocking story of a bridge group which had started off with tea and a snack, and then, each member trying to outdo the others, had ended with a hot turkey dinner.

The games always took place in Birch House, partly because three members of the four lived there, and the fourth, Miss Peake, drove a Mini, and partly as a concession to Mrs. Armitage's knee which was rather more of a handicap than the word "bothersome" suggested. Miss Peake had recruited a fourth player to take dear Alice's place. Her name was Mrs. Sawyer, and when it was her turn to provide, she was allowed to bring small sausage rolls, because as she said with absolute truth, she could not cut bread evenly.

Mr. Goodchild was first to arrive, and he said, almost immediately, "Well, I've seen our new neighbour. She looks a decent body enough, but I'm damned if I could understand a word she said. Either she's foreign or has an impediment."

Mrs. Armitage laughed. "That is what is known as Good Old Suffolk. And I'll bet you five pence you weren't wearing your aid."

"As a matter of fact, I wasn't. I am not deaf—as I have said before. It's just that you ladies will mumble so, I'm obliged to pander. . . . Have you seen what it pleases her to call a dog?"

"I have indeed."

"It's a donkey covered in a hearthrug! And quite vicious."

Mrs. Armitage, who had been obliged to change her jersey and then spend some time removing long black, white, and tan hairs from her skirt, said, "Oh, do you think so? To me he seemed over affectionate."

"Ah, a dog of good taste."

Then Miss Peake and Mrs. Sawyer arrived, and the euphoria of bridge took over. Mrs. Armitage had never played bridge until she came here, still shattered by bereavement and the threat of homelessness. But dear Alice had said that if you really gave a card game your full attention, you couldn't think of anything else. And she had been right.

The invitation to take tea at six o'clock came two days later. Mrs. Armitage knew what village people regarded as tea and was not surprised to find, in the severely crowded room, a well laden table. Almost a whole ham, and where else but in a shop did one see such a thing nowadays? A bowl of salad—what that must have cost, in March! A plate of new bread rolls. At least half a pound of butter in a dish. And Mrs. Corder, bringing in a vast brown teapot, brought also a tureen heaped with fluffy mashed potato. "The tea'll draw time I carve," she said. She carved very well and so generously that Mrs. Armitage was obliged to say, "Please. That is enough for me." She took two crisp leaves of lettuce and one small tomato and helped herself lightly to the mashed potato. Mrs. Corder helped herself liberally and then poured the tea, which had brewed itself very strong indeed. The ham, she explained, and the butter had been given her by Mrs. Wyckham. "She'll miss me. I used to go and lend a hand up at the house from time to time. But she'd never seen this place. That ham won't go in what they call a larder. I hev to keep it in the oven. Built for midgets, these places are, and all that waste space outside."

She then tackled her piled plate with vigour.

"I always understood," Mrs. Armitage had been well trained in the delicate art of eating and making conversation simultaneously, "that the balconies were supposed to provide a place for old crocks like me to take a little exercise in bad weather—or to sit out in good. And those troughs along the railings provide a little gardening space for people who find stooping difficult."

A wave of sadness rose. Alice had planted the ones outside these two flats with daffodils, now almost in flower, and though nobody wished to be morbid, it was *sad* to think that she . . . Oh, stop it!

Mrs. Corder devoted herself to eating. She loaded her fork to capacity, opened her mouth and threw in the food somewhat with the action of someone loading hay or feeding a machine. She munched audibly and rhythmically, took a long drink of tea, and began again. . . . Mrs. Armitage remembered that only animals should eat in silence and like a good guest said, "I do admire your dresser." Innocent words, instantly regretted.

Mrs. Corder said, "Too big!" and ejected a spray of half masticated morsels from her mouth. Flecks of ham—pink—hit the butter; lettuce—green—landed on the ham.

Mrs. Armitage watched with the fascination of horror. She was naturally squeamish, and years of experience had failed to harden her. For years she had taught a Sunday school class and had always gone armed with a box of Kleenex. Once she had said to Arthur: "Well, I may not have explained Abraham's willingness to sacrifice Isaac very satisfactorily, but I did get five children to blow their noses." Poor Arthur had looked rather hurt, as he always did if she criticized, however indirectly, his beloved parishioners.

She'd done worse. Told white lies to avoid the inevitable cups of tea, offered in cups not properly washed since last being used. "Thank you so much. I've just had one," or "How kind, but I'm trying to avoid tea just now. It seems to provoke my indigestion."

And was there something in transference of thought, even between the unlikeliest people? Mrs. Armitage had only just remembered that evasion when Mrs. Corder said, "Do you suffer from your stomach?"

"Oh, no."

"Well, you don't eat very hearty. Maybe you don't care for home-cured."

"I think it is absolutely delicious. And lettuce at this time of the year is a real treat."

"And not easy to come by, either. I tried the shops you spoke of. Very poor in my opinion. So I took a taxi."

Taxis, even three and a half years ago, had been hideously expensive; now they were exorbitant. A taxi to buy a lettuce!

Once again there was that sidelong response from Mrs. Corder.

"I'm pretty well placed. Jake always bought his stamps, so I get the Widows' which is better than the Old Age. And he'd got more insurance than I knew. Also Mr. Wyckham come down very handsome, being upset at seeing me kicked out so to speak."

"How lovely for you," Mrs. Armitage said, without any genuine envy because part of her mind had gone flitting away and was wondering about Mrs. Corder's mediumistic abilities. In appearance she was just right. Mrs. Armitage had never seen a medium, but she had read, and she had seen pictures. Fattish, without being fat, clad in black, rather soiled and dusty. And with a motherly expression. Certainly Mrs. Corder's face was motherly.

And yet again Mrs. Corder seemed to catch on.

"D'you hev any family?"

"Unfortunately no." Mrs. Armitage never elaborated upon her really terrible miscarriage. Her squeamishness extended to many physical functions; to her, "bladder" and "bowels" were disgusting words, "womb" she disliked and "diarrhoea" was detestable.

"I've got two. My daughter went and married an American, and my son settled in Sydney. So I've got grandchildren I've never seen. Still, we live in hopes. D'you do the Pools?"

"No. I know it sounds completely stupid, but I could never understand the forms."

"Sure you won't hev a touch more? Well, I've got nice afters."

Nice indeed. Young pink rhubarb, stewed, and that stumbling block for poor cooks, an egg custard. Perfectly made.

"I never could make one," Mrs. Armitage confessed. "And I must have tried hundreds of times. . . . Sick villagers seemed to expect them. Mine invariably curdled."

"They must never boil," Mrs. Corder said, somewhat like a priest rebuking a cardinal sin.

"Very little for me," said Mrs. Armitage. It was morbidity in another form to wonder had Mrs. Corder perhaps been eating anything and talked to the dog as she cooked. "I'm really not accustomed to such sumptuous meals."

"No. You don't look what I'd call well fed." Mrs. Corder helped herself liberally and stirred the fruit and custard vigorously together. The result looked like—horrible thought, but however much one might shudder away from a thought, once it was thought, it was thought—bloody vomit. Both horrid words.

And now that to her outraged squeamishness was added her vague feeling of Mrs. Corder being on the same thought-wave, she felt definitely uneasy. For although she sometimes expressed violent feelings—"The man should be flogged!" or "Such people should be decapitated!"—she was at heart a woman who would not willingly have hurt a fly, far less a fellow human's feelings. Almost frenziedly she wished for the time to arrive when she could decently go.

In Nettleton when people took the trouble to drive or walk to the gamekeeper's cottage to eat a substantial tea, they'd settle down afterwards for a good gossip and a drink—port, cider, or beer; Jake had had his expansive and his parsimonious phases. But when Mrs. Armitage glanced at her watch and pretended surprise and dismay and said she must go, Mrs. Corder did nothing to detain her. For she sensed that Mrs. Armitage no more liked her than she liked Mrs. Armitage. Nothing wrong. A very decent woman but not easy company. Because of that likely to be an untroublesome neighbour.

"I'll bring something through," Mrs. Armitage said when Mrs. Corder had agreed that it was time she took Jumbo out. Mrs. Armitage lifted the butter dish and the Pyrex in which some of the egg custard remained.

And there in the kitchen, Mrs. Armitage's regrettable squeamishness received a final shock. Jumbo was tethered to the rail, intended for tea-cloths, at the side of the sink. Mrs. Corder said, "Give him that dish. He's a good washer up."

He had already washed the two meat plates and the tureen.

Mrs. Armitage had not lied when she said she liked all animals. She and Arthur had owned a dog themselves and more than once provided temporary homes for animals whose owners had had to go to hospital. So she knew how they washed up. They left a peculiar slimy coating on their own food bowls, which had to be diligently scoured with wire wool and then well rinsed before being fit even for a dog's use.

A horrid feeling—the best word for it was nausea—stirred at the thought that Jumbo had probably washed up the plate from which she had recently eaten. But she controlled herself, said, "Thank you so much," and got away.

Never again!

Yet, despite this unpromising start, the two women became good neighbours. Never quite friends. Not compatible. But neighbourly. Mrs. Corder would rap on Mrs. Armitage's door and say she was going down to the shops or the town, and ask if there was anything she could fetch. And when Mrs. Corder was stricken down with a most unseasonable cold, Mrs. Armitage, braving the difficult stairs, walked Jumbo three times a day. Mr. Goodchild, who suffered no disablement, might have undertaken or shared this task, but he affected to be scared of the dog. He could be gallantly generous at times, but he was fundamentally a selfish old man.

Mrs. Corder, wary as she was of neighbours who might become nuisances, had her gregarious moments, and these she spent in the local public house, once she was certain that Jumbo was welcome there. In what she inelegantly called "the boozer," she made many acquaintances but no real friends, and she never invited anyone home. Nor was she ever actually the worse for drink, just a little noisier than usual and less inhibited in the terms she applied to Jumbo. Though, as Mrs. Armitage said to the bridge players, to call a dog a son of a bitch was not really an insult. The adjective which accompanied this definition Mrs. Armitage could not bring herself to repeat.

It was from a drinking session that one evening in late August Mrs. Corder brought rather disturbing news. Both the families downstairs were moving away, the Arbons to the house they had at last succeeded in buying on mortgage and the Wrights back to London. Everybody hoped that the new downstairs people would be quiet and have no teen-age children. "Teenager" was rapidly becoming as frightful a word as "highwayman" had once been. Elderly people in both Beech and Hawthorn had recently been terrorized by gangs who were noisy and abusive and not above a bit of pilfering if opportunity offered.

There were children downstairs when the new families moved in, but rather too small, everybody agreed, to be teenagers, and since the weather was still reasonably good, they did not use the upstairs balcony as a playground. Indeed the first intimation that there might be an undesirable element downstairs—admittedly a mild one—came one evening when a boy with really vivid red hair mounted the stairs carrying a chipped enamel bowl. For some reason of his own, he started his operation at Mr. Goodchild's flat which was the farthest from the head of the stairs. Mr. Goodchild looked warily from his kitchen window on to the balcony— thoughtfully lighted by the council—guessed his caller's errand, and decided to be very deaf indeed. The boy then rang Mrs. Armitage's bell, making her jump. But she went to the door, and the boy said, "Can you lend me mum a cup of sugar?"

"I have none," Mrs. Armitage said truthfully. She did not use it herself, and she and Mrs. Corder had long since, with no word spoken, agreed to avoid each other's undrinkable tea, and Miss Peake who had always taken two lumps had recently gone on a diet.

To the red headed boy a household without sugar, except in such emergencies as this, was inconceivable, and he expressed his disapprobation, "Bloody mean bitch," and passed on to Mrs. Corder's.

This was the very last thing that her niece had so feelingly described, and she had dreaded; but there was nothing mean in her nature and for some reason she had always been peculiarly susceptible to redheads, had indeed almost married one. A most lucky escape!

But even as she poured rather more than a cupful into the bowl, she made herself perfectly clear.

"I don't lend," she said. "You can have this. I don't want it back. But remember, I don't lend."

He did not acknowledge the warning, nor did he thank her. He said, "Me Dad's waiting," and scampered off.

Next day a woman, much made up and flashily dressed, carrying a pound packet of sugar, rang Mrs. Corder's bell and angrily addressed her: "My name's Dodd, and I don't like rude messages. I ain't no borrower and don't you dare hint that I am! Anybody can accidentally run out once in a way. Here's your bloody sugar. Go on! Take it! Stuff it up your arse!"

Mrs. Corder was not a woman to take such treatment lying down. She retorted with spirit—and in the same idiom. The row about nothing became a slanging match. The contestants were well matched.

Mrs. Armitage could have avoided hearing more than the opening salvos, but only by withdrawing to her sitting room and switching on the TV. But she was hard boiling three eggs for the evening's sandwiches, and even for that simple operation care was needed; get them too hard, and they did not mash very well. So she stayed, her eyes on the egg timer, and listened to the ear blistering epithets.

She had no knowledge of the altercation's origin, but she was inclined to side with Mrs. Corder whom she knew, whose salt she had eaten, with whom she had exchanged small favours. There, she knew, she was morally wrong. Arthur would have said one must hear both sides and try to be impartial.

Mrs. Corder seemed to have the last word.

"I'll show you what I think of your frigging sugar. I wouldn't use anything you'd handled, you floosie!"

In the stunning after silence Mrs. Armitage realized that, although she had switched off the heat at the correct moment, she had not immediately run cold water over the eggs, so there'd be that nasty dark line between yolk and white. Oh dear. Too late to remedy that now, but she ran the cold over them—it made them easier to shell. And as she stood at the sink, Mrs. Corder did an unprecedented thing, she tapped on the window and then tried the door. She was too thoroughly enraged to remember that familiarity was a thing to avoid.

As Mrs. Armitage opened the door, Mrs. Corder said, "Well, did you hear *that?*"

"I'm afraid I did."

"What a way to repay a kindness! All I did was . . ." She related what she had done, what she had said and concluded, "Still I give her as good as I got. And I chucked her sugar over the balcony."

"I think you were quite right." Mrs. Armitage said this so heartedly that Mrs. Corder's tepid opinion of her warmed, and she became confidential.

"Mind if I come and set for a minnit? I don't make a song and dance about it, but I gotta dicky heart. Not bad. Valvular lesion they call it. I always hoped I'd go afore Jake. . . . But I'm all right, till I get upset. Now I am. And now perhaps you see what I mean about neighbours."

"I do indeed."

Certainly, even now that she was seated, Mrs. Corder looked a bad colour, the red on her wide cheeks gone patchy.

Perhaps a drink. And fortunately Mrs. Armitage could offer it. Mr. Goodchild's really, left over from last time when he had been host. He'd never quite liked to carry the bottle away with him, but he had succeeded in making it clear that a bottle should serve two sessions.

Mrs. Corder accepted the small measure of unfamiliar and indeed rather unpalatable stuff. Mr. Goodchild's own taste was astringent, and he bought a brand of sherry called dry. Still, it was restorative, and Mrs. Corder felt better.

"You ain't heving one?"

"Later," Mrs. Armitage said. "I am expecting friends." A statement borne out by the card table with its baize cloth and the four spindly chairs.

"I'd better be off then."

"There is no hurry. They don't come until six."

"But just listen to that blasted dog."

Jumbo was putting up his usual protest at being left alone. "Thanks for the drink. And I'll say right here and now—what I said about borrowing don't go for *you*. Anything I got you're welcome to."

Mrs. Armitage was genuinely touched.

During the evening's tea break Mrs. Armitage regaled the company with the whole story, bowdlerized by the substitution of "blank" and "blanketty" for the more pungent words actually used.

Mr. Goodchild, a lifelong bachelor, had not always lived in a council flat, but he had vast experience of boarding houses, private hotels, and privately owned flats. And he said an ominous thing: "Let's hope this won't turn into a feud."

The feud broke out overnight and at first centred, not upon Mr. Goodchild who had not answered his door, nor upon Mrs. Armitage who had failed to provide, but upon Mrs. Corder who had lent but in lending had given offence. She woke next morning to find her door and her window sprayed with black paint.

Mr. Goodchild advised nipping this kind of thing in the bud but was a little uncertain as to who should do the nipping, the police or the council. Mrs. Armitage was too much shocked to give any advice at all; she kept saying, "Oh, how spiteful! How could they?"

"It wasn't *they*," Mrs. Corder said. "It was that redhead, egged on by his bitch of a mother. But I don't reckon anybody can *do* much, and we don't want people poking about, do we? I'll just get it off as best I can."

"Let us hope it is an isolated incident," said Mr. Goodchild.

Had only the door been sprayed, Mrs. Corder would have ignored it, blue door, black and blue door, what matter? But paint on the window made her kitchen dark, so she took a taxi and went into town, explained her predicament in three shops, and in the third was sold a can of the requisite solvent. All afternoon she worked with vigour, and by early evening the window was quite clear, the door almost so.

Two nights later the enemy struck again, and this time at them all.

In a place where concrete was so prevalent, the window boxes—those substitute gardens—had afforded a welcome note of life and colour. Mr. Goodchild did not go in for bulbs; he planted polyan-thus which, dead flowers removed, retained green leaves until it was time to set out begonias. Then it was time for small, shrubby, almost hard chrysanthemums. Less expensively, dear Alice and Mrs. Armitage had followed daffodils with pansies, which had long lives if properly tended. After that they had simply moved into the window box—balcony box—the potted hardy ivy which usually stood under and around. Mrs. Corder had been lavish; after the daffodils, night scented stocks, French marigolds with heads like yellow and bronze sponges, and then, as the weather cooled, small pointed evergreen trees, the greens varying.

All, all wantonly ripped out and destroyed. Soil all over the balcony, most of the cherished plants flung out, others broken and dying.

Mrs. Corder swore luridly. Mrs. Armitage wept, largely because Alice had grown those ivy plants from cuttings. Mr. Goodchild, at last fully involved, said, "Don't touch anything. Braddock comes today. Let him see."

Baildon was still old fashioned enough to employ rent collectors who were also expected to act as liaison officers, reporting such things as broken windows, faulty taps, doors which, swollen with damp, opened and closed with difficulty. A good-hearted and ex-tremely handy man, he had once carried, in addition to the rent bag and book, a few tools with which he could effect at least a temporary repair. But the maintenance department had heard about this and registered a strong protest, and Mr. Braddock had been reprimanded. Some union nicety was involved. After that he had confined himself to carrying a few spare fuses in an inside pocket. It was really astounding how many old ladies could not replace a blown fuse.

Faced with the devastation on the upper floor of Birch House, he was, of course, helpless, able only to sympathize, promise to report it, and ask if they had any idea. . . . Mrs. Corder had more than an idea, she had certain knowledge—but of course no proof.

The councillor most responsible for the layout and assembly of the four double-story buildings at the end of Elmwood Avenue was an idealist. He had strongly advocated the mingling of elderly and young. He had spun his fantasies: mutual help, the young gladly running errands, the elderly baby-sitting. "A replica of family life," he had said. He'd carried the day, only to be defeated later when detailed plans were being discussed; he thought that the accommodation for the elderly should be on the ground floor. Then somebody had mentioned young mothers with perambulators. And presently all had agreed that if the stairs were made shallow, covered with some non-slip material, and provided with stout handrails on both sides, all would be well.

So far all had been well at Birch House; now there was trouble there. Most disappointing! But what could one do? This bit of vandalism was trivial compared with the destruction in telephone booths, and what was done to public conveniences was quite unspeakable.

This kind of thing reduced the idealist almost to tears, but he had both an explanation and a solution. Boredom lay at the root of the problem, and he suggested that the entry fee at the Leisure Centre be reduced from 10 to 5 pence. Including as it did a heated swimming pool and space for almost every known game except golf and polo, as well as a non-profit-making cafeteria, the Leisure Centre was already a burden to the rate payers, but the idealist had a blind spot where they were concerned.

However, he felt for what he called "the old folk" in Birch House and suggested that the head of Parks and Gardens should be asked to plant the window boxes. That canny man returned a threefold refusal: He had enough on his hands; he had no plants suitable for bedding out at this time of year; whatever went into those boxes would only be uprooted again.

Despite the lowered price at the Leisure Centre, the downstairs

children of Birch now took to playing on the balcony both on
Saturdays and in the evenings, until a well directed ball put the
lighting out of action.

They couldn't all be Birch House children, Mr. Goodchild argued, unless the downstairs flats were statutorily overcrowded.
There were seldom fewer than six, sometimes as many as eight.
Two owned transistor sets never, even by accident, tuned in to the
same station. It was noticeable that whatever ploy was in hand, the
leader, the boss, was the red headed boy. A miniature Genghis
Khan, he had his subsidiaries, both girls and both distinctive; one
wore plaits, rather rare these days, and one had a bad squint,
which by all accounts should have been rarer. Was there not an
operation?

The children made a playground of the stairs, too, and it was on
the stairs that Mrs. Armitage was hurt one Saturday morning.
Ordinarily she would not have ventured forth on Saturday, but on
Friday the little shop in Briarwood Avenue had no eggs, but expected some tomorrow. And eggs were a necessity, not only for
the sandwiches, but for her modest midday meal at least three
times a week.

The stairs were clear when she went down, but on her return
were occupied by three girls, making the interesting experiment
of seeing who could jump down most stairs at a time. Mrs. Armitage stood and waited for a break in this game, but it never came;
so she said, very clearly, as she assured everybody, "Would you
allow me to pass?"

She was half-way up, rather slow, this was weather unfavourable
to bothersome knees, when the girl with the plaits launched herself from the top. In the collision Mrs. Armitage fared worst. She
had, most fortunately, kept a grip of the handrail, so she didn't go
down, but she was swung round, her arm almost wrenched from
its socket and her knee—the bad one of course—striking the side
of the staircase. From her other hand fell the bag containing six
fresh eggs.

Plaits said, "Silly old cow! You spoilt my jump!"

In more agony that she would have thought supportable, Mrs.
Armitage hauled herself up and along the balcony, where other
children were playing, and as far as Mrs. Corder's window sill,

where she paused and clung for a moment, telling herself that nobody died of severe pain in the knee.

Mrs. Corder, most fortunately, saw her, helped her in to her own flat, examined the knee, now the size of a melon, and said, "I'll tend that in a minute. Just now I've had enough!" She went into her own flat and came out with a broom.

"Be off," she shouted, striking about. "Clear off, the whole bloody lot of you. If you come back here again, I'll set my dog on you."

Physical violence they recognized.

"It could be water on the knee. A knock'll do that," she said, coming back, the clearing operation completed. "You might hev to hev it drained. Who's your doctor?"

"Oh, no. Please. It isn't necessary. And Dr. Tomson is never there at weekends. Besides, once before I suffered the same thing. . . . We laughingly called it Housemaid's Knee. I had some pills."

They were there, carefully saved, in the neat bathroom cabinet, and Mrs. Corder contributed her own palliative, half a glass of whisky.

Quite soon the worst was over. It was Macaulay, wasn't it, who at the age of three, scalded, said, "Thank you, madam, the agony has abated." The reference would have been wasted on Mrs. Corder, so Mrs. Armitage said, "Really, it is much better now. . . . But my eggs were all smashed."

"I'll get you some more when I take Jumbo out. Bit of a joke ain't it, me threatening to set the dog on them. Bless the daft thing, all he wants is to get out and play with them."

Afterwards Mrs. Armitage often thought, Poor Jumbo. Poor innocent victim!

There was an interval of comparative peace, but punctuated by nasty little episodes. The flats all had rather outsized letterboxes, and a variety of unpleasant objects began to appear on the kitchen floors. Mr. Goodchild and Mrs. Armitage suffered this form of persecution, but Mrs. Corder bore the brunt of it; for every one horror the others received, she had at least four. Somebody displayed a degree of inventiveness which in another sphere would have been admirable. The objects varied from harmless wrappings from fish and chips, to lumps of horse dung, to toilet paper which, as Mrs. Armitage delicately said, "had been used," to some revolting entrails culled from a slaughter house. Mrs. Corder also received a dead mouse.

Mr. Goodchild wrote to the housing officer, a man of experience. He decided to visit Birch House—an entity hitherto trouble free. He noted that the ground floor tenants had recently changed, Dodd and Hopkins having replaced Wright and Arbon. He also noted that the Dodds were now three weeks behind with their rent.

He asked each upstairs tenant in turn if there had been any dispute. To this Mrs. Corder cagily replied that the opposite was the case; she'd lent some sugar, and it had been returned.

Mrs. Armitage thought it no part of her duty to contradict this statement and contented herself with saying that, even when jostled on the stairs and quite hurt, she had uttered no word of reproach. "In fact I was quite speechless with pain." Mr. Goodchild said he had never set eyes either on a Dodd or a Hopkins, but that life in Birch House was now unbearable and that he wished to be moved. This was a very usual request from people on the upper floors of the four model buildings, and it received the usual response: "I will make a note of that and see what can be done." But he did add that he would speak to the people downstairs, meaning only the Dodds, for people who fell behind with their rent were, in his opinion, capable of almost anything.

Mrs. Dodd was at home, and she had a story to tell, oddly at variance with the upstairs one. It cast a different light—at least upon Mrs. Corder. Such language as never was heard. Throwing good sugar over the balcony and lashing about with a broom! Gary had had a lump as big as an egg on his head and several others had received bruises.

Nor did Mrs. Armitage escape censure; the other old woman upstairs had pushed against Vanessa Hopkins so roughly that she narrowly escaped a fall on the stairs.

This kind of thing was the housing officer's daily bread, and Our Father which art give him patience! Presently he managed to mention the outstanding rent and warned Mrs. Dodd that the council could, in these hard times, not allow more than a month to be outstanding. People who couldn't or wouldn't pay for this very superior accommodation were moved out into a big, almost condemned house, often housing nine such families and far from the town centre. And not only rent defaulters, tenants in other ways undesirable, dirty, destructive, or quarrelsome.

"You can have the money now," Mrs. Dodd said. "I only got behind because my husband's a heavy vehicle driver, mostly on the continent." She produced the money, and the housing officer hesitated only a moment. Rent collecting was no part of his job; on the other hand if he refused it, and she spent it, everybody would agree that she'd be entitled to another month's leniency. He took it.

Mrs. Corder had spoken of lending sugar to a red headed boy, and both she and Mrs. Armitage, speaking of the rough games— the balcony light was again out of order—had said that a red headed boy seemed to be the leader. Both had said that he was about twelve years old, but the housing officer, running into this easily identified character in the Dodd doorway, knew better. At least fourteen, probably more, but small for his age. Too small to be accepted in a teen-age gang, preferring to lord it over his juveniles. The boy's face was far from childish. In no time at all he would need to shave—or grow a beard. Were schoolboys allowed to sport beards?

Jumbo's routine was now well established; since his basket was too large for the kitchen, he slept in the sitting-room, under the Welsh dresser. Mrs. Corder, used to country hours, still rose early, and while she made her first pot of dark tea, she let him out to water the railings of the balcony. He would never run away, he was far too fearful of being abandoned again; in fact he did not like her to shut the kitchen door. After this little run he came in, had a bowl of tea and as many biscuits as Mrs. Corder felt like dispensing. Mrs. Corder ate a solid breakfast, Jumbo washed up while she dressed. She then walked him around the adjoining playing field until he had done what she called "a serious job." He had another, shorter walk at midday; then, if Mrs. Corder went to the boozer, as she did with increasing frequency, he went, too, and was regaled with bits of biscuit, potato crisps, and similar snacks.

There came a very dark December morning, just a week before Christmas. So far as Mrs. Corder could see, nothing had been pushed through the letterbox during the hours of darkness. But, as she later remembered, Jumbo was one leap ahead of her. She opened the door, and he bounded out towards the nearest railing. She made the tea, allowed it to brew, opened a new packet of biscuits. The door was already ajar, but when he did not come, pushing at it, she went and opened it fully. The kitchen light streamed out and showed Jumbo staggering, his legs at odd angles, trying to be sick, and then toppling over.

She ran to Mr. Goodchild's flat where the nearest telephone was. She knocked, she screamed; she took off her slipper and hammered. Eventually roused, Mr. Goodchild came in his pyjamas.

"Ring a vet. Oh, please. Ring a vet. Jumbo's dying. Poisoned. Oh, quick, quick."

Mr. Goodchild kept his head. He knew of no vet, but he dialled 999 and was asked which emergency service he required: Police, Ambulance, Fire.

"Police . . . Oh, hullo. We are in desperate need of a veterinary surgeon."

There was only a slight pause; the police had known stranger requests. The calm, steady voice said, "2680. Or 82661."

Mr. Goodchild dialled the former number. The vet was up and alert, having just returned from a night call to a difficult calving. He came at once and found Mrs. Corder sitting on the balcony with the dead dog's head in her lap.

For a lonely woman bereft of a pet—and in such cruel fashion— she was remarkably controlled. She described what had happened, and it certainly sounded like cyanide poisoning. She called it prussic acid, and she was well informed. It was often used, she said, to keep down the rats and mice, which would otherwise have infested the place where pheasant food was stored.

The veterinary was a kind man, and he offered to take away the body. But she said she intended to give the dog a decent burial, "in the place where he had his happiest days." She asked, "What do I owe you?" and he said, "Nothing. I didn't do anything." He then proffered a piece of advice which he knew to be good. The very best thing she could do was to get a new dog immediately. And he knew of some lovely little Cairn puppies.

"They'd only kill that, too," Mrs. Corder said.

She lapped Jumbo around and around in the patchwork quilt made by the same grandmother as had owned the Welsh dresser.

At each end of the parcel she tied string, so that Jumbo, smaller in death than he had been in life, bore a horrible resemblance to a Christmas cracker. She took a taxi and drove to Nettleton, where she borrowed a spade and dug a grave with her own hands in Layer Wood, where Jumbo, restored to human company, had so happily played. And all this she did in a kind of icy calm which Mrs. Armitage found more disturbing than tears or hysterics. Mrs. Armitage had been called upon to comfort many bereft people in her time, and she knew that people were capable of crying even over the death of an aged and totally unwanted relative. And she had often noticed that with the tears a kind of healing process set in. She wished that Mrs. Corder could weep.

Her completely stunned grief was surprising, for she had never addressed Jumbo in affectionate terms; she often called him "a bloody old nuisance."

Four days before Christmas, she announced her intention of going to the police. "After all, what was done to Jumbo was a crime. And I know who done it."

Mr. Goodchild said, "Very difficult to prove, I'm afraid, Mrs. Corder."

And so it proved. With little of her old spirit, she reported what had happened at the blasted cop shop.

"The first one I talked to was all right. He said he was sorry; he liked dogs hisself. But he passed me on to a real bugger. Talked to me as though I'd broke all the rules in the book. How did I know it was poison? Had I called the vet? Which vet? Had there been an autopsy? Why did I suspect Gary Dodd? And I looked like a fool. Didn't even know the vet's name. Did you catch his name, Mr. Goodchild?"

"No. I was given a number which I rang as quickly as possible."

"D'you know the number?"

"No." That was untrue, he had scribbled down both numbers; but he wanted no involvement, for he was preparing for his annual treat—four or five days in a little private hotel down in Bywater, which broke the lean season of winter by offering accommodation and excellent food at much reduced terms at Christmas. There he could always be sure of a bridge game and the undemanding company of people of his own kind. And though the seaside might sound cheerless at Christmas time, it was frequently warmer than it was inland. He had been going regularly for seven years, and on four occasions had been able to sit in a shelter on the front for an hour. When he went back into his flat to resume his packing, he destroyed the paper on which he had scribbled the two numbers.

Despite the police lack of enthusiasm, some slight action was taken, less about Jumbo's premature end than about the general outbreak of vandalism and thefts from shops which had recently afflicted the estate in general and the Elmwood Avenue area in particular. A little show of uniform might be no bad thing, and since Mrs. Corder's chief suspect was, she said, "no more'n twelve but as wicked as they come," a woman police constable was despatched to prowl about a bit.

Mrs. Dodd, not without reason, was allergic to police uniform. Her husband was under close scrutiny, suspected of drug smuggling, and she knew that Gary stole. He'd always been a bad boy and at the age of ten had been removed from her care and sent for two years to a special school, from which he had returned rather worse than ever. She did not want him removed again, since that would mean losing the child allowance. So she spoke very severely to Gary and said that if he got into one scrap of trouble during the Christmas holiday, she'd tell his dad. And Gary knew what that meant—a belting. (One day—and not too far distant a day—Gary was going to avenge himself on his father.)

Mrs. Armitage went, as usual, to spend Christmas Day with Miss Peake, Mrs. Sawyer, and another lone woman. It was a communal effort at merrymaking. Miss Peake cooked a turkey—a gift from her brother who reared them; Mrs. Sawyer brought mince pies and a cake; the other lone woman contributed a bottle of table wine and one of port, and Mrs. Armitage took a Christmas pudding in a foil basin with a foil lid, which needed only to be heated through.

And what would Mrs. Corder do about Christmas?

"Sweet damn all. Don't you fret about me. When I think of last year—I had Jake and Jumbo. . . . I can do without Christmas, if I live to be ninety!"

The Day itself was inclement, not the white Christmas of the song or the cards, just a dull, lowering day, with an unkind wind and flurries of sleet. Miss Peake, leaving her two other guests to see to the turkey and lay the table, fetched Mrs. Armitage in her Mini.

Mrs. Corder went to the Maypole, was treated and in turn treated, and presently produced from her vast, shabby handbag a brand new dog collar, red leather with bright brass bosses.

"Anybody here got a decent sized dog? I'd got it for him for a Christmas present."

Softened by drink—and by the season—they all repeated their commiserations. The joker must have his little joke. "On my old bitch," he said, "it'd act as a chastity belt. And not before needed!" But he again promised Mrs. Corder the pick of the puppies due in January. The collar went to a man who had an Alsatian. Mrs. Corder went home, had a little nap, woke up sober, and at six o'clock set out for the Maypole again.

Miss Peake brought Mrs. Armitage home fairly late, when the sleet was thickening. It had been for four lonely women, resolutely banishing memories of happier days, a wholly successful day. Mrs. Armitage was still enjoying the glow of the final mince pie and glass of port, as she got out of the car.

"Don't get out, dear," she said, "it's such a filthy night. And the lights are working again. Thanks again for a lovely day. . . ."

The stairs were in two flights, at right angles to one another, and as Mrs. Armitage gained the little half landing and turned left, she gave a cry of dismay. Mrs. Corder lay sprawled on the stairs, face downwards, and a pool of blood was gathering on the step where her head lay.

Because of her squeamish nature Mrs. Armitage had never practised First Aid much, but some experience had been forced upon her, because even in these heathenish days people were inclined to turn to the rectory in emergencies.

Mrs. Armitage removed her gloves, felt for a pulse, then for a heartbeat. She then took a small looking glass from her bag and held it before Mrs. Corder's nose and mouth. The surface remained unclouded. To the amateur Mrs. Corder appeared to be dead. But she was still warm, blood was still issuing, though more slowly, from the ugly gash on her temple, and possibly more expert attention might resuscitate her. Telephone! Ambulance. Keep the patient warm.

Mrs. Armitage had Mr. Goodchild's key, so she had access to the telephone. Asked which service she needed she replied firmly, "Ambulance and Police and as quickly as possible. There has been a dreadful accident at Birch House in Elmwood Avenue. Somebody is dying. . . ."

(And this was no hoaxer making merry on Christmas Day. One could tell by the voice.)

Mrs. Armitage then went into her own flat and took a blanket from her bed. It would have saved a moment to have taken one from Mr. Goodchild's, but it was likely to get soiled, and he would be displeased.

It was very cold on the stairs, and it seemed to Mrs. Armitage that in just that short time, the body had lost heat.

She then did a strange thing. She replaced her right hand glove, picked up Mrs. Corder's conspicuous handbag, and carrying it to the balcony railing, cast it forth into the night.

"It has been—as you may imagine—a terrible shock to me," Mrs. Armitage said, looking pale, frail, and shaken, but controlled. However, to the pleasant police sergeant, the control seemed to be maintained with such an effort that he wondered was it really necessary to inform her that the victim of the accident was dead.

"It must have been," he said sympathetically. "You were friends?"

"Hardly that. We were neighbours—good neighbours."

The sergeant thought that Mrs. Armitage had behaved admirably; she'd wrapped the neighbour in a blanket, called help, stayed there until the ambulance and the police car arrived simultaneously, and then not danced about, asking questions and getting in the way. Just "I saw exactly what happened. I'll wait in my flat."

What had happened was easy to guess. An elderly woman with the soles of her shoes slippery—and a strong aura of whisky about her—had slipped and fallen forwards, inflicting a wound on her head and probably fracturing her skull. One of the ambulance men, by a gesture, a change of expression, had indicated that the woman was dead. That being so, the policeman had felt justified in removing the blanket and returning it to its owner.

"You knew her name, of course."

"Oh, yes. Mrs. Corder. E. I think for Emily."

"Ah," he said, "I'd been wondering where I'd seen . . . Didn't she lose a dog recently?"

"Her dog was deliberately poisoned, just a week ago. I find that most sinister—in the light of what happened this evening."

"You mean—the accident?"

"Sergeant, that was no accident. It was a vile, cowardly attack. Premeditated. And committed for gain."

She spoke these damning words in a gentle but incisive voice.

"You saw this attack, madam?"

"As I said, I saw exactly what happened."

"And are prepared to make a statement?"

"Of course. I should prefer not to go to the police station in this weather."

The rules governing police behaviour had grown stricter as those governing the general public had grown more lax. It was as well to be careful. People said things and then tried to withdraw them, saying they had been frightened, threatened, hysterical, or even drunk. The sergeant thought it wise to summon his colleague who was in the police car, smoking and wondering why the hell Sarge was taking so long to return a blanket.

Mrs. Armitage greeted the newcomer with grave courtesy and then fixed her candid, blue, unwavering gaze on the sergeant again.

"Would it be in order for me to ask one question? Did you find Mrs. Corder's handbag?"

"Did she carry one?"

"Invariably. She kept all her private papers in it. And often quite large amounts of money."

The police constable, young, slender, and good looking, said diffidently, "Lots of ladies don't carry bags now. Not since the bag snatching started."

"Mrs. Corder always carried hers. Oh, dear. It may sound trivial, when she is so hurt . . ." The two policemen exchanged a swift look, warning, acknowledgment. "But it does irk me to think that They have profited. That I was too late. Though I went at once . . ." Her voice faltered, though her eyes remained steady. Both men sensed that she was now forcing herself to recall something painful. Something she would have liked to forget.

"I had just come home," Mrs. Armitage said. "I was in my

kitchen, filling my hot water bottle, when I heard a sound. A sort of scuffle on the stairs. Perhaps I should explain, both other tenants are away. And Mrs. Corder always came in very quietly. So I thought . . . Well, frankly, this may sound cowardly, but for months we have lived on such a knife edge of terror. . . . Then she cried out. I recognized her voice and went at once. I wonder now that I dared. . . . She was standing then, defending herself with her handbag against two of them. Then the third struck her, and she went down. I screamed, and they ran away." She closed her eyes, and a slight shudder shook her. "Quite awful."

Her distress was so obvious that the next question seemed cruel, reminding her, as it must.

"Did you see the weapon, madam?"

Pulling herself together with a visible effort, Mrs. Armitage said, "Yes, I did. It was a broom handle or something very similar. It struck her on the side of the head."

Both men could visualize the ugly scene and felt sorry for the woman who had witnessed it.

"I must ask just one further question," the sergeant said with apology in his voice. "Did you see any of the assailants clearly enough to recognize him again?"

"Oh, yes. I know them all. I have seen them often enough. One I know by name." For the first time she lost her composure. Her gaze flickered, and she put one hand to the modest little string of pearl beads about her neck.

"I dare not tell you. You see, they also know me. If I identified . . . If they were so little as reprimanded, I should be the next victim."

She looked back at the sergeant, and there was no mistaking the genuine fear in her eyes.

Nor was there any mistaking the soundness of her argument. Thousands of people withheld vital information because they feared reprisals.

There was a long silence in the pretty little room. The sergeant thought of many things: what a horrible proof of the breakdown of law and order, a citizen's duty, the word *"premeditated,"* the death of the dog. And he wished that he could be Home Secretary for about six months. When he spoke it was in the voice of one who wishes to reassure himself as well as his hearer.

Radford Public Library
30 First St.
Radford, VA 24141

"Robbery with violence—possibly fatal—gets more than a reprimand, madam. If you can positively identify those men, they'll be put away for quite a long time."

Mrs. Armitage said, "But they were not men. They were children. You would hardly believe how vicious." And she straightened up a little, facing the worst, which was to accept Miss Peake's repeated invitation to go and share her home. "One," she said clearly, "is a boy with red hair; his name is Gary Dodd, and he lives just below. The others are girls—but almost as bad. One has plaits. I think her name is Vanessa, and the other has a most disfiguring squint. . . ."

3

Saving face

Outside in the lane the bicycle bell rang and went on ringing. Somebody wishing to attract her attention. Kathy withdrew her hands from the mixing bowl, rubbed them on the towel, and went to the front door. The dusk was thickening, but she could just see Nico standing astride a bicycle.

"Mum, look! Isn't it *beautiful?*"

"Yes. Whose is it?"

"Mine! I won it in the draw."

"You lucky fellow."

The wind blew sharply, tunnelling along the lane.

"Bring it round to the back. Right into the kitchen."

She turned and went back into the house. From upstairs Mr. Fraser's loud strong voice called, "Mrs. Dawson. Mrs. Dawson. Miss Ayling wants you!"

Kathy sped upstairs and into the bedroom on the left. At the sight of her, Miss Ayling began to cry.

"Oh, dear, oh, dear. I am *so* sorry. Now you'll have to change me again. I did try . . . I did ring. Oh, this is the most humiliating. . . ."

"Never mind. You were well padded." It was indeed humiliating for a woman who, when merely crippled with arthritis, had been as fastidious as a cat. A stroke had robbed her of all control. "Just relax. I can lift you easily." The poor old thing could never believe that and made a simple operation more difficult by clutching, as drowning people are said to do, hindering their rescuers. But soon everything was done: clean night-dress, fresh draw-sheet, a spirit rub on the pressure points.

Kathy prided herself that never once in six years had any patient of hers suffered the added pain of bedsores.

"You are so kind. And I'm such a nuisance. I wish I were dead."

And the shocking, the really horrifying thing was that Kathy should think, Yes, that would be best.

She said, placing a book on the neatly turned down sheet, "You can't go and die without finding out whodunit."

Miss Ayling could still read and was addicted to mysteries. Kathy often wished that Dick Francis could produce a new book every week.

She had always tried to keep the more squalid side of things from Nico; so now she went to the bathroom, put what was to be disposed of in a close-lidded bin, what was to be washed in a wicker hamper.

And, damn and blast, Mr. Fraser had left the hot tap running again. To judge by the heat of the tap and the amount of steam, it had been running for quite a while. With oil the price it was! It is like my life-blood running away!

She whisked across the landing, assuming a different personality.

"You really are very naughty. You left the hot tap running again."

"Maybe I did," he said truculently. "I happened to be washing my hands when Miss Ayling began calling. Which is more important? The twist of a tap or a fellow being in distress?"

He was completely unpredictable. He could be vague, incoherent, and forgetful, almost senile, and then, as now, sharp, almost shrewd. Sometimes she almost suspected that his silliness was feigned—a form of escapism. Not that one could blame him, poor old devil; he must find his present life too tedious and dreary for words. Such an active, such a very outdoor man. She remembered

him as almost a neighbour, an oldish man, eking out his already
debased pension by keeping fowls, keeping bees, growing vegetables and fruit. She had always been one of his customers. Then,
rather more than two years ago, he'd been up a ladder, gathering
his superb Cox's Orange apples, when he'd fallen and broken his
ankle. A Pott's fracture. Heavy with plaster he had come here, for
at most six weeks . . . But when the plaster was removed, it revealed a quite useless foot, flaccid as a fillet of fish and set at a
curious angle. "And why the hell didn't they take it off and have
done with it! I could have managed a tin foot," he said furiously.
Then, as though a useless foot were not infirmity enough, all the
more unpleasant reactions from the change from an active life to a
sedentary one crowded in: thrombosis, gout. Then came the
mental retreat.

She said, "You know that to that question there is only one
answer. You did the right thing."

"If you say so."

Hurrying, indeed almost slithering, downstairs, Kathy thought
bitterly, At the utmost, I was out of the house for three minutes!

Nico was in the kitchen, wearing an aggrieved expression.

"Well, now can you look?"

She accepted the rebuke meekly, actually refraining from pro-
ceeding with her pastry making, sitting down and giving full attention while he demonstrated the wonders of his new possession.
Obviously a very superior article, better than the one she had been
saving up for to give him at Christmas.

"Which draw was it?" There were so many just at this season.

"Oxfam. The one with the fifty pence tickets."

"It certainly is a beauty! Everybody must be pea-green with
envy."

"I thought of that. So I made the least display. . . . I waited till
nearly everybody had gone. Mr. Soames called my number two or
three times and then said, 'I think 742 must be an outsider.' Then I
went up with my ticket. And then I rode straight home."

"How extremely tactful!" She would have liked to kiss and hug
him, to run her hand through his bright, crisp curls, but she restrained herself. He was eleven. And the way widows ruined their
only sons was notorious.

"Everybody will know tomorrow."

"Umm. Well, I rather thought I wouldn't take it to school until after the hols. Christmas present. See? Or would that be a lie?"

"Only a white one. As a matter of fact I did intend to get you—nothing like such a splendid one, of course. And Nico . . . I was going to ask you, as a token of gratitude, not to go on that busy bit of road until you've had more practice. So not taking it to school just yet suits me very well."

"I got on fine this afternoon. Still, all right."

"Your tea's on the dresser."

He went to inspect it. "Gosh! My favourite. Drumstick. School dinner was lousy."

"What a change!"

He grinned and gnawed away at the chicken leg like a puppy.

She finished the pastry and covered two pies which, with a square of gingerbread and sponge cake, filled the oven. Such petty, indeed trivial economies had long ago become second nature.

Miss Ayling rang her bell, and this time she had forestalled an accident.

"There you are. You see, you are getting better."

"I wish I could believe that." Professional false jollity had little effect on her genuine gloom.

From across the landing Mr. Fraser shouted, "Look at that! No picture at all."

"You've been fiddling with it again. I do wish you wouldn't."

"You know I should be much better in my own home. I could have my bed downstairs and get into the garden. No bloody stairs." Stairs defeated him. On the level, supported by a stick with four feet, he could limp and shuffle fairly well. "I want to go home. Can't you arrange it?"

"I'm afraid not."

"You could if you weren't such a hard bitch."

"When you are yourself again, you'll remember that you sold your house a year ago."

"I was not consulted."

Let that pass. She righted the last control.

"There you are. Bright and clear."

He now liked children's programmes. For him a daily *Blue Peter* would have been ideal.

The focus of his mind shifted again. "May I ask what's for supper?"

"Scrambled eggs."

"And very nice too."

Downstairs Nico had upended the bike and was going over each glittering spoke with a duster.

"Can I keep it in the old scullery?"

"I think that would be the best place. You'll have to move it soon. It's Pat's night, and I shall want to get to the freezer."

"Right! Mum. Don't tell her about it. She'd only sneer and say it was just my luck. She doesn't like me."

"There I think you are mistaken. Though I must admit that you've never done much to endear yourself to her."

He stilled the whirring wheel and said in an unchildlike way, "I only approve of people who approve of me."

"Don't you find that a bit limiting?"

"I don't mind your teasing me. But she thinks I'm spoiled."

"She'll think so all the more if she thinks I gave you that splendid job."

She withdrew the pies and the sponge cake and placed in the oven the mutton-chop casserole for the day after tomorrow. It was almost amusing to think that thirteen years ago, in this very kitchen, she'd taught herself to cook, aided by a book designed for beginners.

She whisked the eggs for scrambling, cut the bread for toast. Set the trays. Then, after a second's hesitation, she took from a cupboard a bottle of whisky and a glass not much larger than those used for medicine. She set it on Mr. Fraser's tray, thinking, Poor old boy, he tries so hard to economize, and what pleasure has he left? She wished she could so easily provide a tiny treat for Miss Ayling, but she had probably never been a drinker and now seemed to take little interest in food.

She heard Pat's Mini arrive and went to the door, ready to help with the haulage, wondering as she did so how she could possibly manage if this tried good friend had not offered to do the marketing when the good little village store finally closed its doors.

Thirteen years before, when she and Hugh settled in Lane's

End, Nettleton had been a self-sufficient little village with a butcher, a post office and general store, and a school for children under eleven. It had also, she thought with a twinge, had a very useful garage which belonged, in part at least, to Hugh Dawson. All was changed now.

Two laden carrier bags, a smaller one, and Pat was still diving into the car.

"Put that down!" Pat said in a voice of authority. "You take this. And one carrier. Leave the rest for me."

"This" was undoubtedly a bottle.

Laden, they struggled into the warm kitchen, and Pat immediately struck a wrong note.

"Where's your dear boy? He could have helped."

"Homework, I think. But we managed, didn't we? Isn't it cold?"

"Too cold for snow, as they say. Still, it's doing its best."

Together, not speaking much, they disposed of a week's provisions: meat and fish into the freezer, other stuffs into the larder. They had always worked well together, even when they were both student nurses in a past as remote as the building of the Pyramids.

"Pat, you know I can never thank you. . . . The coffee is just about ready."

"Leave it for a moment. I've brought something to try out on you. Get a couple of glasses. . . ."

She reached for the bottle which Kathy had carried in and stripped off its wrapping, revealing a squat green glass bottle, with a golden label and a neck capped with gold foil.

"It's the very latest 'in' drink. Low alcohol content. I think you could drink half a bottle and still face a breathalyser. But it has a kick. It says it contains herbs. I wonder what, exactly."

She poured as she spoke a clear, faintly green liquid.

Before she could taste it, Kathy heard Miss Ayling's bell and, unguarded for a second, said, "God! It isn't three quarters of an hour. . . ."

When she came back, she feigned an animation that she did not feel. "Well, that's that. I've given her her Nembutal." She took up her glass and sipped.

"Lovely. Somehow I expected mint. A kick, you say . . . Lord, do you remember when we thought Pimms Number One was

harmless lemonade? Drunk as muck. A wonder we weren't both
sacked on the spot."

"Think what they would have lost! Look, Kathy, at the risk of
offending you again . . ."

"But, Pat, you never did. You argued and advised. But even
when . . . I mean, when you said I was a bloody fool, I wasn't
offended."

"You are about to be. Do you realize that sirloin is two-fifty a
pound and even stewing steak one-seventy-five. Fish goes up every week. Cheese, and you get through three pounds a week, is
one fifty. Old people shouldn't be fed like fighting cocks."

"It's the only pleasure they have, Pat."

"That is quite beside the point. Do you know, quite a modest
bed-and-breakfast place in Baildon charges seven fifty a night?
And, besides food, think what your old crocks are getting: practically round-the-clock attention, expert attention. And you should
think, too, what you could be earning. During that 'flu epidemic,
we had to fall back on chance help. I drew a girl absolutely unqualified—she'd failed the first exam twice. Her English was quite
unintelligible. She romped off with eighteen pounds."

Either the slight alcohol content or the mysterious herb in the
pretty drink with the pretty name—Green-Gold—was at work in
Kathy. Hitherto her reaction to Pat's mild bullying had been a
passive acceptance combined with an obstinate adherence to her
own way. This evening she said, with some firmness, "There is
another way of looking at it. Here almost all expenses—food, heating, rates, repairs—are legitimate expenses, tax deductible. I know
that just at the moment, I've got myself clobbered with two cases
needing attention all the time and both hard up, but that can't last
forever. It was just bad luck. And look at what I have achieved.
Kept my home—even reduced the mortgage a little. And above
all, *prevented Nico from being a latchkey child.*"

"Melstead Junior School has been known to take boys at six—in
exceptional circumstances. I found out for you."

"I know. I thought it was too young. And I wanted to keep the
house because . . . Oh, God! It can't be true! A Nembutal should
hold her for two hours."

"I'll go!" Pat sprang to her feet and bounced out of the room.

Kathy thought, We're both thirty-one, but she still moves like a girl. I don't. I hurry, but I have no spring left.

Going up the stairs, Pat knew that if Kathy had been allowed to finish the sentence, she would have said, "Hugh put so much of himself into it." Which was true; Lane's End had been a neglected wreck, long empty but cheap. And Pat had seen it grow into a thing of beauty, had even been allowed to slosh about with paint and distemper. For the pretty girl's marriage had not resulted, as sometimes happened, with the discarding of the plain girl friend. Pat had always been welcome at Lane's End.

And now she was doing her best to repay. On two occasions she had taken charge so that Kathy could have a holiday, once to take Nico to the seaside, once to London, a whirlwind visit: British Museum; Natural History Museum; Changing the Guard; Hampton Court.

With Pat—brisk, competent Sister Grimwade—temporarily in charge and Green-Gold exercising its magic, Kathy could enjoy a moment of real relaxation. The only trouble was that in such a state memories would take over.

Happiness for so little time.

I blame that bit of new road! Everybody admits now that mental stress can bring on a coronary. The bit of new road, nothing very much, not even a proper bypass, had diverted traffic from the through-village road and ruined the garage first of all; for people could still *walk* to the store, the butcher's, and the post office. A garage depended upon cars, and naturally they took the new road, saving a few minutes. Saved for what? Whatever they saved, was it worth a young man being worried into a coronary at the early age of thirty? God, if ever we meet up, You'll have a bit of explaining to do to me! My faults may be many and various, but I've never yet been brutal. . . . How daft! She had relinquished all belief long before that. Reading about the eighty—was it eighty million? I was always so bad at figures, say a vast number of Jews—deliberately and often painfully exterminated. Why not a thunderbolt?

Pat came down with her buoyant step.

"Poor old thing. She really is incontinent. But I've fixed her. And of course the old devil roared as soon as he heard me. So I went in. Kathy, I was horrified. He was trying to light his pipe. Striking matches one after the other and dropping them, some still alight. I simply took them away." She set the box on the table with a decided little rap.

"It's the pipe," Kathy explained. "He is trying to economize, so he gave up cigars, and can't seem to get his pipe started. He has set fire to the rug a few times."

"Do you want to be burned in your bed?"

"I always take away his pipe and his matches last thing at night."

Pat refilled the glasses.

"He should be at Waddington. In a ward with similar cases and under constant supervision."

"The very thing he dreads most. I couldn't do it to him. He's such a brave old boy. I'll admit, if he became bedridden, I couldn't cope. He's too heavy."

"And not likely to lose weight, the way you feed him."

That reminded Kathy that she had not yet paid Pat for the shopping. Then, as she handled the money, a thought struck her. She would not now have to spend her hoard on a bicycle. Of course she would give Nico another present, but nothing like so expensive. She'd have a little money to splash around. And splash it she would.

"Have you seen the Christmas rota yet?"

"I have. And it couldn't be worse. For me. Off on Christmas Eve, on for two days, off for one . . . Which makes York impossible. Could you do with me on Christmas Eve?"

"Do with? I'd love it. And we'll keep Christmas that day. With turkey."

"Turkey? Have you come into money?"

"No. At least . . . Well, let's say I've been spared an expense which I was facing. You might call it a windfall."

"Perhaps it's a sign that your bad spell is over. I hope so with all my heart."

Pat's idea of better luck for Kathy would be the removal—not death—of her present residents and the reverting of Lane's End to what it had been in the early days. Not a nursing home, just a place where people who needed some care, some nursing, could come and be looked after. Pat could remember when Kathy's patients could get downstairs, sit in the garden, eat at a table.

Nico said, "Mum, is it all right with you if I get a holiday job?"

"That would rather depend upon what it was. And upon whether, at your age, you are allowed to take a job."

"Just for a day or two. Casual. Obliging a friend. It only means riding around on my bike—which I should be doing anyway."

"Where? Sorry, Nico. Not in Baildon. I truly do dread that bit of new road—until you've had more practice."

"It's Clevely. Just delivering things, extra Christmas things, for my friend Joe's dad. At the shop. Joe generally does it, but he's had his appendix out. So I said . . . I said I'd ask you." She heard the slight hesitation and deduced that he was already committed. And she could find no real fault with the arrangement.

Clevely had fared better than Nettleton. It had been unaffected by that stretch of new road, which had strangled its neighbour. In fact it had gained something. Several real old diehards now trudged to Clevely, taking a short cut through Layer Wood, in order to cash their Old Age pension vouchers or buy a postal order.

"It sounds all right to me, darling."

"And it counts as a social service."

That was a valid argument, for the disappearance of the errand boy, that cheerful, whistling bringer-of-goods, had inflicted great hardship.

Nico earned, incredibly, a pound a day. And there were what were called "fringe benefits" too. Joe's dad, whose name was Weatherall, was always offering bargains and occasionally downright gifts.

"I always look in the tub where the bargains are," Nico explained. "And being early, I get first pick. Some aren't real bargains—down at the bottom, I mean. But all I could see wrong with this was a scratched label."

Small things. But Kathy could imagine the tub, "TODAY'S BARGAIN," awaiting the unwary and being inspected first by a hawk-eyed eleven year old.

In addition, as the season of goodwill drew nearer, people were inclined to tip the handsome, smiling boy who delivered what for them would have meant heavy loads. Nico became bitten with the desire to earn, speculating as to whether, in the New Year, he could find a regular Saturday job. "Or I might baby-sit," he said thoughtfully. "I could see that brats didn't murder each other *and* do my homework at the same time."

Christmas Eve being Pat's Christmas, they celebrated on that day, with a formal exchange of presents as soon as the visitor arrived. This year there was a bit of a contretemps.

Pat presented Kathy with a pretty pink cardigan and what was obviously a bottle.

"Is that Green-Gold?" Nico demanded, glaring. Pat nodded. "Bugger all!" Nico said. "Just what I'd got her." Pat had left the other bottle behind, and Nico had asked, "Do you like that stuff?" and "Is it your favourite?"

With many people the swear word would not have mattered, especially followed by the explanation, but Pat looked severely disapproving.

Kathy thought, Out of his poor little earnings. And could have wept. Instead she said gaily, "But, darling, what could be nicer? I shall be able to have a Green-Gold every evening till Easter. Thanks a million, both of you."

Kathy had bought a new five year diary for Pat and a small transistor radio for Nico. Both these things could be found in a catalogue and ordered by a telephone call to the local agent. Pat now gave Nico a very superior Biro.

Miss Ayling rang her bell. "I'll go," Pat said. "You stay with that turkey."

"Are you angry with me, too?"

"Not irretrievably. Though it's not a very nice word. I know I swear a bit myself, but I try to draw the line."

"Anyway, remember, mine is the one with the bow on it."

"That should make it taste much better. But, Nico, you shouldn't have spent so much. Too generous."

"Well, I got a bit of discount. Mr. Weatherall has a licence, you know."

When Pat returned, making the grimace that informed Kathy that the bell had rung too late, Nico gave her a bottle of bath essence and apologized rather prettily, Kathy thought. So goodwill was restored and reigned for the rest of the day.

The New Year came in. The new term began. And when it was four days old, the telephone rang. A man, asking for Mrs. Dawson.

It was Mr. Mortimer, Head of the far-too-large comprehensive which Nico attended. He wondered if Mrs. Dawson could come to see him. As soon as possible.

"Is it urgent?"

"*I* think so."

"I'll come as soon as I can arrange transport—and somebody to look after my patients. May I ring you back?"

Lane's End, taking only two patients, was not governed by the rule applying to larger establishments—that at all times a qualified person should be in charge. There was in the village a reliable, kindly woman called Mrs. Wade who in the past had obliged Kathy for brief spells—almost all connected with Nico, for Kathy, in addition to not wanting him to be a latchkey child, had been anxious to be, and be seen to be, a Good Parent, turning up at prize givings and sports days. Mrs. Wade was willing to oblige once more, this very afternoon, from two-thirty till five.

Kathy rang the school and said she could be there at three.

"That will suit splendidly."

"Can you tell me what it is about?"

"I should prefer not to discuss it on the telephone. Three o'clock, then."

Now for the taxi place in Baildon. A girl with a very bad head cold informed her that there was a surcharge outside the two mile limit.

Kathy dressed carefully and, for the first time since the sports day last summer, really looked at her reflection, and decided that she looked awful. Pat had said now and again, You can't go on like this. You're heading for a crack-up. God, you're thinner than ever! And things of that kind. And now she thought, No wonder! I look fifty and a wreck at that.

Rattling along in the taxi, she was not unduly worried about this interview. Mr. Mortimer knew that Nico was due to go to Melstead in September, and unlike many men in his position, he did not resent the losing of a reasonably bright boy at twelve. What he wanted to discuss with her was, she felt certain, Nico's prospects of passing Common Entrance—even the modified form applying to boys coming from State schools, who knew no Latin. He would probably suggest a little extra coaching in maths. And that could have been done on the phone. Except that the man was a born fusser. It was a curious thing, but she'd noticed that the tendency to fuss varied according to size; the smaller the person, the more the fuss—it was the same with dogs.

And hadn't somebody said that all men eventually achieve a position beyond their ability. She'd always felt that about Mr. Mortimer.

This time he fussed hardly at all. He said, "I'll come straight to the point, Mrs. Dawson. A week before the end of last term, a well spoken boy went into Grafton's to choose a bicycle which his mother was to give him for Christmas. He chose one and then asked could he try it. The manager agreed. The boy mounted and rode away. Naturally the . . . theft was reported. Next morning a policeman came—in plain clothes, of course—and inspected all the cycles here. The stolen one was not amongst them. Nor could Grafton's manager, invited to do so, identify the boy. Of the six boys absent on that morning, one was in hospital, one confined to bed at home, and four already on holiday. It looked—and certainly we all hoped so—as though the boy who stole that bicycle was not a member of this school. However this morning Grafton's manager asked permission to inspect the cycle shed. The stolen cycle was there, and your son . . . Mrs. Dawson! Mrs. Dawson! Are you all right?"

All right in the sense that I am not dead or unconscious. All wrong that I am in a state of total shock. I can't speak or even make a reassuring movement with my hand.

This is paralysis.

This is the crack-up that Pat predicted.

She had closed her eyes, and the darkness behind the lowered lids threatened, not unpleasantly, to spread and engulf her. It would be so easy to give up.

But Nico needed her now as much as ever in the course of his life. With a great effort she forced open her eyes, saw Mr. Mortimer's face, a mask of concern.

And if I can move my eyes, I can speak.

"I'm all right. A trifle overwhelmed at the realization of my own stupidity. Poor Nico! What he said was substantially true. I did intend to give him the bicycle. I told him to choose it. I should have sent a cheque next day, but I forgot. I'm naturally forgetful, and just at the moment entirely responsible for two very sick people. In fact," she glanced at her watch, "I should be getting back. So I wonder . . . If I give you a cheque now, would you be so kind as to give it to Nico and tell him to call at Grafton's on his way home?"

She opened her bag, took out her chequebook and Biro. Oh, hand, be steady! Writing in what she could, she missed the dubious, almost suspicious, look directed at her by Mr. Mortimer. There was nothing actually wrong with her story; it was in her reaction that the discrepancy lay. Why had she almost fainted? Come to that, why had the boy almost wept?

A certain amount of cynicism about boys, about parents was the natural result of his long experience. It did not seem impossible to him that mother and son had conspired over this matter. Even so this was certainly the most easy and pleasant solution, satisfying everyone.

He thought that he would feel more certain if Mrs. Dawson completed the cheque correctly. For surely people conspiring to cheat would know the worth of their loot.

Kathy looked up. "Do you happen to know the price, Mr. Mortimer? If Nico ever mentioned it, I've forgotten."

"The price of that particular model is one hundred and forty-two pounds. Grafton's manager mentioned it more than once. The incident itself made him appear careless—and I think he gets commission on sales."

She filled in words and figures and mustered the light, the appropriate remark: "For a bike! Why, even ten years ago, a decent second-hand car . . ."

"Yes, indeed. The inflation is quite frightening."

She closed her bag and stood up. Knees not too steady. But she managed one last gesture. "I am so sorry to have made so much trouble for you all. And poor Nico must have been terribly upset. I wonder, could you possibly make it look as though I had not had to be prodded into remembering? If you could just say that I did remember and sent the cheque along. He'd understand."

"I think I might just about manage that," Mr. Mortimer said. He'd managed more tricky things in his time.

Had the interview concerned anything less deadly, Kathy had intended to telephone Pat, trying first the hospital, then the little flat in Friargate. She could have cadged a cup of tea, possibly even a lift home. But she couldn't face Pat just now.

The question was, Could she face Nico?

Her son, her dearly beloved, had stolen a bicycle. And probably a number of lesser items. What about the things out of that Bargain Tub? And the extravagant Christmas presents. All that brief happiness, smirched and smeared.

Nico is a thief. And I have connived. And he will know. He's no fool.

Young thieves, unexposed, unreprimanded, went on and became worse. Became train robbers . . .

The awful thing was that she knew that Nico had meant well. He was too close to her and too observant not to notice that she was short of funds and couldn't really afford the bicycle she had as good as promised.

Would it have been better to have done as Pat suggested, let the house go, let Nico go, and gone out herself to earn a steady living?

She defended herself feebly. Is it my fault that I just happened to land myself with two patients who simply can't pay more? And who, because of their pitiable state, can't be got rid of?

It *is* my fault that I have let slip incautious words about rising prices, about not being able to afford . . . But to whom else could she have said such things?

And did all children whose parents admitted to being hard up go out and steal bicycles?

She was back before she had expected to be. Mrs. Wade said, "Just in time for a cuppa." It was a quarter past four. Nico would be on his way home.

Mrs. Wade said, "They've both gone downhill a lot since I was last here. Her bell rings every twenty minutes—and too late, more often than not at that. And he didn't know me—he thought I'd come to take him home."

"I know. It's all very sad," Kathy said, but her mind was not upon Miss Ayling and her incontinence, or Mr. Fraser with his delusions. They'd both had their day. She was thinking of Nico, now on his way home. And how to be greeted?

Mrs. Wade said, "How you manage I just do not know. And, to be honest, you don't look all that perky yourself. . . . And, you know, if you want me, you have only to ask."

"I know, and I'm most extremely grateful to you."

"Not," Mrs. Wade observed shrewdly, "that you look any better for your little outing. In fact worse."

"I've been house-bound so long that I find that outer world completely exhausting."

Mrs. Wade collected the upstairs trays, dealt with Miss Ayling once more, and then prepared to leave. "I know I said I could stay till five, but it really wasn't very convenient." It was then just twenty to five. Nico would be home any minute now, and Kathy still had not the faintest idea of what to say to him. He'd know that she knew, and however unreproachful and understanding she was, the old easy camaraderie between them would be gone forever.

She washed the tea things, reset the trays, put Nico's plate in its usual place, and now it was five o'clock, and he was late. Ashamed to come home. Or had he . . . ? No, that was too melodramatic a thought! Boys didn't. Nico wouldn't. Yet one did read of cases of children committing suicide over less drastic things than being found out in a theft and some lies. And she knew that under the good health and exuberance lay a sensitive boy.

In a frenzy she telephoned the school and asked for Mr. Mortimer only to be told that he'd been gone for half an hour. Could the voice give her his home number? The voice said, "He's in the book!" So indeed he was, but nobody answered the phone when she rang.

What next? Police? They'd laugh. Silly old cow in a tizzy because a boy was twenty minutes late home from school! All right, let them laugh. She could at least ask if an accident had been reported.

She'd dialled the first nine when she heard him in the scullery. She turned hastily from the dresser where the phone stood, back to the table where the supper fish awaited attention. She must minimize the whole affair by not seeming too much upset.

He came in reluctantly, dragging his feet and—after one furtive glance—avoiding her eye. He looked awful, very pale, dejection writ large in every line of him. Even his hair, always with him—as with his father—a sure barometer of health or otherwise, had changed, the curls lying flat, their brightness dulled.

And suddenly inspiration sat on her shoulder.

"Hullo, fellow clot! They fooled us properly, didn't they? The people who organized that damned raffle should be thoroughly ashamed of themselves. It was nothing but a cheap, low-down advertising stunt." She heard her own voice, a trifle too highly pitched, otherwise all right. "Making it look as though that bike was the prize, when it was just a ten pound voucher off the price. And I'll bet they slapped ten pounds on before they took it off."

She had seen a pot plant, flagging for lack of water, revive almost visibly when given what it needed. Nico was making just such a recovery. The hangdog look fell away, and he was looking at her, a bit baffled but interested. She turned over the inoffensive fillet of plaice and dashed breadcrumbs at it and went on with well simulated anger: "When I heard, you could have knocked me down with a crowbar! I've heard of some dirty tricks in my time, but never a worse one. And wasn't it lucky that I had been saving and could send the cheque right away? I mean it could have happened to somebody truly poor. I wonder what they would have done then."

"Taken it back," Nico said. "Mum . . . I am truly sorry. I know it was more than you meant to pay."

"You can say that again! But never mind. You've got a better bike. Your tea's on the dresser."

He went towards it, less like a boy who had had a lousy school dinner than a boy who had not eaten at all.

"Oh, good. Cold sausage. My favourite."

"Lunch lousy, as usual?"

"I didn't go in. I'd just heard, you see. About all that money . . . But, Mum, I swear, I will pay you back. . . ."

"So I should hope. With compound interest."

He threw a smile, a bit watery but still a smile.

She sat down suddenly and lighted a cigarette with unsteady fingers. She knew that she had done everything wrong. Her conduct was downright immoral, open to criticism from every quarter. But she was not penitent. For out of a touch-and-go situation she had retrieved something fragile as a bubble and of infinite value—a happy relationship.

4

God's own elect

"It would be"—Mrs. Harper's fingers hovered above the keys. Parents must be coaxed, not coerced—"desirable for all girls taking part in the concert to wear dark skirts and white, short sleeved blouses."

Afterwards she could not for the life of her think why she had stipulated short sleeves. Perhaps a memory of her own girlhood when short sleeves meant summer with all its accompanying delights. And she wanted the concert to be a joyous occasion. Fifty years and rather more than her share of misfortune had not diminished her inclination to take joy in little things.

The Jacob Wise School for Girls had never gone in for uniform as had so many other schools when upgraded from elementary to secondary modern. The ideas behind uniform—identification with and pride in one's school and a desire to conform—were dead, and parents considered uniform expensive. Not that the Jacob Wise served an impoverished area; transistor sets, expensive cameras, and new bicycles abounded.

Fifty copies of Mrs. Harper's letter went out, and reaction was minimal. A decently written letter saying, "I am sorry, Angela doesn't own a skirt of any colour, and I have spent all I can afford on her winter outfit."

Well, that was easily solved. One of what Mrs. Harper mentally dubbed "the good families" would lend, or at a pinch the things could be bought, listed as Scenery for Concert, which, Mrs. Harper thought with a slight smile, in a way it was.

The other repercussion took the form of a personal visit from a parent, a father, who tapped on Mrs. Harper's door and marched in, saying with that faint air of aggression often cultivated to disguise shyness, "My name's Bolton."

She greeted him by name and asked him to sit down. He was a small man, very thin, rather pale. Even his eyes were pale, and he appeared to be regarding her with disfavour. Inside her shell of competent and esteemed headmistress, there lurked a soul sensitive to any form of criticism, and she wondered if her appearance displeased him or whether something had been said or done for which he held her responsible.

"I've come about this. The letter you sent. It was the first I'd heard about the concert. Neither Deborah nor Miriam had said a word about it."

Bolton. Deborah. Miriam. The biblical names clicked in her mind. Very well behaved neat girls with plaits. Both musical.

"Perhaps," she said placatingly, "there was no time. The final decision was difficult. So many girls with some talent, and our stage . . ."

"Stage?"

"A platform, really. With very limited space."

"There was time to send this letter. I'm inclined to think they didn't want me to know. They knew I shouldn't approve. Is it a public concert?"

"Oh, no, Mr. Bolton. You could call it a family occasion. Miss Wentworth, who for many years has taught music here, is retiring. The concert—just pupils and relatives—is in the nature of a farewell party."

Rather early because almost immediately Miss Wentworth would be busy with the carols and the Nativity play.

"No play acting?"

"Oh, no. One of your daughters sings very well. The other plays
. . . I think, the recorder."

She was condemned in his eyes—and in her own—for lack of
exactitude. She said, "I leave everything on the musical side to
Miss Wentworth."

"But you wrote this. Then can you tell me what does it matter
how long sleeves are?"

"It doesn't matter. I was probably thinking that white or light
coloured blouses are summer wear, and so have short sleeves.
Does the length of sleeve matter to you?"

"It does indeed. To me short sleeves mean indecent exposure."

"He said it so solemnly," Mrs. Harper said, reporting this gem.
"Bearing in mind what the term usually means, I almost laughed."

"I probably should have done. Or asked him not to use obscene
language on school premises," Miss Hogarth said.

They were sitting together, sipping dry martinis, in Julia Hogarth's supremely comfortable home. Julia was that rare thing, a
teacher with ample private means.

"There was something rather intimidating about him," Kate
Harper said. "Quite small but intense."

"I've always felt sorry for those girls. For one thing I don't think
they're properly fed. They seem to me to subsist on lentils,
oatmeal, and potatoes."

"How on earth do you know that?"

"Well, as you know, I don't take orders from Whitehall. I still
hold that children should learn the alphabet—how else can they
use a telephone directory? And I still set the old fashioned essay.
'My Family.' 'How I spent last weekend.' That kind of thing. I learn
a lot. . . . Pa Bolton, for instance, is a religious maniac."

"Jehovah's Witness?"

"No. Something far more way out. The Elect of God . . . Something like that. And most exclusive. In the whole of Baildon there
are only fourteen members. They meet in the Bolton parlour, and
Pa Bolton expounds on the will of God as revealed to him on his
latest visit to Mount Sinai. Sorry, Kate."

She had forgotten that Kate, in religion as in so many things, was
conformist, went to church at least once a month, and greatly
admired the rector of Clevely, the village in which she lived.

"There's no copyright on the word 'Sinai,'" Kate said. "And, anyway, I don't think you could offend me, even if you tried."

It was true. There existed between these two women a sound tried friendship, based upon a mutual respect. They were different in almost every way, in temperament, background, circumstances—even in appearance. But they'd taken to each other at their first meeting, and that was eight years ago.

"Let me top you up," Julia said.

"Thanks. Better not. They do fuss so if I'm late."

Julia thought, The old people may fuss, but I bet Eddie nags. Poor old Kate! She lifted a white bowl in which an azalea was growing, a neat shrubby plant with some pink flowers already in bloom and a mass of buds. Amongst her many other blessings, she could count a heated greenhouse and an old gardener with two green thumbs.

"For me? How perfectly lovely! Like a little rose tree. Really you are too kind."

"And don't worry about those blouses. I'll go to the trusty Marks and buy a couple."

"Oh, but suppose Mr. Bolton comes to the concert?"

"He won't. On Thursday there is a prayer meeting."

Kate entered her home by way of the back door, which gave upon a lobby where dim old clothes hung upon pegs, and footwear, some long ago discarded, stood about. She thought for the thousandth time that she should do something about it, make a clean sweep, but she never had time, and to change anything would mortally offend Eddie's father, always an arbitrary old man and now living entirely in the past. He still knew Eddie, but always spoke to him as though he were about ten years old and not overbright. Kate he affected not to recognize, often calling her "that woman," and Kate had a suspicion that as such he had always regarded her, even when she entered the house as a bride, twenty-two years ago.

She crossed the kitchen, very cold, and pushed open the door of the general living room, which was at least warm. She was actually not very late and usually at this time they had the TV on. Tonight it was silent, and she sensed a distinct atmosphere. Only Kate's own mother managed any kind of a greeting. She said, "Hullo, dear," but in a voice that spoke of impending complaint.

Eddie eyed the azalea and said, "Offering from Rich Bitch?"

He hated and resented Julia, but in an oddly impersonal way. He really hated all Kate's outside life, necessary though it was, being the mainstay of the household, but Julia, whom he had met only once, served as a focus.

"Julia gave it to me, yes," Kate said and cleared a space on the cluttered table. It was amazing what two old people and a cripple needed always within hand's reach. There lay Old Mr. Harper's three pipes, a bunch of pipe-cleaners, the knife with which he sometimes savagely scraped the pipe bowls, the big ugly ashtray and a box of Swan vestas, the only match he would use. Kate's mother had contributed a piece of knitting, a sewing box, a shirt which she had been mending, and half a bar of milk chocolate. On Eddie's end of the table were a radio, two paperbacks with lurid covers, a box of tissues, and two bottles of pills.

The table also held things common to all, kept there to save unnecessary steps. Salt, pepper, a bottle of the sauce without which old Mr. Harper thought any meal incomplete—lately he'd taken to lavishing it on milk pudding or jam tart. There were also four table mats, pretty ones, decorated with Redouté roses, and four table napkins of puckered, easily washed nylon, each in its distinctive ring.

Eddie said, "The TV's gone again."

Kate's mother said, "It was all right. He *would* fiddle with it!" A sharp, accusative glance identified the offender.

Eddie instantly said, "He was doing his best."

Kate's mother rose and said, "I made a shepherd's pie. I'd better look at it." With a jerk of her head she indicated that Kate should follow her into the kitchen, and once in that chilly sanctuary, she said, "Really, Kate. Something must be done. He went wandering off this morning. *With his flies undone!* I had to go after him, in my slippers. And it rained. One day I shall catch my death of cold. He should be put away."

"Oh, Mother, don't! You know how Eddie would feel. And you know that I did make enquiries."

"Not very diligent ones. I don't think you brought enough pressure to bear. Nobody can tell me that in these days there is no provision made for somebody in his state."

"He's harmless. And the distance he can walk now, he'd be unlikely to meet anybody."

Lane End Farm was rightly named. It lay two miles from the village. Except for the post office van occasionally, and Kate regularly, the lane was virtually unused.

Mrs. Marlow went to the oven, stooped with some difficulty— she was far too fat—inspected her pie, adjusted the switch a little, and stood up.

"Kate, I have to say this. I'm reaching the end of my tether. When I came to make my home here—to help you, as I thought—I did not expect Eddie to be so downright disagreeable and ungrateful, or his father to go demented. I'm seventy-three. . . ."

And although she accused Kate of not trying hard enough in Mr. Harper's case, she had noticed everything with the sharp eye of self-interest. There might be no place for demented old men, but for people able to manage on their own—people like herself— there was accommodation which sounded delightful. Little flats, right in the centre of Baildon. And with a warden.

Kate said, "I know. I think you've been marvellous to stick it so long. The time has certainly come for you to consider yourself."

In Kate's mind, the thought arose—and was quickly dismissed: Has she ever done otherwise?

Kate's reaction to what was indeed a threat was not what her mother expected. No tears, no pleadings, or protestations of gratitude.

"And how would you manage?"

"Get another Mrs. Pearson. Perhaps Mrs. Pearson might come back. She should be over the change now!"

That had been Mrs. Pearson's stated reason for retirement, soon after Mrs. Marlow installed herself. Before that, Mrs. Pearson had come from Muchanger, taking a short cut through Layer Wood, and looked after Eddie and old Mr. Harper. She'd managed the old man very well too, with a rough jocularity, almost a hint of flirtatiousness. If in her time he'd appeared unbuttoned, she'd have said, "And now what do you think you're up to, you old rascal?"

From the living room Eddie called, "Kate! Kate!" and as she

hurried back he said, still nastily, "I suppose your rich friend plied you with champagne, so you don't need sherry. But we do."

"Of course. I was just about to get it."

Old Mr. Harper took up the word.

"Sherry? Yes, I like sherry."

She poured three glasses, abstaining herself, since she was watching her weight. Despite hard work and a multitude of worries, unless she was careful, she'd end up like her mother.

Eddie said, "Take a look at that, Kate." He nodded towards the TV set. "There was a programme I wanted, later on."

What fiddling about could put out of action, more fiddling about could restore, and suddenly the screen came alive, and there was a blast of noise.

"Oh, God!" Eddie said. Kate lowered the sound, and into the quiet the old man said; "When I was out this morning, I saw three gulls on Four Acre. To be so far inland so early is a sign of rough weather."

It was such a rational statement. Really you couldn't dub him idiot and consign him to the one place which seemed willing to accept him.

"Four Acre?" Eddie said. "It was put down to beet this year, wasn't it?"

"And poisoned with yellow virus. I never saw worse."

Between them they'd farmed the two hundred acres, not very profitably—which was why Kate had kept her job and deferred the business of childbearing. The place simply gulped down the money. She'd paid for the new roof, the installation of electricity, some proper plumbing.

This year, next year, sometime, never, as children chanted counting plum stones. In her case, never.

She had actually paid for the new tractor, which was to make such a vast difference. Eddie drove it just a fraction of an inch too near the edge of a ditch, the thing had lurched.

Oh, why think of it now? Surely in twelve years . . .

Give the old man his due, while she had worked away to provide the wherewithal, he'd dragged Eddie about from specialist to specialist; he was indomitable, or his mind refused to accept the fact that a man in the prime of life, whose legs had not been injured at all, would never walk again without crutches. Near miraculous operations were performed in New York and in Switzerland; there was a blacksmith who combined bone setting and faith healing in Devon. To help defray the astronomical cost of some of these expeditions, the old man had sold some land. But not the whole. As a final, touching proof of his faith in Eddie's ultimate recovery, he had leased the remainder and some outbuildings on a very short lease—therefore a very low rent. "It'll be waiting for you, Eddie, when you wake up one morning as good as new."

But the strain and the repeated disappointments told on him. He'd begun to go queer. And it might be an unkind thought—because it could be mere coincidence—he'd grown much worse since the coming of Mrs. Marlow and the consequent departure of Mrs. Pearson.

Mrs. Marlow's attitude towards him was unfortunate because it was ambivalent. He was a silly old lunatic whose proper place was the asylum—and yet she held him responsible for what he said and did.

It is not surprising that Kate took refuge in her work from this troubled household and was, as Julia Hogarth often said, over responsive to ideas suggested by authority. In fact if someone had dreamed up the notion that all good headmistresses should stand on their heads for ten minutes every morning, Kate would have done her best to comply.

And if the JW was a temple of refuge, Julia Hogarth was its high priestess. Irreverent, sardonic, independent as a cat, she was just what Kate needed.

Even before she received her astounding legacy, Julia had shown signs of being better off than the average. A more expensive car, a mink coat, a very expensive flat. And holidays well outside the range of any package deal.

Then one day she'd said, "People will never cease to surprise me. I once dared to light a cigarette in my Uncle Timothy's presence, and he never spoke to me again. Now he's dead and has left me all his hoard. Quite a bit, even in present day's debased coinage."

Kate thought, And now she will go, and I shall be bereft.

She was on good terms with all the members of her staff—it took a bit of doing, calling for tact and good humour, with the emphasis on the *good.* Humour was singularly lacking.

Julie said, "And now I can buy The Croft and make it habitable."

Kate said, "Julia, I warn you. Old houses can be hell. I've done my best with Lane End. There are islands of warmth. But long stretches in winter when you need to call out the St. Bernards with their little brandy flasks on their collars."

"That I will try to avoid," Julia said. She did not mention resignation. And once she had said, "I quite like bridge and golf and skiing, but I couldn't devote my life to them."

"What about marriage?" For Julia was still young and very pretty. And now rich.

"That would be mixing pleasure with happiness," Julia said. "Fatal combination! Anyway, I happen to *like* teaching. We sow the fields and scatter. . . . Stony places, thorny places—but there is the occasional fertile patch." So she had stayed and done everything to The Croft that Kate would have liked to do at Lane End.

And now it was Thursday, the nineteenth of November, and Miss Wentworth's farewell concert was about to begin. Kate studied the platform appreciatively, thinking how nice the girls looked. And the platform itself, banked in front by pot plants, all lent by parents. Miss Wentworth, whose evening this was, looked very well, too. She'd had her hair styled and set and with her small neat figure did not look like a woman about to retire.

It was rather a pity, Kate reflected, that Miss Wentworth had expressed a wish that no outsiders should be present. This was the kind of occasion which impressed visitors and proved that a school need not be large to be effective. The huge school which would eventually swallow the Jacob Wise Boys', the Jacob Wise Girls', and another which already catered for both sexes, was being built on the outskirts of the town. Soon small, personal units like the JW would be only memories.

Miss Wentworth, who managed to combine extreme republican sentiments with a respect for those unfortunate enough to be born royal, held that the National Anthem should be played before, not after, when people were struggling into overcoats or pushing towards exits. So the Queen (Poor girl, what a life! Worse than a circus animal. The whole system should be abolished) rapped with her baton and, still standing, struck with her left hand five unmistakable notes. Everybody stood up and, dominated by that section of the choir which specialized in unaccompanied song, some sang. Then everybody sat down, Kate thankfully, in an obscure place to the far right of the second row.

Everything went exactly according to the programme, designed in the art class and reproduced on the photostat machine which had replaced the old duplicator and which had not been bought by government funds. The JW could always raise limited sums of money—once they'd even had a whist drive.

Kate noticed that Julia had kept her word about the disputed blouses; Deborah Bolton, to the rear of the platform, and Miriam, in the very front row of the choir, were wearing white blouses with elbow length sleeves and modest little Peter Pan collars. Their flaxen plaits had been looped up and tied with bows of pale rose pink ribbon.

Even the unrehearsed item went well. In the interval, half-way through, there was some shuffling and laughing at the rear of the platform, then the head girl stepped down and presented Miss Wentworth with an enormous bouquet, staying in the parrot voice of the very nervous, "With our love and thanks, and we're sorry you're going."

Almost eclipsed by the flowers Miss Wentworth just managed to say, "Thank you, dear girls. Thank you, everybody." She then laid the bouquet along the piano top, thus disobeying her own rule that nothing should ever be placed there, took up her baton and prepared to conduct the unaccompanied choir as they sang "Where the bee sucks . . ." the offering which had gained top place at the South Suffolk Music Festival and missed by only two marks an appearance at the Albert Hall.

In the clapping that had followed the presentation, nobody noticed that the outer door had opened and closed. Or that Miriam's pallor had changed to chalky white. Everybody saw her fall from the platform, bringing down several pot plants, and striking her head on the corner of the piano. Some girls screamed.

From an ill chosen position in the very middle of a row, Dr. MacBride got to his feet, saying, "Let me pass. I am a doctor." Kate by that time had picked the child up and was carrying her to an adjoining classroom.

There were the beginnings, not of panic exactly, for no danger threatened, but of commotion. Miss Wentworth asked herself quickly, What can anybody sing? She sat down and began to play "Rule Britannia." Aptly enough, also composed by Thomas Arne.

Scalp wounds bleed very freely, and amongst Kate's weaknesses was a pathological horror of blood. She could only hope that she would not disgrace herself. Her sleeve and the front of her frock were soaked. Dr. MacBride had his bag—he never went anywhere without it. He took a gauze pad and applied it to the wound, just on the hairline.

"This needs stitches," he said. "Hospital. Where's your phone?"

The JW was such an old building, added to so many times, that directions were rather difficult to give, though the actual distance was not far. Oh, if only somebody else could come—preferably the gym mistress whom blood did not affect at all, or the highly unusual caretaker.

"Press, but not too hard. The poor little thing may have a fracture," Dr. MacBride said, handing over as he prepared to follow her instructions to cross, to turn.

Then help arrived, Julia coming in quickly from the far door of this classroom.

"All under control," she said. "Anything I can do?"

"Hold Miriam while I show Dr. MacBride . . ."

She led him to the phone, and he spoke with brisk authority. Setting it down, he said, "I decided against the ambulance. It takes time. I'll take her in my car. But somebody must hold her."

Julia said, "I'll go, Kate. Maybe you should show yourself. *Gown.*"

That was clever. Gowns, hardly worn in youth, but only worn on very special occasions because it made people not entitled to them feel resentful, hung in a cupboard in this very classroom, so handy for the main hall. Kate hauled hers—to which she was fully entitled—out and donned it. It did conceal the worst of the damage that the blood had inflicted on her best dress, and it lent authority.

A group of Britons, almost as varied as could have been found anywhere and all enslaved to some degree, by rates, by taxes, by the planners, were still declaiming that Britons, never never would be slaves. . . . Kate went to the front of the platform, and Miss Wentworth struck a loud chord.

Kate said, "The little girl who took a tumble is quite all right. So, shall we proceed?"

Dr. MacBride's authority stopped short at the hospital door. He carried Miriam in, laid her down on a kind of stretcher in the casualty reception room, spoke briefly to a doctor who looked very young and a nurse who looked competent, and then turned to Julia.

"Will you come back with me?"

"No. I think I'll hang around for a bit."

She was wearing her black velvet trouser suit with a frilled shirt, the whole effect rather cavalierish and now bloodied. She found a cloakroom and cleaned up as best she could with hot water and paper towels. She went to the reception area, the one place where smoking was allowed. It was now eight o'clock, and the public side of the hospital was closing down. Most of the lights went off. Not for the first time Julia felt that special eeriness which comes upon places ordinarily populous and busy when the human element is withdrawn. It is quite different from the emptiness of an ordinary dwelling. The *Marie Celeste.* That deserted lighthouse on Flannan Isle.

There was, just inside the main door, which now seemed to be closed, a kind of cage, well lighted and occupied by a man who now and then lifted a telephone and jabbed what looked rather like typewriter keys. Julia thought, No harm in asking. He was a kind person and, when she had explained, jabbed the keys with enthusiasm.

"Your little girl's all right, so far," he said at last. "On F-four, in one of the side rooms. You know how to get there?"

She knew. She rode up in the lift and then followed signs, reached F4, and there was the sister's desk, at the moment un-manned, and in front of it two very angry men. One large, one small. The small one was talking.

". . . Until you're black in the face. I say no. It's a matter of principle. And this is a free country. Or supposed to be."

"But the child needs a transfusion. She has lost a great deal of blood—and what she has is of poor quality. I don't wish to be dramatic and say life or death, but the need for a transfusion is urgent."

Over the small man's shoulder, the big man saw Julia and said impatiently, "Yes?"

"I came to enquire about Miriam Bolton. I helped to bring her here. I'm one of her teachers."

"She's alive," the big man said. "Only a hairline fracture. But her general state . . . She does urgently need a blood transfusion."

"And I forbid it. We don't believe in it, so we don't give any, so any she got would be heathenish. . . ."

The big man gave Julia a despairing look.

Julia said, "Mr. Bolton, would you be willing to put your objection in writing? That would exonerate everybody."

"I'll do that. Willingly." He rounded the sister's desk, found a sheet of paper and a Biro, and wrote in a large, bold, yet unformed hand: "I forbid, for religious reasons, my daughter, Miriam Bolton, to have a blood transfusion. W. R. Bolton."

"There you are," he said. "And now I'm going to sit in that room and see nobody goes behind my back."

The sister in charge had come silently back. She evidently knew what the dispute was about, for she exchanged a despairing look with the doctor and then said, "Oh, no! About visitors out of hours I am allowed to use my discretion. You must wait downstairs."

He was plainly not a fond father, he did not go towards the little side room to look at the daughter he had just condemned. On a matter of principle.

While he was still on his way to the exit, the doctor said, "Bloody bigot! The child is not concussed, but still unconscious. A transfusion . . ."

Julia slipped away.

She was on the ground floor in time to see Mr. Bolton shake the closed main door. It resisted, and he turned to the man in the cage.

"How do I get out?"

"Can't you read?"

There, plain for all who could read, was a notice on an easel; "EXIT" it said, and an arrow pointed. Mr. Bolton went that way. Julia counted up to ten and then went to the cage herself and said in her most beguiling manner, "I wonder could you lend me a piece of paper—and something to write with?"

"Only printed."

"All the better."

He was fundamentally a kind man, and he had a good memory.

"Little girl all right?"

"I hope so."

"Kids are tough," he said encouragingly.

She took the paper to the nearest table in the reception area and wrote in as good an imitation of Mr. Bolton's hand as she could manage, "I hereby retract my refusal to allow my daughter to have a blood transfusion. W. R. Bolton."

The lift seemed unbelievably slow. In the corridors she ran and arrived on F4 panting. The sister was still at her desk, but now talking to a junior nurse who held some charts in her hand.

"Look!" Julia said.

The sister looked. She put the two papers together. She then gave Julia a long, hard, but understanding stare, straight into the eyes.

"Dr. Stevens will be relieved," she said. "All is ready. I can set it up myself."

At the JW the Bolton sisters had never been popular, always seeming to prefer each other's company, and a bit odd. But custom was custom, and it had long been the habit, when a schoolmate was ill enough to be in hospital, to subscribe for gifts of flowers or fruit and to write letters or design Get Well cards. And because Miriam Bolton's accident had been dramatic, almost ruining the concert, contributions reached a point where they could not be expended on grapes and apples. By adding almost nothing, Julia was able to buy something of which Miriam seemed to be in need, and something calculated to cheer any convalescent—the prettiest possible dressing gown. A dark maroon enlivened by embroidered flowers and butterflies. Made in Hong Kong where women stitched themselves blind for wages minuscule by English standards. But if nobody bought what they made, how could they earn even that little?

Miriam was delighted with it, stroking the embroidery with loving fingers. "Deb would like this."

"Has Deb been to see you?"

"Not yet. Not till I'm better. And on Saturday I am going to Bywater. To a different sort of hospital. For convalescent people."

"Oh, I'm sure Deb will come before that."

By this time Julia was on excellent terms with Sister Anderson, the day sister on F4. She had described in vivid terms the terrible fuss Mr. Bolton had raised when he discovered that Miriam had received a blood transfusion after all.

"And, really, young nurses are odd. They exasperate me past bearing at times. But when Mr. B. called Dr. Stevens and me downright liars, and threatened to sue everybody up to the Minister of Health, look what they produced."

The statement read, "We the undersigned wish to testify that we were present when Mr. Bolton gave written permission for the transfusion to take place." It was signed by four names with the rank of their bearers from staff nurse to student nurse. "If it comes to the point," Sister Anderson said, "the suggestion that all four were in one place and free to observe Mr. B. reflects badly on the way I run my ward. Still, it was well meant."

It was from Sister Anderson that Julia learned that neither Deborah nor Mrs. Bolton had ever visited Miriam, and that Mr. Bolton had, since the morning of the row, confined himself to telephone enquiries.

Miriam had remained staunch to her vegetarian diet. She was—as Julia had suspected—very anaemic and should now be plied with good building up food, but she refused all meat, all fish, anything but vegetable soup and would not accept a cup of Bovril. Sister Anderson said, puzzled, "Yet when I suggested the obvious alternative, Marmite, she seemed never to have heard of it. And no doubt whoever draws up these menu sheets thought it clever to say 'Sherry trifle,' so the poor child jibbed at that. Terribly well indoctrinated. How right the Jesuits were. And Hitler . . ."

Miriam went to the convalescent home in Bywater, where it so happened she was the only patient under sixty, and could have been badly spoiled. And at the JW the winter term ran towards its frenetic end.

Julia went skiing in Austria. Kate had something more like a traditional Christmas, with the village bellringers trudging to Lane End and consuming vast quantities of sausage rolls, mince pies, and a kind of punch—lemonade, hot water, and a scant measure of rum. She also cooked a turkey and invited the rector, his wife, and his son and daughter—two formidable *avant garde* students—to share it.

Her mother had said no more about moving, and old Mr. Harper had managed to keep himself properly buttoned. . . . Peace on earth and goodwill to all men.

Then the New Year, and the new term. And a rather severe warning in the professional teachers' journal. Somewhere in the Midlands a child playing tag with others in a cloakroom had contrived to knock its eye out. A lawsuit was pending. Cloakrooms should be supervised.

Lingering about, playing about in classrooms had never been much of a problem at the JW. There were better places in which to play. A fair proportion of the girls were collected by parents in cars who must not be kept waiting; others mounted bicycles and fled; for others there was a walk through the Abbey Gardens, where a section had been laid out as a play area.

Julia who was on cloakroom duty one bleak January afternoon was quite surprised to find a loiterer. Miriam Bolton. She said, "Hullo, Miriam. Are you waiting for Deb?"

"I have to allow Deb a good start."

"Is it some sort of game?"

"No, Miss Hogarth. You see, I don't . . . belong any more. And I never did anything bad—except wear that blouse. . . ." Misery overcame her, and she began to cry in a subdued, very forlorn way. Julia, not a very demonstrative woman, put her arm around the small, shaking body and said, "I know. We'll go and have tea at Palmer's."

"We are not allowed tea, Miss Hogarth. And I am an outcast already."

"In what way, honey?"

"I don't belong. I have to eat alone and sleep in the box-room. And not speak to Deb. My blood is tainted. . . . And that dressing gown. I didn't know. I didn't know. It was breaking a commandment. Father put it on the bonfire."

"I agree it is monstrous," Kate said, looking worried. "But I can't see what is to be done. Interference might even worsen matters. I think I read something about that sect or a similar one. Some man joined it, and his wife didn't, so he banished her from bed and board."

"The poor little mite did say don't tell anybody. But, Kate, I feel so bloody responsible for it all."

"You? Why?"

Better that poor Kate should not know. She'd only worry, and God knew, she had worries enough.

"Buying those blouses, like a meddling fool. But they would have been so conspicuous. . . . Their blouses weren't even white. But how could I guess he'd come creeping in and frighten that child into a faint."

"You did what seemed for the best, dear. Try to forget it."

"I can't. It's mental cruelty. As bad as the other kind. I suppose you wouldn't consider going to see Mr. Bolton?"

"I don't think it would do any good. In fact, harm. Miriam asked you not to tell anybody."

"There is that. Could I go on some concocted excuse—something about Deb, perhaps?"

"Julia, I don't know. He's really rather a terrible little man." She did not know that Julia had seen him being terrible indeed. "I don't say he would assault you or be abusive in the ordinary way. He might . . . upset you. And Miriam's banishment probably has a limit. A biblical one, forty days and forty nights."

The little smile that accompanied these hopeful words was very half-hearted. In fact this afternoon the dry martinis were not having their usual cheering effect.

"Or it could be tackled from the medical angle. That child has definitely lost weight. And so pale. Could we send her and a couple of camouflage subjects for a check-up at the clinic?"

"Now that is a feasible idea. She might get some vitamins or something. . . ."

Dear Kate was dodging the issue as she often did, Julia thought. In her own mind she considered the possibility of having a word with Deb—she was two years the senior, yes, fourteen, old enough to have some sense. Julia visualized the approach: Deb, have you and Miriam quarrelled? I notice you no longer walk home together. That would not betray the younger child's confidences.

Then perhaps the suggestion about mercy being a Christian virtue. Query, were these people Christians?

Sometimes as she brooded, Julia's habitual self-confidence dwindled. Look what she'd brought about by her original meddling! Ah, yes, but think of that further bit of meddling which had undoubtedly saved the child's life.

Mr. Bolton was feeling bitterly frustrated. It was possible for him to dismiss the first lawyer he consulted as a deliberately stupid fellow, but he had now tried three, equally stupid. They wouldn't listen, they wouldn't understand; they actually asked: Was he not grateful that his daughter was alive and well? And to his claim that his permission had been forged, they one and all gave scant attention or said, "Very difficult to prove. Who stood to benefit? And no two handwriting experts ever agree—and juries are suspicious of them all."

Finally one fellow, younger and quite frivolous, had made the most insulting suggestion. "You were under stress at the time, Mr. Bolton, and probably hardly knew what you wrote. I have been in touch with the hospital. One sister and four nurses on the relevant ward at the time are willing to take oath that you gave your written consent."

"It is a plot. Everybody is against me."

The caretaker at the JW Girl's was a man named Stephen Laker. He was nearing sixty but trim and active and still surprisingly handsome. He was, everybody understood, a widower with grown children who occasionally came to stay in the neat house on the other side of the playing field. It was also known that he was one of the survivors of the Battle of Britain; his legacy from that was a limp and a small disability pension.

In earlier days he would have been an integral part of the Empire, but the Empire had foundered under him. He'd once grown good coffee in Kenya, but his unadaptable mind would insist upon looking upon Jomo Kenyatta as an ex-gaolbird and a leader of the Mau Mau. So he'd moved to Rhodesia and for a time grown good tobacco.

And all the time he had been acquiring knowledge and skills. In lonely places a man had to be a jack of all trades, ready to deal with any emergency. He was a good carpenter, plumber, electrician, engineer, and he had the knack of getting the best out of school cleaners, that arbitrary breed.

He had a bad temper which he made no effort to control, but he had a beautiful voice even when he was rebuking sloth and slovenliness, and all the cleaning ladies thought him a real proper gentleman.

He had an obsession about litter and always carried a stick with a spike at its tip. Some of the older girls had been known to drop things well within his view for the pleasure of focusing his attention and being scolded in that exquisite voice.

Two days after Julia had talked to Kate about Miriam Bolton and before any action had been taken, Mr. Laker made his usual evening round, taking the shortest path between his house and the school building. He checked the central heating plant and the level of oil in the tank which supplied it and adjusted the thermostat. This evening there were no messages on his particular corner of the notice board, drawing his attention to a cracked window pane, a leaking radiator, or a non-functioning cistern, but this absence of directives did not deflect him from his duty.

The cleaning ladies worked—rather flexibly—from six until eight. They had all remembered him at Christmas, the poor lonely man, and had presented him with cakes, puddings, and mince pies. It would have caused them some mortification to know that he did not distinguish between them, except by function, each doing her own area. But of course he had thanked them all equally and extravagantly, saying, "It absolutely made my Christmas." Judging by the way they cleaned, being paid and under supervision, he had the gravest doubts about their kitchens and had actually disposed of their goodwill offerings and some others, plus a monetary offering, to the rector of St. Mary's who knew many poor old people.

On this evening he had found nothing wrong and nothing to complain about. And on his spike he only had four bits of litter. He extinguished all lights, locked all doors, and prepared to go home by another route which included the path which skirted the swimming pool. Provided by good parents, the pool was unheated and could have been emptied at the onset of cold weather, but one of the parents who had contributed both in money and labour was deeply interested in birds. There was one breed of duck which until 1920 had wintered in England and had not been seen since. This the Good Parent attributed to the dearth of still water, and he hoped—almost prayed—that by some mysterious means the duck population would receive the message and choose the JW pool.

The water did not constitute a danger either to the children or anybody else, for it lay in a corner between the end of the school building and the wall which separated the school grounds from Schoolhall Lane. It was reached by a path, neglected during winter by everyone save Mr. Laker, who occasionally found that paper had blown there. As it had done this evening. Not on to the path, but on to the water. As he approached the pool Mr. Laker saw a pale blob on the surface. He swore softly and exotically because he would need a tool longer than the spiked stick.

The corner was lighted by radiance from a lamp in the lane, and as he neared the pool, Mr. Laker saw that he had something other than litter to deal with.

He jumped straight in, got the poor little creature to the side, clambered out, and went through the drill, remembered from his Service days, of restoring the apparently drowned. Nothing, not even the kiss of life, did any good. When he finally gave up, he was shivering, chilled to the bone. At sixty, one is less resilient than at eighteen, one cannot take risks, so Mr. Laker ran to his own house and gave himself a brisk rub down and donned his dressing gown before telephoning the police.

He had noticed the time as he left the school building: eight-twenty precisely. His watch, not of the waterproof type, had stopped at eight-twenty-two.

One of the two policemen, himself a family man, said, "School stops at three-forty-five. You'd have thought somebody would have reported a missing kid by now. She can't be more than seven."

Nobody reported a missing child that night, nor in the morning, and Miriam Bolton remained unidentified until well on into the first hour of the school morning, when she and three other girls were found to be absent without explanation. Most parents sent notes or telephoned or gave messages to other girls.

Very soon the three other absentees were accounted for, which simply left Miriam. Yet—a macabre touch—Deborah was at school as usual.

Neat, pallid, and, Kate could swear, totally ignorant, she answered questions, unwittingly revealing a strange state of affairs.

No, she knew nothing of Miriam. She'd last seen her at school yesterday, in the recreation time.

"Not at home? At any time in the evening?"

"No, Mrs. Harper. I haven't seen much of my sister lately."

She'd gone home, she said, helped her mother to get the room ready for the meeting. Then there'd been the meeting. Afterwards it was bedtime. And she had not seen Miriam or expected to see her this morning. "Miriam gets her own breakfast nowadays."

It all knitted in with what Julia had said, but Kate had hoped—and continued faintly to hope—that the child found dead in the pool might not be a JW girl at all. Whoever it was, it was awful, of course, but if a child had strayed in by way of the playing field gate, or even climbed the wall from the lane, there would be no possible reflection on the school, no unfavourable publicity.

As a possibly bereaved father, Mr. Bolton was treated with marked consideration; the driver of the police car sent to collect him even offered him a cigarette, refused with unnecessary vehemence. But it was in the morgue that Mr. Bolton truly showed his mettle.

"Yes. That was my daughter. Miriam Bolton. She was twelve years old." No sign of any emotion whatsoever.

It was not their function to ask more at this stage. The coroner would do that at the inquest. What they could and did do was let Mr. Bolton *walk* home.

Julia said, "I'm sorry, Kate. I do see your point, but somebody must expose that little fiend. And who can, if I don't?"

"I know. I know. I see your point. But, Julia, nothing can bring that poor child back to life. It's bad enough that it should be one of our girls. . . . I really do feel that for a member of the staff to go to the inquest and volunteer such accusations would heighten the drama and attract bigger headlines. Also it could give rise to a very nasty question. If we knew all this, why did we do nothing about it?"

"I wanted to," Julia said and instantly regretted it. Poor old Kate

was having such a hideous time. The season of goodwill had been
brief; old Mr. Harper had irretrievably offended Mrs. Marlow by
saying of some food she had prepared, "This is only fit for pigs,"
and going in search of the swill bucket which had once stood
outside the kitchen door. Mrs. Marlow had again mentioned moving and, because Kate did not instantly protest, had taken to bed
with what she called a nervous breakdown, brought on by circum-
stance. Mrs. Pearson, piteously appealed to, agreed to come back
on condition that Mrs. Marlow stayed out of her way. She would
also work shorter hours, and her charge had almost doubled.

To Julia, Kate now said, "I know. I blame myself very much.
Perhaps if I had let you interfere . . . Julia dear, I meant inter-
vene. Really I hardly know what I'm saying. This has been a hideous day."

Narrowing her green eyes slightly, Julia asked, "You'd really like
a verdict of death by accident, wouldn't you?"

"Frankly, yes. And if we didn't know . . . what we do, it would
be easy so to regard it. Suppose she had forgotten something and
come back in the dark and found the main entrance locked. Could
she not have thought of finding Mr. Laker and taken that path to
his house?"

"Kate, that really is wishful thinking. We do know what happened, we know why she felt life wasn't worth living. If there's a
suspicion of suicide, they do ask about mental condition, don't
they? I could tell what I know. You see, I think showing him up
might deter others."

"Mary Baxter's father went to gaol for ill treating her. How
many did that deter?"

"Really, Kate! Who can say? We only hear about those who were
not deterred. Anyway, I think cruelty allied to such sheer bloody
nonsense should be exposed. Don't you? In your heart?"

Kate emptied her glass.

"How I feel about the thing itself," she said, "is different. I mean
as a private person. As head of JW my instinct is against any further
involvement. But, my dear, I think you must judge." Suddenly she
said, in a voice near breaking, "For God's sake, let *us* not quarrel."

But already their happy relationship had undergone a subtle
change, like a leaf changing colour in the course of an autumn day.

Julia knew what Kate was anxious about—the eventual headship of the grand new school. And of course it mattered to Kate, because two old people and a cripple were dependent upon her. The State helped, of course, giving Mrs. Marlow what used to be called the Old Age pension, and Eddie permanent sick benefit of £22.50 a week. Old Mr. Harper had somehow slipped through the net; maybe he'd never bought the requisite stamp, and he still owned property.

I mustn't judge, Julia thought, and I will not judge. And I don't want Kate worrying all through the weekend.

"No, of course we shan't quarrel. Look, I won't just wade in baldheaded. I'll have a word with my lawyer—a grandiose term for the man who did the conveyancing when I bought this place. Nice old boy. I'll tell him all and see what he says."

Blatant compromise.

"I may just catch him," Julia said, looking at her watch and then at the telephone. It was only ten minutes after five, but Kate, looking at her watch, felt, despite the good martini—with some brandy in it—that sinking feeling. . . . On her new contract Mrs. Pearson left at three. The fire would have died down. Oh, God!

Julia sat down by the telephone and presently realized that this was Friday when men of law went home—or wherever else—somewhat early. Her dialling evoked only one answer; in some deserted office a voice said hoarsely, "Hallo, Liz. How is he?" A pre-arranged call and anxiety on the listen. She said, "Sorry. Wrong number," and was rewarded by a very ugly word indeed.

Obviously nothing could be done tonight. She poured out the remaining contents of the jug in which she had mixed the martinis and surveyed her glass critically. So little. Top it up with brandy. Put another log on the fire. Find your book. . . .

Her doorbell rang sharply. She was expecting nobody, but at the moment any distraction was welcome, for her book had failed to hold her, and she'd been back with Miriam Bolton. She ran to the door and opened it eagerly. The Croft had a deep porch. In its shadow stood two smallish muffled figures. One just recognizable. Deb Bolton and—just possibly—another sister of whom she had heard no mention.

Deb said, "Miss Hogarth. May we come in?"

"But, of course." Julia saw then that beyond the shelter of the porch, slanting against the light of the street lamp, snow was falling. Their hats, their shoulders were white.

Deb said, "Miss Hogarth, this is my mother."

What now?

"Do come in, Mrs. Bolton." What else was to be said at just this moment? Usually so articulate, so fluent, so poised, Julia could find nothing to say except "I can't tell you how sorry . . ." and leave it there.

The hall at The Croft was warm, and on the table in its centre stood a bowl of hyacinths in full flower, extremely fragrant. Deb and her mother struck an incongruous note, and the light, flaky snow began to melt immediately. "Do take off your wet things and come to the fire," Julia said. She saw now that, although Mrs. Bolton was very little taller than Deb, she was old and dressed in archaic fashion: a brown mackintosh, practically ankle length, and a curious, squashed looking hat.

"On the chest, there," Julia said, indicating it. "What a horrible night. Do come in and get warm."

Mrs. Bolton said in a surprisingly deep, rather rich voice, "I've come to ask your help, Miss."

"And you shall certainly have it. Anything I can possibly do."

And, God, she'd been taken by surprise again, for Mrs. Bolton was wearing, over a colourless dress, an article of clothing nowadays never seen, almost unrecognizable: a white apron, stiff and shining with starch.

Mrs. Bolton had once had that same flaxen hair as her daughter's, dulled and greyed now and severely dressed, a centre parting and a severe knob at the back of her head. She was pale. Her eyes were bluish, slightly protuberant, and over wary. The eyes of a hunted hare, Julia thought, and then, at once, What sentimental tosh! Whoever got near enough to a hunted hare to observe its eyes?

She pushed a sofa a little nearer the fire and said, "Do sit down." They sat, side by side, stiff and ill at ease. Shyly observant, though, darting swift little glances about the pretty room.

Julia turned and gave the fire some unnecessary attention and wondered rather wildly what hospitality she could offer. They were not allowed tea, so presumably coffee was also forbidden. Cocoa? Hot milk?

"We need your help, Miss, but I'm not asking for charity," Mrs. Bolton said. "A bed for three nights and just a small loan. I can work. I was a good cook once." She looked down at her hands, reddened, clean scrubbed, and looking too large for the thin, frail wrists. "I'd pay you back."

"You can have whatever you need," Julia said. "Now, I think we all need a hot drink. What would you like?"

"Oh, if I may . . . A cup of tea. Of all things, I've most missed tea." So might an old roué, on a diet, have spoken of vintage champagne.

The tray, the china, all beflowered, would have provoked Mr. Bolton to destructiveness, but since his wife had asked for tea, presumably she would drink from a pretty cup. As indeed she did, avidly. Deborah lifted her cup, set it down again, and left it standing.

"Go on," her mother said. "It's lovely. But of course you have to get used to it." She gave Julia an apologetic look. "Mr. Bolton didn't allow tea or coffee. He said they were stimulants."

He may have been right, for half-way through her second cup, Mrs. Bolton became stimulated.

"I'll be honest with you, Miss. I've left Mr. Bolton. I've borne it and borne it till I can bear no more. He lost me my first—my boy. There are injections now against whooping cough and diphtheria, but Mr. Bolton didn't hold with them. So my boy got diphtheria and died. I should have left then, but Deb was on the way. And after that, Miriam. And he killed her as surely as if he'd axed her." Deborah gave a little whimpering sound, and Mrs. Bolton touched her arm, gently but awkwardly. "I *know* it is an awful thing to say, but then it was awful. If he'd had his way, she would never have had the blood she needed to save her life. But somehow she did get it. And ever since she's been treated like a leper. . . . And the worst thing, yes, the very worst was that when I tried . . . and I *did* try to make it not so bad. If I so much as spoke to her, to my own daughter, or saved her a bit of extra bread, he'd know—and take it out on her. Miss, I can't describe, nobody could." Her shifting gaze had steadied itself and fixed on Julia's face, but in an unseeing way, as though she were looking through and beyond and into Hell.

"But I shall describe it. At the inquest on Monday. I don't know much about inquests, but I think they try to find out why. And I can tell them. Exactly."

Julia's first thought was, Then I need not go and run counter to Kate's wishes. And coming from the child's mother, it will carry far more weight. What a relief.

Mrs. Bolton drained the now tepid tea and said, "I shouldn't unload all this on you, Miss. Just because you were so kind about the blouses. But where could I turn? I had to save Deb. You see, if I stand up and say what I intend to do and just go away myself, then he'll take it out on her."

"I'm sure you are doing the right thing. And you needn't bother a bit about the future. I have plenty of room. You and Deb are welcome to stay as long as you like."

"That is kind, but it wouldn't do. He'd be after Deb and get her back somehow. That I simply could not bear. No, I think my best plan is to get away. Clean away. Out of his reach . . . He'd stop at nothing."

"You are quite right," Julia agreed. "And perhaps I can help."

She knew several people, relatives and friends, one as far afield as Cornwall, who would see in Mrs. Bolton, with her white apron, something the equivalent of the Archangel Gabriel.

Deborah stood up suddenly and said, "May I be excused?"

Julia said, "Just across the hall, dear. The door immediately opposite."

Mrs. Bolton said, "They were so close—not being allowed to associate with anybody else. But, believe me or not, Deb wasn't even allowed to cry."

"I do believe you," Julia said.

Deborah came back, wearing her outdoor clothing, the long blue coat, the knitted cap. She looked even paler than usual.

She said, "I'm going back to Father."

Hunted hares when brought down screamed, it was said, with a human voice. And Mrs. Bolton did so scream. A terrible sound.

Julia said, "Deb, wait." But the girl had already turned and gone.

After a few minutes which had lasted several centuries, Mrs. Bolton raised her stricken face and said, "So now I have nothing. Sixteen years of absolute hell, and in the end, nothing, nothing."

5

Gateway to happiness?

In the beginning Steve Bowyer and I were forced into a kind of proximity because we were the only boys, in fact the only children in the little hamlet of Crowswood, which consisted of one farm in which the Bowyers had lived for generations and six cottages once occupied by people employed at the farm: the horseman, the cowman, and the ordinary labourers. There had been no dearth of children in those days.

But times had changed. Steve's father, with the aid of a young man who came up from the village on a motor bike and some fearsome looking mechanical devices, grew sugar beet and various cereal crops, and the six other dwellings were leased or sold to retired couples who had always dreamed of life in the country with roses round the door, or to young people who commuted to Baildon and postponed having families until they could afford them.

We, that is my parents and I, moved into the country for a definite reason; my father, young, tragically young, had been smitten with multiple sclerosis, a deadly, progressive nervous disease. Either no cure was known or none worked for him. He'd been self-employed, so the State didn't want to know about him except that he should not starve; so he obtained, after a bit of wrangling, something called Permanent Disability Allowance, and my mother, country born and bred, thought that she could keep hens, grow potatoes, perhaps even start a little business in home-made cakes. In our better days, when she could afford to be charitable, her contribution to events in aid of good causes had always been cakes, scones, and delectable looking pastries.

Rose Cottage was most admirably suited to our purpose. It was larger than the other cottages, with two ground-floor rooms, one for Father and one for Mother, who must always be within call. The kitchen was spacious enough to serve as work place and sitting room, and the garden was bigger than one woman could easily manage. I was nine when we moved and very anxious to be helpful, but I was short for my age and not very husky.

I remember being startled and very envious when I learned that Steve Bowyer was in fact a month younger than I. To me he seemed enormous. But so indeed did most of the children in the village school of Minsham St. Mary's, which during our year there was on the point of being made redundant. They were all typical East Anglians, with hair almost the colour of straw, eyes of blue, varying from periwinkle to cornflower, and had thick muscled necks and limbs. They were what breeders would call true to type, for even after communication had become easier, like tended to marry like. Steve's father and mother could easily have been cousins.

Among these children who—apart from my not very happy home—made my life at that time, I was a foreigner and could all too easily have suffered at best ostracism, at worst mild persecution. Even my speech, standard Londonese of the more refined kind, was subject to mockery, and I was useless at all games. However, always behind me stood Steve Bowyer. . . . I never actually saw him strike a blow; there was no need. "You wanna clout?" he'd ask. And that was enough.

Nor was this entirely a one-way traffic. He was far from stupid; he could do sums in his head with dazzling rapidity. I often thought I could see his mind working, Click-click, click. But he couldn't deal with words except those needed for the most basic exchange of the most basic ideas. So we used to cheat. He'd do my sums, with just an error or two to make it feasible that I had done the work, and I wrote his essays and any other exercises that demanded a facility with words. Needless to say our examination results were disappointing; however by that time terms unknown to earlier pedagogues were coming into use, and Steve and I were said to be victims of examination nerves.

We usually did our homework at the farm where there was room to spare, with a fireplace where we could have a fire in winter (if we collected the wood), and naturally we walked to school together. But during the weekends and holidays we saw little of each other, for ours was far from being the carefree existence that the words "country boyhood" evoke. I had a bicycle of antique design equipped with an errand boy's basket, and on it I rode briskly about delivering stuff to Mother's growing number of regular customers. Then I returned more heavily laden with most of the week's stores. After that I helped in the garden, cleaned windows, and scrubbed the kitchen floor. Steve always swore that he spent all his spare time hosing down and polishing whatever was polishable on the machines which had replaced men in the fields. But he had one consolation: he was often allowed to drive one, quite illegally.

At the age of eleven all the children within a wide area left their village schools and went to a huge new comprehensive on the outskirts of Baildon. There was, in the very centre of the town, an ancient grammar school—it really did date back to Edward VI. In the frenzied scramble for egalitarianism, it had managed to remain independent, but of necessity the fees had gone up, and the entrance examination was stiff.

Steve and I got in without lifting a finger. The clever old woman who with the help of one assistant had run the Minsham School for almost forty years thought that Steve and I showed promise in our differing ways, so she went diving and delving and came up with a prize, the now almost forgotten Hartley Trust. An old grammar school boy, Robert John Hartley, having made his fortune in India, had heavily endowed his alma mater and founded a scholarship which enabled two boys at three year intervals to enter the school without examination, to pay no fees, and to receive an allowance of five pounds a year for clothing and other necessities. The one condition was that the boys should live in one of the five villages,

Clevely, Muchanger, Nettleton, and the two Minshams. Nobody had applied for or even thought about the Hartley Trust until our dear old mistress saw two very ordinary—and rather dishonest—ducks as swans and bestirred herself on our behalf.

After the change of schools Steve and I saw more of each other than ever, for though there was a conveyance known as "the school bus," it was geared to the timetable of the comprehensive pupils. So on our bicycles, his brand new and mine divested of its errand boy basket, we rode back and forth together and talked about everything under the sun. I still preferred him to any other boy I met in my now widened circle; he was that rare thing, a person with no streak of malice, and except for the little matter of cheating at homework, dead honest. And now there was no longer need to cheat, for even the ancient grammar school conformed to new fashion by having two "sides" called, of course, Classics and Science. Steve was no longer required to write essays, and everybody soon realized that the binomial theorem was for me an unsurmountable hurdle.

Except for worsening conditions at home, those were for me happy years. Steve acquired and tinkered with an old car, which we could drive on private property—that was the farm—well before we were allowed on the highway.

Then the inevitable parting came. We were both seventeen. Steve had planned his course and was going to a place, just over the border into Essex, in part a rather posh agricultural college, in part an experimental place, with a laboratory devoted to the study of seeds.

My future was different. I had to set about earning as much as I could as soon as I could. I joined, if that is the appropriate term for general dogsbody, the firm of Buxton and Hall, Auctioneers and Estate Agents, 8 Market Square.

To understand Buxton and Hall, one must understand Baildon, for nowhere else in the world could a firm run by two old men, one often drunk, have survived for a week.

Doubtless in the course of history there had been other firms plying the same trade, but they had vanished, leaving Buxton and Hall the monopoly. Newcomers had pushed in and soon retired, discouraged by lack of custom because there seemed to be a feeling—amounting almost to superstition—that if you bought or sold anything except through Buxton and Hall, some ill would befall the transaction.

Both the old men were femininely coy about their age, but judging from their reminiscences they must have been at least nearing eighty, and they most definitely needed an assistant— there was actually work enough for two! There'd been several before me, and if between them they had owned a single good quality, I never heard it mentioned. Their manifold faults defined guidelines for a bright boy to observe. Never contradict; never push yourself forward; never despise a menial job; never try to tidy up the incredibly muddled office. "I know I'm not spick and span," Mr. Buxton said, eyeing his collection of what looked like waste paper. "But I could come in here, in the dark, drunk or sober, and find exactly what I wanted. When that young bastard had finished meddling, I couldn't find anything. Some things I never did find. I believe he threw them away."

Incredibly, both the old men still held driving licences, but preferred to be driven. Thanks to Steve, I could drive and, accompanied by one or both and displaying my L card, was able to act as chauffeur, getting what speed I could out of their vintage cars. "Made when cars were *made,* not just blown together," as Mr. Hall said. And it was true that neither ancient vehicle ever broke down or failed its MOT.

It was interesting to me to see how both their minds functioned on two different levels so far as finance was concerned. They were both sharp enough to recognize inflation when it affected the price of a bungalow or a bullock, but privately they were not merely pre-decimalization, but pre-1939, or even—dare one think it?—pre-1914. They paid me, by the standards of the day, a beggarly wage and exploited me shamelessly. I could have laid bricks or slapped plaster on walls, maybe even cleaned windows, at a more immediately remunerative rate per hour. But there was the slump with its superfluity of young men with no training and no special aim beyond the next pay packet.

And I was, in effect, serving an apprenticeship. I was qualifying to become something. And it could be done without leaving home. I managed to squeeze in a few sessions at the College for Further Education, and I took a correspondence course. It was hard going,

on top of all else, but it enabled me to live at home and help
Mother to deal with Father.

In due time, having taken and passed my examinations, I was by
law entitled to conduct a public auction and call myself a house
agent. Both my masters congratulated me warmly, but there was
no hint of an increase in pay. I waited a fortnight and then suggested it myself and for one horrified moment feared that with a
simple request I had brought death on two apparently indestructi-
ble men. Mr. Buxton's intake of spirits had never reddened his
face but my request turned him purple; Mr. Hall, normally rubi-
cund, paled. They spent a day mumbling and muttering together,
and I agonized over the prospect of being made redundant, the
civilized term for getting the sack.

I had two not very substantial lifelines: Mr. Buxton, whose last
driving licence had been granted for five years, had just been
refused a renewal, and Mr. Hall had some time back decided that I
could describe a property in rather more arresting terms than he
could. He had actually said, "Well, I suppose after sixty years one
tends to get into a rut. In future, you do it. But bear in mind that
'dominated by a fine cedar tree' is wordier than 'in mature
grounds.'"

Nobody could argue with that, but "dominated by a fine cedar
tree" made more impact. I was still being handy with words or
what words can imply.

They emerged at last and agreed to pay, not quite what I had
asked but near enough to be an acceptable compromise, and as a
sop to Cerberus Mr. Buxton threw in his old Morris Isis. A bit of a
white elephant to me, for its consumption of oil matched its mas-
ter's of whisky. Even had I not liked Steve as well as I did, I should
have welcomed his visits home, for on a farm as mechanized as
Crowswood, oil and petrol were to be had for the taking. Steve
always filled me up.

He'd really changed very little during his time at Willingford. I
thought him handsome—and obviously girls found him attractive.
Whenever there was something special on in Baildon, he'd bring a
girl home—never the same one twice. Mrs. Bowyer said she became quite confused, since three in succession were called Helen.

He was obviously very good at his mysterious calling; he was
asked to stay on a third year, more or less as a member of the staff.

Then he reached the stage of being sent on visits to other experimental places, Holland, Germany, Mexico, and California. Before he left he said to me, and he was not joking, "By the time I get back you'll be a partner." I doubted it. My masters pushed more and more work on to me, but still regarded me as the office boy. I did once suggest hiring either a youngster or an elderly man just to clean windows and paste labels saying "SOLD" when a property was disposed of. This caused almost the same catastrophe as my request for more salary had done, but eventually Mr. Hall, the slightly less rocky character of the two, said he had thought of a way of easing my lot; he'd undertake the job of tea making. This was an absurd concession, since when I was at the market or showing a potential client over a house, tea was skipped altogether. I entirely failed to see how Mr. Hall's making tea did me any good, yet perhaps, in a backhanded way, it may have done.

One Market Day afternoon I was auctioning bullocks and doing rather badly because fog was already with us, and dense fog had been forecast. Buyers and sellers alike were anxious to get home. Back in the office Mr. Buxton dozed in his chair, and Mr. Hall made the tea, carrying it in and saying—as he himself told me—"Wake up, you lazy old devil." When he realized that his friend and partner of so many long years was beyond the revivifying effect of tea, he too collapsed and died two days later in the intensive care unit at the hospital.

Both had left wills, made at the same time and years before I was born. Mr. Buxton had been married, but his wife died, and he had no children. Mr. Hall had never married. Each had left to the other everything he owned, apart from some bequests to charity— and they were identical. Some of these worthy causes had survived and were still household words, others had long vanished.

Mr. Hall, however, had added a brief codicil as recently as two years earlier. In it he named me as his heir to his half of the business known as Buxton and Hall and his share of the property known as 8 Market Square.

Mr. Turnbull, the solicitor, eyed me with an expression as near sympathy as his stern face could assume. "You will finally benefit, but unless you have some capital—or access to some—things may be a trifle difficult. The laws applicable to charitable bequests are very stringent. You will be obliged to buy the other half of the building—that is, if you wish to remain there. The clause about half the business, can, I think, safely be ignored. There used to be an asset known as goodwill but that is seldom considered in these days. And in any case you may be assumed to have it. You have been here how long?"

"Eight years."

"And for the last four virtually singlehanded. Strictly off the record, what do you think the property is worth?"

"That depends entirely upon the purpose for which it is needed. The building as a building is in such bad repair. It should be completely reroofed. The wiring is so old as to constitute a fire hazard, and there is a sinister bulge over the side door. But, of course, as a site it could fetch an astronomical figure. Smack in the centre of the town . . ."

"Where do you park your car?" he asked, with seeming irrelevance.

"On the Square, near the War Memorial."

"And your clients?"

"Well . . . I suppose the same—or they use the Hawk in Hand. I must admit I never gave the matter a thought. Why?"

"It has a certain bearing upon purpose—and thus upon value. Surely, Mr. Forbes, in the course of your work you must have observed the *position* now matters much less than car parking space."

I knew that. The ugliest, most jerry-built house with a garage sold more easily than an elegant Georgian house, "near shopping centre" and without one.

"We will get the place valued," Mr. Turnbull said and allowed himself a little frosty joke. "I'm sure the Medical Mission to the Upper Congo, if I can ever locate it, will welcome a windfall."

I went home, thinking sourly that had Mr. Hall truly wished me well, he might have considered my position a little more thoroughly. I had no money; I had never earned enough to be able to save. I wondered whether the bank would regard my half ownership of the premises as security enough for a loan to buy the other half.

I had no one with whom I could talk things over. Mother had enough to worry her; Father grew worse almost daily and was now beyond our care. We were lucky to have help—a village woman who had been a nurse before she married. She was competent and kindly, but had a very proper sense of her own value. She charged by the hour and, had she worked the hours I did, would have earned about three times as much.

Apart from Steve Bowyer I had no friend. I had never had time. No, maybe I wrong Mr. Turnbull. Or perhaps the task of tracing down beneficiaries on whom the winds of change had blown disposed him to favour the one on the spot. He found a valuer who took a very poor view of 8 Market Square. His report read as though the whole thing might collapse at any moment: damp rotted beams made the upper floor unsafe. There was dry rot, woodworm, death-watch beetle, no rear or side access except to a space big enough to hold a dustbin, and the doorway outside which the dustbin stood was definitely dangerous. A thorough man, he commented upon the sanitation in most unfavourable terms.

(Perhaps I should here remark that things formerly concealed are made public in obituary notices. Mr. Buxton was ninety-two, Mr. Hall eighty-seven. Once, no doubt, regarded as a dangerously go-ahead young man, with a flush water closet near which on the wall, for the benefit of the ignorant, was a little china plaque saying: "Pull and Release." As though some innocent, if uninformed, might stand holding the pretty china handle until death intervened.)

All in all, he judged this deplorable building as worth four thousand pounds.

"As it stands," Mr. Turnbull said, looking not ill pleased, "you can hardly demolish your half without lessening the value of the remainder. Multiple ownership. I have counted sixteen and tracing them may take years. If you could produce two thousand pounds . . ."

"I can try," I said. And I thought, Try—that about sums up my life, so far; try, try, and try again . . . and again.

By this time the year had turned, and the days were lengthening. John Drinkwater had written a poem called "January Dusk"; my memory had cherished it, perhaps because it sounded a faint note of hope. I thought of it then, walking round from Mr. Turnbull's office to Market Square with hope little more now than a dusty memory. And there, outside the office which was half mine, was a ~~oar~~ car, and getting out of it, Steve Bowyer.

And we might have parted the day before.

He said, "Hullo. I thought I might catch you."

I said something about being surprised. "I didn't think you were due back till Easter."

"Well, that was the general idea, but I reckoned it was time to get to work. And maybe I was a bit homesick. And sick of being, well . . . not bossed about exactly, but nothing of my own."

I used my keys, smelt the dry rot, the damp rot, and faintly the defective sanitation. I said, "Come in, but mind how you step. Only half is mine." I certainly had no rightful claim to the whisky in Mr. Buxton's cupboard. He had always believed in buying ahead. I poured liberally.

I had always been the talkative one and in no time at all had told Steve my position and my problem.

"Poor old chap," he said, "you do have luck! First that old car. Now this!" He sounded, as always, just right, sympathetic, but not pitying, slightly amused.

"Quite apart from the two thousand—which might as well be twenty—I need some cash. I can't conduct a sale or show somebody a house, and tend the office. And though that surveyor man exaggerated a bit, the damned place will fall down unless something is done soon."

"You could do with three thousand at the very least. And not bank money—if that can be avoided."

I laughed with no great merriment. "All I got from the bank was advice. Doubtless sound. Let the demolition men move in. Unencumbered by the building, the site would be valuable."

"You mustn't move," Steve said quickly. "The people around here are so hidebound. If you moved just across the Square, they couldn't find you! They put tabs on pigs as soon as they're born, Buxton and Hall, Eight Market Square!"

I became aware of the time and said I must be getting back. Worry rode with me. We now needed Mrs. Argent every day. And who would pay me on November 30?

Three days later I received one of Steve's characteristic communications: staccato sentences, written on a postcard, but enclosed in an envelope postmarked Willingford.

"I rustled up the needful. It's at Barclay's in your name. See you at Christmas, if not sooner. S."

Mother had reported that she had had a visit from Mrs. Bowyer who said Steve had simply looked in, stayed a night, and gone to Willingford. She was convinced that he had a girl there.

"She thinks that is what brought him home before time. So she thinks it may be serious. I imagine she's already fancying herself in the role of grandmother."

As she said that, one of the rare but very eloquent changes took place in my mother's controlled face. She was comparing not so much on her own behalf, as mine. I said lightly, "You may have to wait a bit longer, darling. I have yet to convince people that Buxton and Hall is still operative."

Actually that was not difficult. The sheer inertia of the two old men had served me in a way. I was Buxton and Hall at 8 Market Square.

And there was the pre-Christmas fat stock sales pending. By the end of that year I had money in hand, and I had found the perfect assistant: a woman, no longer young but very competent. And she found an elderly man—I think a relative—who did what I had done for so long, sweeping the front, cleaning windows.

Now that I *was* Buxton and Hall, rather than an employee, I went up a notch or two in the hierarchy of small town life; I was asked to join things. Using Father as an excuse, I refused; I was determined to fritter not a penny away until I had cleared my debt to Steve.

He came home that Christmas, bringing another blonde beauty, but nothing came of that, and although he often went back to Willingford in the next year, he said it was only because he could find people there who understood what he was talking about: genetics, chromosomes, and so forth. Still, some people nearer home must have caught the drift, for it was in that year that Crowswood changed its field pattern to one that faintly resembled that old strip pattern of mediaeval farmland: different varieties of the two main crops, sugar beet and barley, growing more or less side by side and all plainly labelled. Steve spoke of "field trials,"

and Mr. Bowyer said, "Barnum and Bailey's," but rather enjoyed
the stir and the visitors, I think. Mrs. Bowyer said she did wish
Steve would settle down.

So, two years slipped away, and I was clear of debt, and Steve
announced that he was about to get married to the daughter of a
Norfolk farmer—quite a landowner—in Norfolk. Mrs. Bowyer
said, Well, she supposed a Norfolk girl was the next best thing to a
Suffolk one, but regretted that the whole thing should be so hasty.

Steve asked me to be best man. I acknowledged the implied
compliment, for he now had many friends, but I had Father to
consider.

Poor Father. He had now reached the stage where the only
movement possible to him was a slight jerk of the head. He lay,
rigid as a corpse, the sheet smoothed across his upper chest. He
still enjoyed a cigarette. Whoever was in charge would place it
between his lips, light it, and put an ashtray on the sheet. He could
just knock off the ash by giving that little jerk of the head. His sight
had failed some time earlier, so the TV set no longer entertained
him. He could still hear—they say hearing is the last sense to go—
but he did not enjoy music. The damnable thing was that inside
the inert hulk his mind remained alert; he enjoyed what he called
a good gossip and liked to be read to. My evening job.

Steve said, "Surely, just once. You are my oldest friend."

The wedding was timed for three o'clock in the afternoon. Saturday. June. It could just be done.

"All right. I'll be with you. But somebody else must go round
kissing bridesmaids and reading those so-witty telegrams."

Steve said he didn't mind about the reception. He just wanted
me there at the crucial moment.

My memory of the whole thing is blurred, but I was left with the
idea that the wedding was as traditional, as near feudal as possible.
White flowers everywhere, the bride rustling and shrouded in
white, a bevy of pretty girls in pale pink, Steve looking unusually
solemn, and almost . . . well, dedicated. So much so that I
thought of mediaeval knights taking vows after an all night vigil.

Then I was hurtling back as fast as the good new car, which I had
bought as soon as I was out of debt, could carry me.

And, of course, too late! Father had been dead for three hours
when I arrived.

"Nothing is there for tears or beating on the breast," I reminded myself. He had lived life-in-death for so long and died without pain or struggle. Sad, but then the whole human condition is sad; better not to think about it.

In the next few weeks I had two surprises. The first came from Mother, who said she wanted to go to Australia. There, it appeared, she had a brother, the Alec for whom I had been named. He had not made a fortune in a far off place, in true black sheep tradition; he hadn't even been a regular correspondent. "But," she said, "we were young together, and he is the only person I now feel I want to see. Apart from you, my dear boy—and God knows, we have seen enough of each other. We both need a change."

My second surprise was meeting Steve's wife when they came back from the traditional honeymoon. Her name was Celia, and she wasn't even pretty. Steve, with his good looks and his fairly certain if not dazzling prospects, had been much sought after. And he had married a slight, insignificant girl with a monkeyish face. Oh, dear, that makes her sound ugly, which she was not; I mean just a trifle flat of nose, wide of mouth and sallow of skin. Not Steve's type at all—perhaps the attraction lay there; and in her eyes, which were large and darker but, there again, monkeyish because of the in-built look of melancholy.

Mrs. Bowyer, come to wish Mother a good holiday and show a sheaf of wedding photographs, said she didn't think Celia looked much of a breeder.

Mother's first letter merely announced her safe arrival and her joy at finding her brother so little changed. Her second gave me a bit of a jolt, for in it she said she intended to stay in Australia. It suited her. Apparently Uncle Alec, though not dazzlingly successful, was sound enough, owning a sheep station, small by Antipodean standards, "though it's bigger than half Suffolk." He employed six or seven men, most of whom had never had a decent meal in their lives. She cooked every evening—no shortage of materials. And she had learned to ride a horse.

I had now to decide what to do about Rose Cottage. So far I'd confined myself to transforming it back into a normal house with beds upstairs. I had wondered if Mother would prefer to live elsewhere, now I had only myself to consider, and found, slightly to my surprise, that despite everything I was attached to the place.

It was near enough to Baildon and to a spur of Layer Wood where the cuckoo called all day in its season. It was also near to Crowswood—though I had not, since Steve's marriage, gone there uninvited.

With very little outlay, I could make Rose Cottage into a rather elegant small house for a single person. I put the work in hand and began to look rather more sharply at furniture I was asked to sell. Even professional dealers sometimes miss a bargain and have a kind of snobbery about things obviously mended.

One evening during the first week of October, Steve strolled across—alone except for one of his dogs. Celia would have come, he said, but had gone early to bed. "She's pregnant." He tried to speak casually and did not succeed.

"That calls for a drink," I said. "I bet your people are delighted." There I was exercising tact, allowing him free expression of his own delight under cover of theirs.

Presently he said, "You know, old boy, you should get married. You've no idea . . . I mean, when I look back, I can see that I was only half alive."

"One day I may run into somebody who makes me feel that way. Up to the present I've not felt deprived."

He was my best, my oldest, and in some ways my only friend, but even to him I could not explain why I should never get married. About what had afflicted Father no one could be absolutely positive. It was not specifically one of the hereditary curses, but nobody knew enough about it to guarantee immunity. I might well escape, but in me it might lurk.

I was taking no risks. Also, quite apart from that, it had fallen to me to clear up Mr. Buxton's personal effects, and he had actually once kept a diary which proved that married happiness could be very dearly bought. He'd been so entirely devoted to his wife— her name was Adelaide—that her death had made him into an alcoholic. I had, of course, burned the diary but I should never forget the last entry. "Adelaide died this morning. I am drunk."

My feeling that non-involvement was best was reinforced two months later when Celia miscarried and almost died. Steve was distraught. He kept saying: "Never again. Never again. I simply couldn't bear it. . . . Let Father go on about the place having gone from father to son since Domesday. And Mother can break up that old cradle for firewood. Never, never again."

Celia recovered, looked, I thought, the better for the experience. Steve took a little longer to get back to normal, and when in February of the next year a peculiarly vicious type of influenza struck, he, who had never known a day's illness in his life, damned nearly died. Both his parents did, their hopes of posterity going to the grave with them.

I chiefly remember the time after Steve's recovery as a time of gaiety. Crowswood was no longer a little out-of-the-way farm where a few experiments were being conducted; it had become a show place, visited at certain seasons by people from many countries, and Steve was never at a loss for a reason for a party. He could entertain pretty lavishly because firms, foundations, trusts, even governments, sponsored him, and Celia proved to be not only a charming hostess but a gifted linguist. Steve always asked me to his parties, though I did not always accept. Once he telephoned me and said with an urgency not altogether simulated: "Alec, come across. Parlez moi Anglais, s'il vous plaît. This place is like the ground floor of bloody Babel!" But he enjoyed it all.

I entertained less frequently, less lavishly, and in far less cosmopolitan style—though it was actually a Korean who christened my gate.

I had had my eye on that gate—a covetous eye—for some time before I possessed it. Most genuine, eighteenth century wrought iron gates would have looked silly in front of Rose Cottage—they belonged with mansions. But my treasure had served as a subsidiary, just one entry to a vast estate which belonged to a man who had inherited so much that the huge decaying house at Minsham All Saints meant nothing to him. I doubt if he ever saw it. Then, for some reason, he decided to dispose of the whole estate and put the sale of it into the hands of a well known London firm with whom I had had a few dealings, since they had the good sense to know that a reliable man, on the spot, familiar with local conditions, could be useful.

I was useful to myself over the matter of the gate. To me had been entrusted the sale of movable articles not important enough to be catalogued. And for the one and only time in my life I cheated. The vultures were already busy picking the bones of what had been a beautiful house, and I simply could not stand up and sell that gate for scrap iron. I "bought it in" at a fair, but not a competitive price.

So, at last, it was mine, and it fitted, just as I had known it would. Only seven feet high, wide enough to take a farm wagon, but beautiful: acanthus leaves and those pine cones which the uninformed call small pineapples. I'd guarantee that the man who wrought that gate had never seen a pineapple.

When it was hung, cleared of rust, painted glossy, Steve rang me asking me to step over and help him out, and I said, on impulse— or is there, in us all, however little we care to face it, that tit for tat instinct?—I said, "Why not come here? I have something to celebrate. Come and help christen my new gate." Then I realized that "christen" was not quite the word for use between friends of whom one has said, "Never again," and the other never even tried.

Steve said, "Well, a little walk would do no harm. But there will be six of us."

"That's all right. I have seven glasses."

"But it's such a mixed bag. . . . Even Celia . . . All right, we'll be over. . . . Thanks."

It was rather mixed. The Korean, very dignified and with a pleasant smile, spoke no English and brought with him a so-called interpreter, very fluent in mangled French and English. There was also a Bulgarian and his keeper, multilingual to some extent. They had been misdirected and seemed to think that they had come to Crowswood to see some new type of machine. But, given enough goodwill and, is it cynical to say? enough alcohol, men reveal themselves as akin. Everybody eventually understood that a new doorway or gateway needed an oblation, an offering to the gods, so that good fortune might step over and in, bad luck be banned. By the time this was understood, we were all pretty drunk, and few entrances, I think, had been more generously christened. Then the man from Korea said something to his interpreter, who communicated with Celia, who, looking a bit confused, consulted with the others. Let nobody feel excluded. She turned to me and said, in the stilted manner of an interpreter, "He asks by what name?"

That caught me off balance. I said, "Well, I suppose Rose Cottage."

She turned and, communicating as much by gesture as by words, conveyed that rather dull message. And then turned back to me and said, "Alec, he says something more personal. Gateway to Happiness. You know what Orientals are for flowery phrases!"

I said, "I think that's rather nice."

On occasions as rare as I could contrive, I went to London, which I had become too much of a countryman to enjoy. In fact I was always glad to get to Liverpool Street station and settle down to a British Rail dinner which I found, perhaps by association, invariably good. It had been a hot, sticky day, and I felt sorry for commuters, now cramming themselves into the already crowded trains.

Suddenly Celia Bowyer came into view, accompanied by a man of whom I took small notice; there was indeed nothing much to notice, a very average man. She looked very smart in a frock and jacket of pretty, floral stuff and with a wisp of gauzy stuff masquerading as a hat. They came about level with the window where I sat, and then drew away a little, so that other people sometimes obscured my view.

Nowadays inhibitions about public displays of affection have almost vanished, but the embrace between the two was so prolonged, so passionate—and somehow desperate—that it seemed almost indecent to watch it. In fact I tried not to, yet was powerless to look away. And alongside my feeling—almost of shame—at being witness to such a display, I suffered a sense of trepidation. How many other people on this train were watching, recognizing Celia? Popping eyes. Wagging tongues. Steve was too modest and good-natured to have made any real enemies, but he had been extremely successful—and success does attract envy. More dangerous because less open.

There wasn't much I could do except make up my mind that if a whiff of gossip ever reached Steve, I would refute it.

There was the flurry, the banging of doors, and the train started. The other seat at my table remained empty. Dinner was served, and people who gibe at British Rail food haven't suffered at the hands of Mrs. Argent and her like. However, tonight nothing tasted quite right.

Celia slipped in. I was sure that she had been crying but had taken time and pains to repair things in the wash room. And she greeted me with apparent pleasure.

"Alec! How lovely! Did you keep this seat for me? I can't eat anything—I had a huge lunch—but I do want a drink."

There were, so far as I could see or guess, no repercussions. Seasons came and went. Then, one typically mad March evening, my phone rang. Steve, sounding as though he were choking, said, "Alec. Can you come? Please come. Alec . . . I've killed Celia."

I was immediately afflicted with what I lightly called The Shakes, something that, in low moments, I regarded as sinister and very difficult to describe, a kind of quiver in the marrow of one's bones. It did not affect my mind. I said, "Steve, put that phone down and just wait. I'll be right over. Just wait. Steve, I'm coming."

I went on foot—far quicker than opening my garage door, my gate, driving down my bit of lane, on to the main road, and into Steve's long drive. I had only to run across my back garden, over the one remaining bit of pasture at Crowswood, jump across something called a ha-ha, a fine name for a ditch, and into Steve's garden. But the wind was dead against me, snatching away my breath and in places the ground was soggy.

Steve was out on his front porch, waiting for me. He looked like a man who had suffered a severe internal injury and was bleeding to death inside. The possibility, the hope that he could be mistaken, died at the sight of his face. He took hold of me and seemed to collapse. I heard myself say sharply, "Pull yourself together, man. Stand up. Let's get indoors." The heavy front door opened easily enough, and then the wind seemed to snatch it, and it closed behind us with a bang.

To the left of the hall, the door of the small sitting room, which they used when alone or entertaining two or three friends, stood open. All the lamps there had rose coloured shades and the carpet was pink; seen from the hall it had a warm, enticing look.

"She's in there."

I then asked my silly question: "You are sure?" Hope dies hard. I

was thinking again that he might have hit her, knocked her unconscious, panicked.

"Look for yourself. I . . . I strangled her."

I braced myself and went into the pretty room.

My experience of people who have been strangled was limited,
confined, in fact, to the horrible sight of a bankrupt who had
hanged himself in his barn. But I had read . . . about cyanosis,
protruding eyeballs and lolling tongues. Nothing fitted here. Celia
lay on the pink covered sofa—her favourite place—her face half
turned into a cushion. She could have been asleep, but for the
slightly odd angle of her head. She was undoubtedly dead, but she
had not been strangled. There was no mark on her neck. And not a
hair of her head was disarranged. (The oddest things will slip into
the mind, and for a moment I thought about a scandal, way back in
the time of Elizabeth I. Amy Robsart, dead of a broken neck at the
foot of some stairs, "and her headdress not disarranged" a fact that
had puzzled everybody at the time.)

On the sofa table was a great bowl of pink hyacinths and on
another table a vase of freesias.

I shall detest the scent of those flowers so long as I live.

I went back into the hall, and Steve said, "You believe me?"

"Yes."

"Alec, I need a bit of help."

"You need a drink. And so do I." He was still acting like a
zombie, so I went into the dining room, pushed him into a chair,
poured two good slugs of brandy, and sat down myself. One thing I
had noticed. When I said, "Put that phone down," he had done just
that, leaving it dangling out in the hall. I set it back on my way
through.

Steve said, "You're my friend. Stand by me, Alec. Don't let them
pry. Say I did it. Say I always had a foul temper. I killed her, and
I'm willing to take the consequences. What I can't face is the *yap*.
All that rot about diminished responsibility—or provocation. I
don't want her name blackened."

"Of course not. I'm with you there."

"I'd hang. I deserve to. Or I could blow my brains out. But it'd
be, Why? Why? You're my friend. . . . And you're clever. Can't
you think of a reason—I mean respectable one—why a chap like
me should suddenly strangle his wife?"

"To begin with, you didn't strangle her. I think you broke her neck."

"Makes no difference. I shouldn't have laid hands on her. No excuse at all. I mean, I wasn't really mad or jealous, the way they'd think. I wasn't even surprised." He hesitated as though wondering how much more to tell me. Then, speaking more quickly than was his habit, he said, "You see, I was so absolutely dotty about her. Awed. It took me more than a week. . . . So I was always a bit dubious about that baby. But I didn't really care. In fact, if she married me because of that, I could only be grateful. There were so many chaps, better looking, better off, more amusing. . . . And this'll show you how daft a man can be! After the baby, this between ourselves, mind, she started having affairs."

It was hardly the moment to say that I knew.

"Never local," he said. "At least I think not. She was never like that. Never nasty. But I always knew. Inside myself. In my bones. Hell! I could tell by the very smell on her. And yet . . . I was always glad to have her back. You may think that despicable, but I loved her."

So far he'd hardly sipped his brandy, now he took two great gulps.

"Tonight," he said. Stopped. Started again. "Tonight she said she wanted a divorce. She said she wanted to marry a fellow called Peel, Bobbie Peel, and he's a proper bastard. I know. At Willingford he was a byword. His wife divorced him, and a messy case that was! And I happen to know that he's not sound financially. Celia's father left her a packet—did you know?" I shook my head.

"Alec, I swear, I was reasonable. I said, 'He's after your money; think again.' And she said I was wrong. It was on account of the baby. . . . She's two months gone. So I said . . . oh, some rot about never mind, something about having been through this hoop before, and we could do it again. But she wouldn't listen, and I said something like, 'Listen to me. I will not have you ruin your life!' Alec, she laughed and said lightning never struck twice in the same place. And I grabbed—to shake her . . . So here we are. Unless you can help. Say you were here. Say you saw me lose my temper. Say I often hit her. Say anything. To make it look decent."

I had, though I say it myself, a lively mind. Never given full rein and now on the rampage.

I said, "Steve, I have an idea. It may not work. But if it did . . . Apart from the heavy stuff, what vehicles have you?"

"There's the Land-Rover." I thought, Too strong! "And the jeep. She had the little Sprite. And there's my Ford."

"We'll take the Ford. Now listen. You must do exactly what I say. And this is your story. I walked over to have a drink with you this evening, and on account of the weather, you drove me home. She came along for the ride. . . ." I then told him how that ride would end.

At first he looked so stupid that I thought he hadn't understood. Then he said, "No. You might get hurt. Damn it all! I've just killed my wife. I'm not going to hurt my best friend. I'll drive."

I argued, bearing in mind what he'd said about blowing his brains out. "You're in no state, Steve. This has to be done in a split second. I shall be ready. I shan't get hurt."

"Either I'll drive, or I don't go." I knew he could be as stubborn as wood, so I gave in.

We had another argument about who should carry out the corpse. He said he couldn't. Couldn't even go into that room.

My physical contacts with the dead woman had been of the slightest and always completely conventional. Best man kissed bride, very hastily; various Christmas parties with token kisses under the mistletoe and then lately the fashion had come in for those quite meaningless cheek brushings between friends. And I was no dancer, because by the time I had leisure for it, I was too old to learn.

So this was the first time I'd ever put my arms round her. I know the difference between live and dead weight, but even dead she was very light for her size. Bones very frail and probably brittle. For a moment I doubted the wisdom, even the necessity of my scheme. Given a pathologist's report, a sympathetic jury and a lenient judge . . . But it was hardly safe to count upon such favourable elements. Besides I could not entirely trust Steve; he was so essentially honest, so conscience stricken, quite unlikely to make a good show under pressure. My way—if it worked—would be best.

So I carried Celia out and arranged her in the passenger seat. Her head dropped, but only as a tired woman's might do. And on such a night, the wind worse than ever and a thin sleet falling, we were unlikely to be seen on our short journey.

Steve, from habit, began to fasten his seat belt. I said, "I wouldn't! It could make just that second's difference."

Steve's drive, the short stretch of main road, my bit of lane, and then my beautiful gate—the Gate to Happiness!

"Stop," I said. "And be ready. Steve, for God's sake be ready!"

Then, as I walked forward, doubt struck again. Steve never ran ostentatious cars, but he always had the best of its breed. The Ford looked big and strong and heavy. My gate, by contrast, rather frail.

However, when I had it unlatched and was pushing it into position, the wind was against me. Or had something happened to me? That shakiness of the bone marrow reaching out to muscle? Was I, in fact, going to end like Father? Not exactly a heartening thought at such a moment, but it angered me, and anger helps. I shoved with greater vigour, got the thing open and stood beside it, holding it back until just the right moment. The ironwork was now as slippery from the sleet as it had been when we had jocularly shared our drinks with it. It was like grappling with a live thing with a will of its own.

The Ford advanced. And just a second too soon the wind wrenched the gate from my grip.

I now understand why no two witnesses of any extraordinary event ever give identical accounts. Look at the Gospels, wrongly termed Synoptic! I was there, more or less in my right senses; I saw, I heard, but I could never describe.

I only knew that what I had planned as a sidelong crash, sufficient to explain why the passenger should sustain a broken neck, had, because of the wind's strength and my weakness, turned into a head-on smash, and Steve had not had time to jump and roll away. As instructed.

The lights went at first impact, and on such a night there was no light from the sky. So it was in total darkness that I set out, after a moment or so of stunned immobility—to grope my way to the house and switch on my porch light. I was partially guided by sound, for after the first tearing crash there were minor noises, creaking and crackings and a belated thump.

My first thought was that nobody could possibly emerge alive from such a mess of wrecked metal, broken glass. An odd simile struck me—it looked rather as though a bull had charged a gate, but in doing so, foreshortened itself. My gate lay athwart the concertina'd bonnet of Steve's car, and it had brought one of the gateposts with it. That accounted for the thump.

And I thought: I no more intended to kill Steve than he had intended to kill Celia.

Then, out of the wreckage, he called. Calmly, all things considered, "Alec! Alec! Lend a hand . . ."

The door on his side wasn't even jammed, but he was in a curious position, the steering wheel so wedged between his chest and hunched up knees that now he occupied less space than he had ever done since he was about fourteen, burrowing under a tilt in the obstacle race on sports day.

He said, "Try the seat catch. I can't reach it."

Incredibly, it worked. His seat moved backwards a few inches, and he cautiously freed first his arm, then his legs.

"All right?" I asked anxiously.

"Yes." Then he attempted to stand, stumbled, and grabbed at me for support. "I think I've busted my left ankle."

"Lean on me and hop."

I got him indoors and on to the couch in my living room. I fetched a couple of painkillers—mild, but all I had available. I poured two drinks. All in the silence of complete exhaustion. I could think of what still remained to be done—inform the police, get Steve into hospital, but at the moment I was incapable of further effort.

Steve recovered and spoke first though what he said was not quite in his usual prosaic style.

He said, "Well, now we can at least mourn her decently."

"Yes," I said. "We can." And that "we" meant more than anybody would ever know. For I, too, had been in love with Celia from the first moment I saw her.

6

The natives are friendly

The new shop attracted a great deal of interest even before it was opened. Nobody knew what it was going to sell, nobody could see what was going on behind the blinds at the two bow windows. The workmen—not Baildon men—were either surly, ignorant, or reticent. All that the most curious could ascertain was that everything that could be painted white was being painted white and that windows were being fitted with awnings, striped rose pink and white. Perhaps a new eating place. It'd last maybe six months and fail, as similar ventures had failed before. Even a Chinese restaurant, run by a diligent family and so without labour problems, had failed in this backward town. Too few citizens or people from the surrounding rural district had holidays abroad and thus acquired a taste for foreign food. And although it was now in the latter half of the twentieth century, there remained the mediaeval belief that foreigners began at the border of Norfolk to the north and of Essex to the south. And all to be profoundly distrusted.

The new shop opened on a Monday morning in mid-June, and somebody must have worked through the brief darkness. On each side of the door stood a tub brilliant with blue salvia and pink geranium. Over the door was a sign that said "Rosa," and under the name was a half blown pink rose. Each of the windows was backed with pink velvet curtains about shoulder high. In the left hand window there were two dresses, displayed not on the lifelike models which Baildon's up-till-now best shop had used but on invisible frames. One was a full length evening dress of black velvet, very sedate and formal, the other a trouser suit in pinkish beige, well cut and sharply creased.

Between the two stood a bowl of roses.

The right-hand window—not by any means crammed—managed to display a number of things designed to tempt women: a filmy night-dress, thrown negligently over a small gold chair, some costume jewellery, a few bottles of scent, and a jar of bath salts. Dominating this display was a bowl of peonies and blue delphinium.

Nothing was priced.

It was generally agreed that the place wouldn't last a month. Who wore toe-length evening dresses now, except of course half a dozen old fossils dragged out to attend some formal occasion? And although the trouser suit was more up to date and admittedly smart, it missed its mark; the unisex generation wore jeans, tee shirts, and thick pullovers.

Practically every female in Baildon who could walk—and one indeed in a wheelchair—came to stare at Rosa's windows that day or the next. But nobody entered the shop. This fact did not dismay Harriet Stone, who had prospected with care before committing herself and her limited capital. This town exactly suited her purpose because—unbelievably—it was without a single shop of its kind. Three shops had dress departments, all upstairs, the ground floor being devoted to utilitarian goods like bed linen, carpets, and kitchenware. Rosa's was an innovation to be approached with caution.

On the third day, at eleven o'clock, the first customer came in. Appropriately enough it was the Mayoress. She was feeling shy and was therefore gruff.

"I'd like to try that black dress."

Her vital statistics were all wrong. And since Harriet's aim was to be exclusive, she could not say that she could supply the same frock in a different fitting.

She said, suitably regretful, "I'm afraid it would be too long."

"Couldn't the hem be turned up?"

"I suppose so. But it would spoil it. It would throw it out of proportion. Did you particularly wish for black?"

"I didn't particularly want. . . . But there it is. Last month Bill —that's my husband—went an got hisself elected Mayor. And I mustn't let him down."

"Of course not. Now, let me think. . . . Yes, I have a dress which would look marvellous on you. It is grey. And slightly more expensive than the black."

It was a cunning, calculated, saleswoman touch and completely wasted on the forthright woman who for a year would be Baildon's first lady.

"Hev I said anything about cost?"

Mentally Harriet added ten pounds to the price of the grey chiffon.

Then came the business of fitting. Helping the Mayoress out of her rather tight fitting dress, reaching down the grey chiffon, slipping it over the tousled head.

Never enthuse.

"I think it suits you. See what you think."

The Mayoress came out of the fitting room and confronted her new image in the full length glass. She turned about gracelessly and gave a grudging verdict. "It'll do." And then she said something touching: "Bill should be pleased."

And all foolery apart, it was a becoming dress, far kinder than black would have been. Harriet *knew*. Black was for blondes or for old white haired women.

"Now," said the Mayoress, "what about something outa the other window to set it off?"

"Nothing that would interfere with the classical outline. I think I know exactly. A pair of earrings. Blue. To emphasize the colour of your eyes."

It was now quite a long time since anybody had noticed the colour of the Mayoress's eyes.

"Less see them," she said. "Might as well go the whole hog while I'm about it."

Then, like a fool, Harriet leaned over the curtained rail, instead of drawing it back and reaching in. And the pain struck.

With the earrings cupped in her hand, she sat down in the little velvet covered chair. Intended for customers.

All wrong, of course. But she held out the glittering, blue-green things, rhinestones, semi-demi-precious, and the Mayoress came forward, took them, tried them on, lifting her drab loops of hair the better to view them.

Harriet said, "You know, upswept hair suits you."

The Mayoress received this piece of information with a grunt and said, "And now, if you don't mind, how about an evening bag?"

There was about the "if you don't mind" a hint of "if it isn't too much trouble." Harriet felt rebuked and tried to make up for the dilatory service by asking the Mayoress to accept the sequinned bag with the compliments of Rosa. She said in her sweetest manner, "You are the first lady in the town this year. And my first customer. I'd like to mark the occasion."

Something in the Mayoress was not satisfied, and reporting to her cronies she said, "It's all right if you can face the prices. But no service. No service at all. She just sets about telling you how your hair should be done. And to get her to shift was like drawing teeth."

Still she was very proud that she had been the first and, for as long as it lasted, used the white carrier bag with its single rose for several incongruous purposes.

Left to herself Harriet swallowed two painkillers and endured a mood of depression. In all the excitement, how could she have overlooked the existence of her old enemy—a weakness of the back which had first shown itself when she was ten and been the bane of her life for nineteen years.

Perhaps her parents would have seen something strange in a child of ten who never jumped or ran or romped. But she was orphaned at the age of three, and her Aunt Grace had always been preoccupied in keeping up appearances and making a penny do the work of sixpence. When, provoked by some activity, the pain was very bad, Aunt Grace had called it lumbago and applied a fierce liniment. Harriet was eighteen, out in the world, earning her own living, before she sought medical advice and was X-rayed. The result was discouraging. A double curvature of the spine. Of some long standing. Surgery was possible, but not recommended. Try corrective measures; a fearsome, heavy surgical belt with steel struts; the left shoe built up, an inch on the sole, two inches on the heel.

This latter device she quickly discarded, for it gave her a club-footed look, and she was as vain as a peacock.

Her infirmity had governed her choice of occupation. Her main interests in life were books and clothes, but to be a librarian or the humblest form of shop assistant demanded an ability to stand. She must have a sedentary job, which really boiled down to typing of the most routine kind. The post of private secretary was beyond her reach, for that one needed to be active and lively. Moreover, the job must be near home, within easy walking distance of Aunt Grace's house in a decayed part of Richmond. The idea of standing in a bus queue or strap hanging on the Underground was quite impossible. She found the job she needed, as opposed to anything she actually wanted, in a house agent's. There, sitting down, she made the window display, mounting photographs of properties—all very desirable ones—and typing in the details alongside or underneath the picture. She also prepared on the photostat machine the pages of description to be posted to enquirers. To type, she sat in a lowish chair with a specially designed cushion at her back. To manage the photostat machine she sat on a high stool, soon painful, but she could organize her own time and drift over to the more comfortable chair.

At the beginning, life had another side; she had several girl friends, who introduced boys, made up foursomes, arranged picnics and outings of various kinds. She was pretty enough, could be amusing, but she tired too easily. Two dances were as much as she could manage in an evening; one game of tennis or badminton laid her flat, even a long walk was too much. And who really could be bothered with a girl whose first thought on entering a bar was to find a comfortable seat?

Girls married young; spinsterhood began at twenty. Friends drifted away and life narrowed down to two rec. one 16 ft. by 12, the other 20 ft. including bow window; four bed; mod bath and kitchen; garage or space for garage; rateable value. . . .

When the office closed, she went home by the shops, collecting food for Aunt Grace to cook. And that, too, was routine. Aunt Grace stuck to her penurious ways even though Harriet now made a full contribution to household expenses. Getting old, afflicted with vague pains which the old fierce liniment did not do much to relieve, Aunt Grace stuck to her programme—or her principles. Harriet soon learned that anything unusual was wrong.

Harriet was twenty-nine when her aunt died, leaving her forty-two thousand pounds on deposit at Barclay's bank. The grim old house in its overgrown garden was bequeathed to a godson, of whom Harriet had never heard.

Now Harriet was free.

So, with caution and discretion, she had chosen Baildon as the place where dreams come true.

Beauty. It was an abstract term but made visible, made concrete in the modest dress shop.

And now. Look, she said to herself—or to one version of herself —Look what I've done for that stubby little woman! And how am I being rewarded?

The bad moment passed. All would be well if she simply remembered to humour her back. And in fact, despite the busy trade that began now, the ice had been broken, she suffered no more pain for a fortnight.

It was at the end of a long, hot market day, and she was tidying the shop when the melodious chimes heralded yet another customer. She turned and saw a man looking not unlike the proverbial bull in a china shop. She greeted him, and he went straight to the point. "Good afternoon. I want a fur coat. My wife's got a birthday coming up."

He had a deep, pleasant voice with a decided Suffolk accent. A farmer, that was obvious, but a prosperous one. His cavalry twill breeches and light tweed jacket had obviously been made to his measure, and although his manner showed that he felt out of place, it also held the confidence of a man who could pay what was demanded of him.

"I have one fur coat in stock, but I could get others."

"Show me."

She went to one of the mirror fronted doors and lifted down the coat. It was of beaver lamb, and though a new process had considerably lightened the weight of that particular fur, it was still heavier than most. She felt a warning pang.

If I sit down promptly, it may pass.

She sat down in the velvet covered chair and spread the coat on her lap so that the lining showed as well.

He thought it a funny way to go about serving a customer, but he took the few necessary steps and reaching out a big tanned hand, touched fur and lining gingerly, as though expecting to be bitten. Then he backed away.

"I'd like to see it on."

Harriet stood up and slid on the garment. It was over-large for her. The pain had not withdrawn, had in fact increased.

He remembered hearing talk between women and agreed that the woman's manner was lackadaisical. There was a grit of impatience in his voice as he said, "Could you turn round?

"Yes. It's about right, I should say. My wife's your height, but a bit stouter. It's ample on you though. What is it?"

"Beaver lamb."

"I meant how much?"

"A hundred and eight . . ." And that includes ten pounds for making me stand in such agony, you big brute!

"Oh, I was reckoning on something better."

"You mean more expensive. What are you prepared to pay?"

Before he answered, he edged past her and seated himself in the chair. He'd had a tiring day. Up at six helping to feed stock, standing in the Corn Exchange selling hay, standing for a pint and a bite in the pub near the Exchange, the pub that boasted that it was the smallest in England and offered no sitting accommodation at all. Then he'd stood at the cattle market watching pigs being sold and stood some more in the auctioneer's office making arrangements to enter some of his own pigs for sale next week.

"I thought more in the region of a thousand."

What ailed the bloody woman? Why didn't she snatch at a chance to do business? After all, she could hardly make such a sale every day.

"I could get down a selection of coats in that range," Harriet said. The black wave engulfed her.

When it receded, she was in the chair with her head bent forward on her knees. Without looking up she murmured, "I'm all right now. I'm so sorry."

"Here, take a swig of this." She looked up. The man, with an expression of acute anxiety on his face, was offering a silver mounted hunting flask. The coat lay in a heap on the floor.

She attempted to drink. The liquid gurgled, but none came out, instead her tongue seemed to be drawn into the flask.

"Funny thing. I never knew a woman that had the knack. Keep your tongue out of the way. Just pour it down. That's better. And again. It can't hurt you. It's sound brandy. . . . God, you had me scared. For a minute I thought . . . Are you delicate?"

The question was not asked impertinently, but rather in an awed and curious way, as one might ask, Can you really speak Arabic?

"Oh, no. I just have a weak back. And," she said defensively, "it is a hot day. And beaver lamb is a bit heavy."

"You know what you want, don't you? A good handy, active girl."

"I know. But not yet. Not until I am sure that I can afford. . . ."

"Look," she was to learn that it was one of his most used words, "is there anywhere where we could both sit?"

"Of course." She glanced at her watch. "If you'd just drop the catch . . ."

While he did so, she hoisted herself to her feet and then led the way to the sitting room, part of the flat which she had made behind the shop.

There he dropped into a chair on one side of the empty hearth, and she took the other.

"Thass better," he said, stretching long legs and surveying his large, superbly shod feet with marked disapproval. "I was a fool to wear new shoes for the first time on a hot day. D'you smoke?"

That business over, he said, "Now about this girl. I hev in mind one who wouldn't cost you much. My own daughter. She's eighteen, just left school and not a clue what she wants to do. Not a clue. She's clever, and her mother thinks she should take up something serious, make a career of some sort. But Olivia—thass her name—is a bit on the flibbertigibbet side. This, being new, she might like. At least for a time. And pay wouldn't matter. In fact, as I understand the new ruling, it now pays *not* to pay the young.

There's some kind of subsidy. And living at home, all she'd want is pocket money. Petrol she just helps herself to—we have our own pump. How about it?"

"Frankly, it sounds rather too good to be true, Mr. . . ."

"Kentford, George. Out at Muchanger Hall. Mind, she mightn't take to the idea. There's no telling. But her mother would. They're devoted to each other, and yet somehow they can't seem to hit it off. When they're together . . . Well, shall we try? I'll send her in to buy something, and you can see what you think. Now don't get up. I can let myself out. I'll hang up that coat of armour for you on my way out."

The girl, Olivia, came next day. A tall, big girl with a good deal of puppy flesh and a leggy colt's grace. Her garb was a compromise; she wore jeans, but they were clean, unpatched, of a pleasant dark green. They should have been accompanied by a tee shirt, but were not. Instead something curiously like an old fashioned Eton jacket with bright brass buttons. She had an absolute mane of fair hair, with a touch of russet. It had to be pushed back to give her a clear view of her surroundings.

To think of puppies, of colts, was not out of order. The girl stood there, pushing back her hair and literally sniffing.

"Hullo," she said. "I'm looking for something for a birthday present. May I look round?"

"Of course."

As yet, Harriet had no proof of her identity, and yet she was certain. She could see a resemblance—and that surprised her for she had not consciously taken much note of Mr. Kentford's appearance.

The girl wandered, lifted and replaced things, and finally sighed. "It is difficult! Mum's a bit on the conservative side, and Dad's worse. He'd denounce all costume jewellery as chicken wire."

"I have some exceptionally nice handkerchiefs. Swiss. Hand rolled hems and initials, not embroidered but woven into the fabric."

Harriet went to a drawer in the white painted cabinet. A pleasant odour streamed out.

"What a nice smell. What is it?"

"Pot-pourri."

"Do you sell it?"

"Yes. In sachets. One-forty each."

"I'll have three. The initial I want is M. Oh, yes. Nice! Can I have six?"

Harriet selected one of the smaller rose decorated bags and slid in the purchases. "The handkerchiefs are one-ninety each."

"That'll be fifteen pounds sixty," the girl said instantly.

"I was reaching the same conclusion, by a slower process."

"I could always do sums in my head." From her shoulder bag she extracted a wallet, pleasantly thick. It had two gold initials in the corner. O.K.

"Parents just don't think," she commented. "I went through school as Oh Kay."

Even when the transaction was completed, she lingered, and Harriet was conscious of being under scrutiny. It did not embarrass her. The crookedness was not visible, she was very slim and had often been called graceful by other females. Today she was wearing a severe jersey dress in pale coffee, cinched in at the waist with a massive looking belt of brown leather and gold coloured metal.

"I like that, if I may be personal," Olivia said, indicating the belt. "But on me it would look like the girth on a horse."

"You'll fine down."

"I fear not. I'm a glutton. Even now, just half past ten, and I'm inwardly grieving for Chinery's. Oh, sorry, Chinery's was the shop on the other side of the pub. They sold lovely coffee and heavenly cream cakes. And inside it was like something out of *Cranford.*"

"What happened to it?"

"Nobody knows for certain, but I have a shrewd suspicion that the new man at the old Hawk bought them out. He's not a live and let live type, and the old girls did offer competition, of a sort. So now if you want morning coffee, you can go to the Hawk or up to Underhill's, which is pretty grotty. Well, I must go, I suppose." At the door she turned back and said, "Thanks for solving my problem."

In the evening it was Mrs. Kentford who telephoned. She sounded brisk and businesslike.

"I know I ought to come and discuss this personally, but I am very busy. It's like this. My daughter Olivia would like to come and help in your shop for a bit. Could you use her?"

"I should be delighted."

"She has no experience. And perhaps I should say that it may be just a whim. But I think that in a shop . . . I mean, she could do no actual harm. And it would give her an interest while she makes up her mind what to do with herself. And she needs only a token wage. In fact I think myself she has too much money. She is our only child."

Harriet imagined the situation. The pretty only daughter, the doting father, the mother slightly jealous.

"Well, if she likes to come along, I can do with some help."

Then began the halcyon days. Olivia was strong and willing, as enthusiastic as a child playing at keeping shop. And within a fortnight there was another element—the slightly embarrassing schoolgirl adoration for an older girl, or for a mistress. Olivia simply could not do enough to show her devotion.

She brought gifts almost every day. The Muchanger garden produced apricots, nectarines, green figs, crops of various apples and pears. Olivia arrived each morning, glowing with health, brimful of energy, laden with offerings. "Mum sent a few eggs. They're free range if you're fussy about such things."

"I do prefer them. But I do realize that few people can afford to be fussy."

"I tell Dad that when he's being so critical. I think you'd like him. He's out of the Ark!" She stopped short, her hand to her mouth. "What a thing to say! Please, don't think I'm implying . . . I mean, you know I think you're wonderful."

Sometimes Olivia's devotion took a maternal hand.

"If you don't mind my saying so, you don't eat enough. Cheese is all very well; it rounds off a meal nicely, but it's not enough in itself. Are you afraid of getting fat?"

"No. Frankly, I can't cook, and I can't be bothered."

Next morning Olivia arrived with a fowl dressed for the oven and a collection of vegetables.

"I'm a bit out of practice, but I once did a course. Do you trust me?"

She really was a most competent girl. The chicken was beautifully cooked. There was even smooth, home-made bread sauce. "It lacks one thing. I should have stuck the onion with cloves."

They shared that meal—the first of many. And at the end of it Olivia said, "There, now I shall know you have something to fall back upon for supper."

If Olivia had had her way, Harriet would have spent her time sitting in the chair and issuing instructions.

"Miss Henderson, do let me try dressing the window. You just sit there and say what's wrong."

Nothing was wrong. Ordinarily her movements were sweeping and vigorous, but in the confined space of the bow windows she moved with the delicacy of a butterfly. And ten times she would tirelessly go out to study the effect from outside and then come in to make some minute adjustment.

The question of modes of address had arisen quite early. "Look," Olivia said, "you can't go on calling me Miss Kentford. My name is Olivia. Most people call me Olly, which I don't like very much— too much like Polly. But I should like it if you'd call me Olivia."

"I will. I think it is a beautiful name." She neatly avoided a reciprocal request. She said, "I have always disliked my Christian name."

"Harriet? Why? What is there to dislike about it? Harriet . . . I think it is a lovely name."

"It sounds to me like somebody's great-aunt."

Olivia brought in a few customers, most of them in search of pretty, relatively inexpensive things. For their meagre spending she was vaguely apologetic: "It's just that we don't have the sort of thing they want, Miss Henderson. Look at these coats from Afghanistan, for instance."

"I prefer not to! To my eye they are ugly, such crude, primary colours. I've had enough of ugliness. Besides, we haven't the space for such bulky things."

The eye of love—however evanescent its nature—can be painfully sharp. One day Olivia said apropos of nothing, "I say, does my hair worry you?"

"Not worry exactly. I just can't see how you can spare the energy to brush it back every time you want to look at anything."

"It's like blinking. Who notices that? Still if it pleases you, I'll do something about it. Shall I get a poodle crop or pin it up?"

"Really, my dear, it is not for me to say. Except don't crop it. You might regret it."

"Not if *you* liked it. Of course what I'd really like is to do it like yours. But I don't want to look like a copy cat."

"Hardly likely. Your hair is so different." Harriet's was dead black and satin smooth, Olivia's midway between yellow and amber, very curly and springy.

"If you're sure you don't mind . . ."

Next day she arrived with a great coil of hair, pinned high. The style was utterly unlike Harriet's rather severe french knot, and it diminished Olivia's resemblance to a pony.

Presently the guns were out at Muchanger, and Mr. Kentford joined the good cause of saving Harriet from starvation, sending partridges and pheasants. Mrs. Kentford continued to send eggs and once a large fruit cake.

"Some competition for the Women's Institute," Olivia explained. "Then that bitch Mrs. Foxley happened to say, 'Of course, you'll win. You always do!' And Mum was so mad she withdrew her entry and said she never wanted to see it again."

One cold late October evening the doorbell jangled. Harriet went along the passage that connected the flat to the seldom used house door and opened it as far as the stout chain would allow. She expected to see somebody collecting for some good cause or perhaps electioneering.

It was Mr. Kentford, not as she remembered him but a sombre figure in the street lamp's light. Black overcoat, black hat, immediately removed.

"Good evening. May I come in for a bit?"

"Of course." She rather regretted that she was wearing a very old wadded dressing gown instead of the less comfortable housecoat. I'm not much of an advertisement for Rosa's! Sloppy old slippers, too.

He smelt very strongly of whisky.

He took off the coat, dropped it on the floor, and set the hat carefully on top of it. He then sat down heavily and said, "Could you spare a cup of coffee?"

"Of course. In fact I was just making some."

"It had better be black."

She was soon back, two cups on a pretty tray, some cheese biscuits in a pretty dish.

"The truth is, I've had one too many. I had to go to a funeral, up Wisbech way. I don't like that part of the country. And I don't like funerals. Not that thass unique." He sipped. "I should be old enough to know that what in the ordinary way I can take and be none the worse for'll go back on me if I'm a mite depressed. As I was. I expect you know that bit about not sending to ask for whom the bell tolls."

She did. She was faintly surprised that he should. He lifted the cup again, and this time drank deeply.

"Another thing too. The police seem to have got it in for the club. You'd think they might find something better to do. But two members have been copped lately. One wasn't even on the move, but he was in charge. . . . So I walked down. Not in charge of a vehicle, an animal, or a child under six . . ." He left the vagaries of the law at that point, rearranged himself in the chair, and said, "I'm all right now. And apart from all else, I did want to thank you for all you've done for Olly."

"Done for her? Absolutely nothing, except perhaps let her amuse herself a bit. And she has done so much for me."

"You've done what two schools—pretty expensive ones, too—failed at. You've civilized her. I don't mean just surface stuff. Deep down, she's changed. A different girl. We both notice it."

"I think she's merely growing up."

"And happy. The main thing, after all. Oh, and another thing. I never really apologized for that day. I thought you were being, well . . . haughty. And there you were, dead on your feet."

"I hope your wife was pleased with the coat Olivia finally chose."

"Madge loved it. The more so when she knew what it cost."

Something in Harriet was alerted. She was not without experience; to some extent the boys of her youth had given way to married men whose opening gambit was usually some criticism, direct or implied, of their wives.

However Mr. Kentford said quickly, "I don't mean that in any fault finding way. It's just that Madge knows the value of money. And she's clever with it, too. D'you know, all these years, I've never had to employ an accountant. Even VAT she took in her stride."

"Olivia does mental arithmetic at a rate that dizzies me."

"I'm glad you find her useful."

Suddenly there was something unreal about this conversation, as though they were putting up a screen of words. Perhaps he felt it, too, for he fell silent. She roused herself to animation.

"In addition to sending me Olivia, both you and Mrs. Kentford have been remarkably generous. Sending me so many delicious things."

"Easily spared. The thing is, I was thinking just now, you don't look a mite the better. . . ." He gave a brief laugh. "There I go again! It's not that I'm finding fault with your appearance. You look fine. But delicate still. I'd rather hoped our air and some fodder with some real goodness in it would have fleshed you up a bit. And thass a cattle breeder's expression!" He laughed again and got to his feet. "I'm all right now. Thanks a lot for the coffee."

He slung his coat over his arm, took his hat in his hand.

At the door he nodded towards the chain. "You can't be too careful," he said. Outside the door he replaced his hat, in order to lift it as he said, "Good night." St. Mary's church clock sounded the three-quarters. Early yet, only a quarter to ten. And it had been an entirely proper visit. There was no reason at all why her heart should be hammering so hard that her fingers shook.

In the morning Olivia came with some branches of carefully preserved copper beech.

"We'll need some flowers, too. But first. Will you come to our party? All Hallowe'en. It's an annual event. Please say you will, or parental wrath will descend on my head."

"Why?"

"Oh, some Victorian idea, probably out of Mrs. Beeton. A first invitation should be written, with RSVP in one corner. I said, 'What rot! You know me well enough. . . .' "

"Saturday week. Olivia, I can't be sure yet. I may be in London."

"Try not to be. I will say for Dad when he gives a party, he gives a party. . . . You know, one night I'll lay in wait for that lout. I'll wring his bloody neck!"

Somebody had taken, with dreadful regularity, to dropping the greasy wrappings of fish and chips on the pavement just outside the shop.

Olivia fetched the tongs and the bucket, collected the main offender and a few satellites, and carried them through to the dustbin. Then she said, "I'll just dash across to Pamplin's." She surveyed the beech leaves. "Red, I think, and tawny, perhaps a touch of yellow."

Pamplin's was a flower shop diagonally across the Abbey Hill from Rosa's. In any other town it would have called itself Flora's or some similarly evocative name. In Baildon it was Pamplin's.

Left alone, Harriet thought about the invitation. Apart from two or three asking her to coffee mornings in aid of good causes, it was the first she had received since her arrival, and part of her easily divided mind urged acceptance. Why on earth not? What but a very warped imagination could see in it anything more than a friendly gesture? But another part urged caution. The policy of non-involvement.

Olivia came back with her arms full of flowers and a curious expression on her face.

"I say! Miss Pamplin says Dad was here last night. Was he?"

"Yes." God, I'd have said I was far past the blushing stage! And what is there to blush about?

"Discussing me?"

"We talked about you, yes. And we drank some coffee. He'd been to a funeral—and that depressed him, so he'd been to the club. And didn't . . . want to drive straight away."

Olivia's face cleared. "That's why he made no mention. He's absolutely morbid about funerals. He's only forty-one and as far as I know has never had a day's illness in his life. And Mum knows he'd have to hold a wake, so she wouldn't worry."

"Oh, it wasn't late. Just a quarter to ten."

"I suppose that would be late by Miss Pamplin's standard."

It was said lightly enough, but it gave Harriet a glance of one disadvantage of small town life. The watchfulness, the reporting, even the invention. She thought, I will attend the party, be seen by all as friend of the whole family.

She said, "I think I can rearrange that weekend. So I can accept your invitation."

"Oh, good!"

"What form does it take?"

"It operates on the principle of something for everybody. There's dinner. Black tie," she said almost apologetically. "So it always was, and so it must be. Until the last dinner jacket has gone to the scarecrow. Then there's bridge or snooker, and," she gave a little skip, "dancing in the barn. Not as oldy worldy as it sounds. It's Dad's barn, but used as a village hall. Muchanger never rose to one. And we round off with kippers."

"It sounds very grand."

"It's practically an institution. I say . . . It might do us a bit of good! If only we could offer a few crinolines—or bustles. . . . I know what you ought to wear—unless you have decided. That kind of Chinese job."

"A bad buy," Harriet admitted. "I thought it might tempt somebody young. It's unconventional enough and very cheap." Made in Hong Kong where wages were very low. On the other hand, if nobody bought the products, there might be no wages at all.

"Too narrow for me. Until I fine down—if I ever do! You'd look marvellous in it."

Yes, I should, Harriet thought. And the proprietor of a dress shop should be an advertisement for it.

"I might." A thought struck her. "Unless Mrs. Blount will be there."

"Who on earth is she?"

"The Mayoress."

"And what has she got to do with it?"

"I once told her that only blondes and white haired women could wear black."

Olivia laughed. "Not to worry. Actually we in the country don't have much to do with the town—socially I mean."

In the intervening days Rosa's sold two dinner dresses, the beaver lamb coat, two lurex scarves—one silver, one gold—and four evening bags. Harriet said, "I wish your father would give a party every month."

"Left to himself, he probably would. Now, you are sure you can spare me all day? Don't do too much. The Allinsons will pick you up at half past seven."

Mrs. Kentford greeted Harriet with a smile and a forthright handshake. "So we meet at last! I've so often meant to look in on you. But this place takes a bit of running, and last time I counted I was on twenty-one committees."

She led Harriet about, making introductions, and added to the normal confusion of too many people being introduced too quickly was the fact that so many of those present had an underlying resemblance to one another. They could almost have been members of the same family. Harriet reminded herself that this part of the country was where the Saxons had settled most firmly. And in the days of poor communications, there had probably been a good deal of intermarriage.

She was, and she felt like, an outsider. Everybody was civil, but conversation was not easy, and they all turned away soon, to greet more warmly somebody known, somebody with whom they shared jokes and memories. The few women whom she recognized as customers seemed to show a faint surprise at seeing her here. At least six people asked if she were related to the Hendersons at Talbot St. Mary. She had a mischievous impulse to say "Yes" and see what the reaction was.

The drinks circulated freely, carried round by a man in a white coat and two girls in overalls; on the breast of each garment the letter W stood out.

Then, when the move to the dining room began, from being an outsider she was made to feel like a usurper, for Mr. Kentford, shouldering his way through, took her by the elbow and said, "You're by me. You're the newcomer."

He was probably obeying a rule of hospitality far older than those laid down in any book of etiquette, but even Harriet, whose experience in such matters was small, knew that the place on the host's right hand belonged to the senior married woman present.

"I got you a cushion," Mr. Kentford said. "I saw you leaning about a bit."

"That was very kind."

The larger table seated sixteen, a smaller one, set at an angle, eight, the smaller table for the young. Both tables were covered with white damask cloths, starched to a glitter, both had banks of greenstuff out of which a few flowers and a great many candles rose, running along their centres. Very pretty indeed, but the big room did not depend upon the candles for illumination. Harriet heard Mr. Kentford say to his neighbour, "I loathe twilight. And I do like to see what I'm eating."

Harriet's right-hand neighbour was rather older than the average, his skin was darker and more sallow, dried-out looking. His dinner jacket smelt strongly of mothballs, a deterrent that few people used nowadays, and he ate as though he had been deprived of food for a fortnight and did not expect to eat again for a similar period. But he had mastered the art of talking while he ate, albeit rather jerkily. His story was not exceptional. Kicked out of East Africa. After thirty years. Lived through all that Mau Mau trouble. Fairly comfortably off out there. Not allowed to bring much out. Tough on the womenfolk. George and Madge had been exceptionally kind.

Mr. Kentford's neighbour was Mrs. Foxley, in all likelihood the one Olivia had designated as "that bitch." No longer young, but unlike many of the faded blondes present, she was putting up a fight. Her hair was tinted, and she wore a good deal of make-up. Her dress had not been bought in Baildon. It said Marshall and Snelgrove or possibly Harrods. She had a sprightly manner, from which her other neighbour derived little benefit since she concentrated upon Mr. Kentford, using his name with great frequency, now and again tapping him on the arm. When he addressed a remark to Harriet, she listened in unashamedly and then interrupted.

From where she sat, Harriet had a good view of Mrs. Kentford, obviously one of the clan, equally obviously Olivia's mother. She was a woman who would look her best in a good tailor made, and she had an air of authority. In repose her mouth had a rather hard line. It was easy to believe that she sat on twenty-one committees and difficult not to suspect that she was chairman of most of them.

It was a substantial meal, lavish helpings of smoked salmon with thin brown bread and butter, even more lavish helpings of roast turkey, two kinds of stuffing, and sausages, three or four vegetables. Service was brisk, for the two girls had been joined by another, and the man concentrated upon keeping glasses refilled.

"I see you're sticking to Warren's, George," Mrs. Foxley said. "Out of our range now, I'm afraid."

"It's cheaper in the end. They take complete charge. Band, everything. And that tunnel between the house and barn. The turkeys were home grown."

After a struggle Harriet admitted defeat.

"Is that really the best you can do?" Mr. Kentford asked with concern.

"George, how extremely rude!" Mrs. Foxley exclaimed, giving his hand a playful tap. "Miss Henderson may be on a diet."

Without turning his head, he asked, "Is that so?"

Answering the faint malice in Mrs. Foxley's voice, Harriet said, "That is one thing I've never had to bother about."

Plates were removed, clean ones brought. The girls offered trifle, foaming with whipping cream, and/or hot mince pies. Harriet's neighbour took a liberal helping of trifle—she could smell the sherry—and two mince pies. She refused both, and Mr. Kentford turned from his discussion about next Saturday's point-to-point, to say, "Oh, but you must. For every mince pie you eat before Christmas, you have a happy month in the New Year. Here's January for you." He lifted a pie and put it on her plate.

For the last ten minutes there had been sounds of new arrivals and of a band tuning up. Now all the young people rose and trooped out.

"You'll be for bridge, I take it, Phyl. I see the light of battle. . . ."

"Madge and Joe gave me and Jim such a trouncing on Thursday. I'm hoping for revenge. It is a pity you don't play."

"A great pity," said Harriet's neighbour. "I've always found that if you take a card game—any game—seriously, it takes your mind off your worries."

"And what would you like to do, Miss Henderson?"

"Just sit somewhere and give myself over to the pleasant process of digestion. Don't worry about me."

In the drawing room three tables were set for bridge, and the would-be players were moving into place. Mrs. Kentford checked and said, "Oh, Miss Henderson. I forgot to ask. Do you play?" She was about to offer her place.

"I never got beyond Happy Families," Harriet said and moved towards a settee by the fire. It was already occupied by a comfortable looking elderly woman, taking some knitting from a bulky bag.

"It's Miss Henderson, isn't it? I rather wanted to talk to you. But do excuse me if I get on. Tomorrow will be November, and I now have sixteen grandchildren." Each one of whom would presumably expect a knitted garment for Christmas. The recipient of the work in hand would be lucky; it would be a sweater in the colour of a ripe melon and worked in cable stitch. The thin, brown speckled hands worked quickly and expertly, then halted.

"That line where one turns needs concentration," the old lady said. "I'm Mrs. Rouse. My husband sat next to you at dinner." She nodded towards one of the bridge tables.

"Oh, yes. We had a most interesting talk."

"Interesting? Well, I suppose if you hadn't heard it before . . . I sometimes think that men don't adjust as well as women. . . . Poor Fred, always looking over his shoulder. Now I'm different. I keep fowls and bees and tame rabbits. And I knit. I understand that you have a clothes shop."

"I do."

"Well, the moment I heard I wondered. Could you sell this sort of thing?" Out of the bag she pulled a sweater, complete except for the sleeve on which she was working. It had the fashionable roll collar, and it was beautifully knitted.

"I'm practically sure that I could."

"Or even just put it on show and say that I was willing to take orders."

"Orders," said Mr. Kentford, coming up behind the settee and putting one hand on the thin, rather bowed shoulder. "Ruth, I have one for you. I want just that sort of thing, but with a V neck, and in a heather mixture. And as soon as you can make it. One of my chaps, and he's weather wise, tells me that an autumn like this is a sign of a stinking hard winter."

Mrs. Rouse turned her head and rubbed her cheek against his hand. She said, with feeling, "Dear George! Unfailingly kind. I'll start on it tomorrow."

He rounded the settee and said, "Would you like to look about a bit?"

"I should indeed." She began to get up, but the settee was very low, very deep, and very soft. Difficult to get up from. She wallowed, feeling undignified, until he reached out, took her hand and lifted her to her feet.

Mrs. Rouse was not too greatly absorbed in her knitting to be unaware. "I shall need a crane," she observed. But above the flashing needles her glance was sharp and cool.

One read of such things, of course, one heard about them, sometimes no physical contact was needed, a glance was enough. But the touch of his hand was like the touch of a live wire, triggering feelings that weakened her knees and robbed her of breath.

"This way," he said, heading towards a door at the far end of the room. He sounded short of breath, too.

They went along a passage and into what he had called a tunnel. It was softly lighted by imitation sconces in the canvas walls, banks of pot plants stood at intervals, and there were a few fragile chairs and small tables with conspicuous ashtrays. The music grew louder as they approached its end. "Jungle stuff!" he said, speaking for the first time. "But the young like it."

Except for the massive beams the place bore no resemblance to a barn. At the far end there was a platform, its curtains pushed back as far as they could go. On it somebody was cruelly punishing a piano, drums of varying sizes hung from a brass stand, a young man strummed a guitar. In the middle of the pale, glimmering floor the young were enjoying themselves thoroughly in a dance as formless as the music was tuneless. They jigged, met, parted, twirled, some leaped in the air, and some emitted loud cries. On the fringe of the floor some slightly older couples were rather desperately trying to dance in more conventional pattern.

One corner, near the entry, was enclosed by a semicircular bar, on which stood bottles of beer and a huge bowl of a pale liquid from whose depths bubbles rose in a leisurely way.

"Cup!" Mr. Kentford said tersely. "Most of them are driving. And that comes well from me, doesn't it, Alf!"

The routine was known. The boy behind the bar had already produced a bottle of champagne.

They went and sat by a table near the wall.

"My father fixed this," Mr. Kentford said. "He was in the war. Prisoner of the Japs much of the time. When he came back, he held the firm conviction that the world owed him all he could grab, and let tomorrow look after itself. Everybody was mad on dancing, so he put down this floor. At one time he even had his own band. Solid oak," he said with a certain satisfaction, "and laid down when you had to get a permit to buy enough deal for a shelf!" It was obvious that he remembered his father kindly and admired him. Presently he said, "Do you dance?"

"Never very much. And not for a long time. Please don't mind about me. I shall be quite happy watching."

"Wait here." He stood up and keeping to the wall made his way half-way along towards the platform. There he halted and said in a voice that carried above the din, "Now play a waltz. If you know one."

They did. They had been warned. They had come prepared. The drummer deserted his post and took up an instrument unknown to Harriet. The pianist forgave the piano and began caressing it. One of the most undermining of all tunes soothed the shattered air: "I'll see you again/Whenever spring breaks through again. . . ." They were both far too young to have heard it in its early days—but it had lost nothing of its magic.

Presently Harriet said, "I'm afraid I must stop. I've just had a preliminary twinge."

"Right. I know what you should do. Come along."

Her head was swimming: champagne and emotions, some uncomfortably resurrected and some mint new. And interwoven a feeling, incongruous and unwarranted, of deep apprehension.

"My office," he said, throwing open a door in the passage and switching on a harsh overhead light. There was a large roll top desk, one swivel chair, and two wooden ones with arms, and along one wall a brown leather couch which Mr. Kentford patted. "And put your feet up," he said. He then gave her a cigarette and was leaning over her, lighter in hand when the door opened and slammed hastily. A male voice said, "Damnation," and a girl giggled.

At the end of the cigarette Harriet said, "Now do go back to your guests. I feel I've rather monopolized you."

"Come and watch the snooker. There's a decent chair in there. And Bob Allinson gets belligerent after a couple of drinks."

The catering staff had departed, so the kippers were cooked and served by the young. The cooking was done in a copper in an otherwise disused wash-house. Accompanied by stacks of bread and butter and gallons of tea, it was a meal calculated to sober up all but the heaviest drinker. Taking leave of Harriet, Olivia yielded to impulse and hugged her. "I do hope you enjoyed yourself, darling. See you Monday."

On the way home Mrs. Allinson said, "Just as good as usual, wasn't it? And it must have cost a bomb."

Made irritable by returning sobriety and some envy, Mr. Allinson said incautiously, "Well, if your wife does your books and is a good cook . . ."

He was not referring to culinary art. Mrs. Allinson made a shushing noise.

All day on Sunday the various Harriets went about arguing. He'd come. Of course he wouldn't. Why should he? You flatter yourself! No, I don't. I know how I feel, and he feels the same. You're imagining things; you're no pin up, you know, damn nearly thirty and infirm at that.

Finally the warring elements declared a truce and combined to ask, If it is so, what are you going to do?

What indeed?

It was almost ten o'clock when he came, as part of her had known that he would. But somehow she had not expected such an open visit—his big black Rover parked immediately under the street lamp. What a treat for Miss Pamplin!

He slammed the door behind him and took her in his arms, almost lifting her from her feet. All the old over worn phrases about melting bones and burning kisses became reality. Reason tottered, doubt fled away. But some nub of sense remained. Even as he said hoarsely, "My God, how I've longed for this! Ever since that first day," she pulled away and said, "Darling, wait!" He repeated the word, amused and triumphant: "Darling! And you've never even used my Christian name before. Now I can say it. Darling. Harriet. Darling."

In the sitting room all the lights were blazing, giving an atmosphere the reverse of romantic. And the Harriet who had been certain that he would come had chosen her dress for the occasion. She had no really ugly clothes, but she looked businesslike in a piqué blouse and a dark pleated skirt. No shining belt, no earrings, the minimum of make-up. Not that it really mattered; she knew enough about infatuation to know that while it lasted, sackcloth could seem beautiful.

He would have embraced her again, but she said, "Please sit down. . . . Have a cigarette. . . . There are things that must be said."

"You're married?" A little of the elated look which had made him seem younger than his years faded.

"No."

"In love with somebody else?"

"No. To say I was would be the easy way out perhaps, but I'm trying to deal in the truth now. . . . You won't like it. I don't like it myself. The thing is, whatever our feelings for each other, anything between us could only end in misery."

"How do you make that out?"

"To begin with, we're neither of us young. I mean not young enough to be resilient. An affair that went wrong—as this must— would scar us for life."

"And why should it go wrong?" He was regarding her with keen interest.

"Extra-marital affairs almost always do. The secrecy, the furtiveness, and the constant fear of scandal don't make for happiness."

He fixed on the word "scandal."

"Scandal. I agree. We mustn't have that. But surely, if we were careful . . ."

"We're being careless at this moment. I'd bet anything that Miss Pamplin has one eye on your car and the other on St. Mary's clock."

"Damn all. I didn't think. To tell you the truth, I haven't thought really straight since that first day. You got under my skin then, like a burr, burrowing deeper every day. And last night. Look, I'm not handy with words. But the truth is . . . All right I'm married, no man ever had a better wife, but I'm talking about feelings. I swear I never felt for Madge or any other woman one thousandth part of what I feel for you. God! I never see anything pretty without being reminded of you. I never have a decent meal without wanting to share it with you. And last night . . . When I put my arm round you to dance, I knew I should never rest until I'd had you—properly."

It was impossible not to be moved by the words—and what they implied—and by the naked hunger in his eyes. So easy to succumb, to take what they wanted and pay afterwards. But the doubts and the arguments which had kept her wakeful last night had lost none of their validity. She gripped her hands together and said, "It wouldn't do. I don't think a bit of scandal would hurt me; the Fallen Woman is always of interest to the respectable. But for you—and your marriage—it would be disastrous."

Momentarily brushing that aside, he said, "Don't you care for me at all?"

"I do care. And that is another thing to consider. In no time at all I should be jealous of your wife."

"Yes. I see that. I should be if it was the other way round. Wait a minute."

He took from an inner pocket an old envelope and a Biro. In frowning concentration he jotted down some words—or figures. When he looked up, his face had cleared. "We could do it. Madge was pretty well provided for when we married. She'd have that and half what I own. We could go to Canada."

This was a turn for which her night thoughts had not prepared her, and she stared, her mouth slightly agape.

"You couldn't possibly. Your beautiful house. The long tradition. Somebody told me there'd been Kentfords at Muchanger for four hundred years. . . ."

He would not be diverted. "I don't mean the cold part. Over to the West. Buy a ranch. I don't mind hard work. And there isn't much about stock I don't know."

She was on surer ground now. "It's unthinkable. The surest recipe for disaster. In no time at all, you'd be measuring what you'd sacrificed against what you had in return—just another woman in a bed. You'd soon hate me."

He floundered a bit. "How can you . . . ? You've got the wrong . . . God, you're hard! Fragile looking as a flower and harder than nails."

"Just sensible. One of us has to be. Very soon you'll be grateful to me."

"And thass your last word? Then I'd best be off."

He stood up, and frustration cried out in her. You've refused the very thing you've wanted, something you've never had, will never be offered again.

She saw him out, went to bed, and cried more bitterly than she had ever done in her life.

Monday, a grey cold morning. Olivia was late. Monday morning was the time for dressing the window. When ten o'clock came, Harriet tackled it herself. Once or twice before she had noticed that an emotional upset could provoke backache almost as readily as overdue exertion. The window dressing this morning was a painful business. Olivia had suggested that it would be a good idea to put a lighted Christmas tree in the trinket window, with gay Christmas present things as decoration. "No need to buy one. We grow them commercially. I'll choose a nice one, not too big, but branchy." She'd brought it, a lovely little tree, and planted it in a bucket. Harriet shuffled it into the shop but dared not even try to lift it the two feet up to the shelf which formed the floor of the window. Presently, having nothing else to do and needing to be busy, she dressed it where it stood, attaching the articles very firmly. She thought, If Olivia is still nursing a hangover—as well she might be—I'll ask Old John to lend a hand. Old John was jack of all trades at the Hawk in Hand. She had stayed there while work was being done on Rosa's, and he had brought her morning tea. A white coat transformed him into a waiter. She'd always tipped him well. Later, before Olivia's arrival, they had become members of the Broom Brotherhood, for he swept the wide frontage of the inn while she swept her narrow one. In a good mood, he'd sweep her pile into his and dispose of the whole.

Olivia arrived at about twelve o'clock. But differently. Usually she parked her fire engine red little sports car on the other side of Abbey Hill. Today she came to the front of Rosa's. The fish and chip paper was there, and she aimed a kick at it, sending it into the gutter. Then she stalked in and stood, looking like the goddess of vengeance. "I'm not staying. I only came to tell you—and to collect a few things."

Rather abruptly, Harriet sat down in the pink velvet chair. And, guessing the answer but needing to ask, she said, "What is wrong?"

"You!" the girl said furiously. "A snake in the grass if ever there was one. *So* prim and proper. Butter wouldn't melt in your mouth, would it? And all the time carrying on!"

The two expensive schools which her father had mentioned had done one thing for Olivia—eradicated all trace of an accent and given her that rather ringing, upper class voice which even mitigated terms of abuse. "A pretty monkey you've made me look! Stringing Dad along. The old fool!"

The awful thing was that there was no defence. She could not profess ignorance: I don't know what you are talking about! Or innocence: There has never been anything between your father and me that the whole world wasn't welcome to see and hear.

"I think you're making a great to-do about nothing."

"Oh! Nothing? Putting you to sit beside him. And Mrs. Foxley said she expected him any minute to offer you a bite from his own fork. Dancing. He hasn't danced for five years. And what about that scene in the office? Grace and Leslie walked straight into you."

"You're putting completely the wrong construction on everything. Your father took me to sit by him because I was a stranger. He did remark about my leaving food on my plate. Also," her voice turned mocking, "he actually helped me to a mince pie. Think of it! And I seem to remember your saying that Mrs. Foxley was a bitch. As for the office, we went there because my back hurt, and there was a sofa. We smoked a cigarette, and your father showed me a few pictures of prize winning cattle."

"Very smooth! And what was he showing you last night?"

"Last night?"

"Ray Hatton saw his car."

Harriet took cigarettes from her pocket. Her hands were not quite steady. Oh, lighter, dear lighter, do for once spark first time! It did. One long inhalation, an even longer exhalation, and she felt very slightly better.

"Olivia, I wish you'd tell me something. When was this nonsense concocted? You and I were on friendly terms at one o'clock yesterday morning."

"I was a bit sloshed. I hadn't taken much notice. Everybody else had and began talking, making a joke in a way. But I," Olivia said sternly, "was not amused."

"I'm not amused either. Only one thing bothers me slightly. I hope none of this silly talk reaches your mother."

"Even you can't be that simple-minded," Olivia said rudely. "The husband may be the last to know, the wife is always the first. All bloody yesterday—the Fosters had a cocktail party in the morning, and the Whitings one in the evening. All seething, good advice, and commiseration. This is what makes me so mad. I've known for a long time that most people were jealous of Mother. She's pretty well off. She's always been smart, and Dad . . . Dad never put a foot wrong. Until you."

Olivia whisked about collecting her belongings. On occasions she had changed here before a date, and she'd bought one or two things for Christmas.

When she was ready to depart forever, she halted by the little Christmas tree. Without speaking, she lifted it as though it weighed nothing and placed it in the window.

Now Harriet was merely back to where she had been at the beginning. Except that then it had been summer and early rising no hardship. And perhaps rather more than four months of Olivia's devoted service had softened her fibre. And of course the shop was definitely far busier now. So clinch the supporting belt a little tighter, produce the welcoming smile, pretend not to notice the sly inspections, the remarks, some genuine, "I thought I'd see Olly . . ." and the feigned "Is Miss Kentford no longer with you?"

One crisp morning, Old John, indicating with his broom, said, "We're going to hev neighbours. And about as mysterious as you was. Even I can't find what it is to be." He meant the shop on the far side of the inn.

"I only wish it could be a place where one could get a cup of coffee and a snack."

"Thass one thing it 'on't be. The Govner bought Chinery's out to stop competition. Could be antiques. We ain't got so many of them as most old places hev." He lowered his broom and said, "Now you're on your own, I'll haul your dustbin out if you like."

It was a kind offer, never made in those earlier lonely days, almost as though he now knew about her ailing back and how dependent she had become upon Olivia.

Still, however prompted, it was a timely and welcome offer, gladly accepted.

Then Christmas, so long looming, came in a rush. Four blissful, restful days. Harriet's preparations for the festive season were simple: three relatively new books from the library, some of that bread which, never having been new, never grows stale, a variety of cheeses, and a bottle of gin. The great advantage of having had a bleak childhood was that one had no sentimental memories of Christmas.

The Day itself fell on Thursday, and the shop was due to open again on Monday. Harriet spent most of Sunday behind drawn blinds removing every bit of Christmas stuff. She pushed the Christmas tree from its place, and it fell on its side, spilling soil and scraps of tinsel on to the carpet. She then rolled it as far as she could, which was just into her sitting room, where it lay looking the epitome of desolation. She then re-dressed the windows with things suitable for the post-Christmas trade depression.

The litter dropper was regular in his habits, and each morning Harriet took her broom, hoping to see Old Jack wielding his so that she could ask him to help remove the sad little tree, which had now begun to shed its foliage, but somehow she missed him until New Year's Day, which dawned greyly, with a slight fog. They exchanged seasonal greetings, and she made her request. "A course I will," he said. Then he gave her a peculiar look, still friendly but not entirely devoid of a delight in drama.

"Seen that?" He nodded towards the shop which had been Chinery's.

It was larger than Rosa's and had two windows. The bigger had room for three dummies. One wore the perfect garb for outdoor winter events: lambs'-wool twin set, tweed suit, beaver lamb coat. At its feet lay a pair of binoculars, half in, half out of its leather case, and a shooting stick. There was, on the second figure, a dress much like one of Harriet's except that it was blue and the belt blue and silver. The third figure wore an evening dress of black lace.

The other window was devoted to the young: jeans and sweaters, some bright anoraks, and two of the coats from Afghanistan, the sheepskin fleece inside and the outsides heavily and gaudily embroidered in wool.

Competition was a natural hazard; it was the prices that stunned

Harriet. Here everything was plainly labelled, at prices which not only precluded any profit but were actually below cost: £30 for a lambs'-wool twin set, when the cardigan alone cost £15 wholesale and retailed at £21; the beaver lamb coat, fully as good as the one she had offered Mr. Kentford, £70. Ludicrous! It did not need the gold stencilled word above the door—Olly's.

"I'll fetch that tree away now," Old John said, curiosity bright in his eyes. In the passage he could no longer restrain himself, "Well, how did it strike you?" With that reserve and self-control which did not make for popularity, Harriet said, "I think it can do nothing but good. It will bring more shoppers into this area."

"Thass one way of looking at it. You know, if you'd watered this tree, it'd have lived."

She gave him a pound and thanked him, smiling.

Then she was alone, for though many people went past and looked into the windows, she had no customers that day. But she was too busy to care. The Kentfords had dealt her a felling blow, but not a fatal one.

Now and then as she calculated floor space—if all fixtures were done away with and the little fitting cubicles and the two windows incorporated again—she suffered a pang almost like a physical pain. How much had he had to do with this vicious revenge? True, she had repulsed him, but surely in a way that had not injured his pride. She had actually said that she cared. She hated to think that he had been associated with something so petty and spiteful. So think of something else. Think. Two tables in the bigger window, one in the other, eight in the main shop. Cloakroom facilities? My own bathroom until I see how the cat jumps. A dish washing machine. And certainly some help . . .

However Rosa's would still be here, and it would still be pretty; she'd have flowered crockery and—since a posy on each table would make work—a little piece of reproduction Staffordshire china, glued down so that the clumsiest customer could not knock it over.

She was still busy with calculations and plans when the shop doorbell chimed.

She looked up and saw George Kentford looking even more out of place than he had on that first day and far less confident. He said, "I didn't know! I swear, Harriet, I knew nothing till ten minutes ago when I dropped in at the club, and somebody asked how the shop was doing. I was never more astounded. Or disgusted. Shocked, too. I'd never have believed Madge and Olly would have stooped so low. You do believe me, don't you? Say you do."

"I do."

He looked quite distraught. The smooth healthy ruddy tan of his face had contracted into patches of dark crimson, high on his cheeks; the rest of his face looked grey except around the nostrils where it was white.

"Look," she said, using his own word, "you mustn't get so excited. It's bad for you. Come and sit down and relax."

She led the way into the sitting room, and he took the chair which she always thought of as his own. He rubbed his hand upwards over his face and over the crisp russet hair, only just freckled with grey.

"Would you like a cup of tea?" Advised in cases of shock, but heavily sweetened—and she had no sugar.

"I'd like a drink, if you've got such a thing."

"Only gin, I'm afraid."

"I can drink gin."

She went to the corner cupboard where the bottle stood. Very low tide indeed. "Neat, or with water?" she asked, keeping herself between him and the bare inch of gin.

"Neat."

"I have water with mine," she said, half closing the cupboard door. She fetched water, poured gin into one glass, water into another and turned back to him.

"Thanks . . . And now I can't even wish you a Happy New Year."

"Why not?"

"Because she's out to ruin you. And I can't stop her."

"Well, I'll wish you one. Happy New Year!" She motioned with her glass, but did not drink—somebody had once told her that it was unlucky to drink a toast in water.

For a seasoned drinker it was a poor drink indeed, but it did something to relax him.

"What I hate and loathe," he said, speaking more slowly, "is this damned idea that I'd been smart, putting my daughter in with you to learn the tricks of the trade and then setting my wife up practically next door. One swine started to congratulate me."

"I suppose people would think that way. You mustn't take it to heart."

"Well, I do. People can be Hell! Ever since that night . . . Snide little jokes. And Madge carrying on as though I was Bluebeard. But then she always was a jealous woman. Even so I never thought she'd go to such lengths."

"It must be wretched for you. I am so very sorry."

"You've no cause to be. You're the only one who comes out of this with a grain of credit. I lost my heart and then my head. Anybody'd think I was sixteen. But you were so dead sensible—and so careful not to hurt her. That sickens me. And all for nothing. Thass what's so bitter."

He looked so abject and sounded so desolate. The very size and strength of him made him seem all the more pitiable. She thought of the brevity of life, the certainty and finality of death. Why not seize a chance to happiness, however transient?

She said, "At the moment I'm not feeling sensible at all."

"You mean?"

She nodded.

He crossed the little space, scooped her up, and held her, kissing her hair, her neck, her mouth, and this time she responded with abandon. . . .

But one of the Harriets stayed aloof and asked: Are you now doing for spite what you wouldn't do for love? Can any good come of that?

7

The horse-leech hath two daughters

Hostility between the two women was mutual, instant, and inevitable.

Charlie said, "Ma, this is Sonja—Miss Armstrong. Sonja, my mother, Mrs. Polstead."

Sonja extended a well kept hand, with dark red nails. She could be as correct as Charlie. She said, "How do you do?" And Mrs. Polstead replied uncouthly, "I do very well. All things considered." Her work hardened, weather darkened hand just touched Sonja's, more of a challenge than an acceptance.

Charlie said, "Do sit down, dear. Ma, we'd like a cup of tea. I'll make it. You sit and get to know each other."

Charlie had often been entertained at 12 Beechwood Avenue and knew that tea meant different things to different people. In the suburbs it was tea, the liquid, with perhaps a biscuit or a slice of cake. In more down-to-earth communities it meant a meal, taken at the end of a working day, say between six and seven o'clock, and was substantial, often called a meat tea, though the flesh consumed might be only a kipper.

"Tea," Mrs. Polstead said pointedly, "is in the oven. A brace of plump partridges. I shot 'em myself."

She was fully entitled to do so, for she owned the four acre holding known as The Snape, and she had a shotgun licence. She grew brussels sprouts and spinach, cauliflowers and sprouting broccoli which customers liked. So did partridges and pheasants, coming out of Layer Wood to feast surreptitiously. A two-way traffic, older than time, a contract between predators. You feed me, and I'll feed you.

Mrs. Polstead had not, momentous as the occasion was, opened the parlour. She disliked the room, it was associated with death; her grandfather, father, and husband had all lain there in their coffins. And the chimney smoked, unless the door was left open. So Mrs. Polstead received Charlie's wife-to-be in the kitchen, which despite its name was rather splendid, having about it the memory of a time when it had been the hall, the main dwelling place of a land owning family, their retainers and servants. It was long enough to contain, in comfort, three distinct areas: that where food was prepared and cooked, that where it was eaten, and that where afterwards one sat at leisure. The cooking area had an Aga, a big white scrubbed table, and some modern kitchen units, bought at different times and not matching. The dining area was furnished with a draw table which, fully extended, would have seated twelve—only one flap was extended now, and the table, shrouded in good damask, was set for three. There was a massive Welsh dresser and some ladder-back chairs. The end now occupied by Sonja and Mrs. Polstead offered comfort, a high backed old settle, a modern three-piece suite, a rocking chair, and a gateleg table. Charlie, making tea at the far end of the apartment, was almost out of earshot.

He did so hope they were getting on together. If not, it would be Ma's fault. Prejudiced against Sonja from the start. A townee, a shop-girl. And what sort of people would call a girl Sonja?

None of it relevant. What was, and Charlie knew it, was that Ma didn't actually fancy his marrying at all. Unlike most ageing women, Ma had no interest in posterity, had no wish for grandchildren. And in the future she had no faith at all. The next Government, or the one after that, would nationalize or commandeer the land. "But you'll have the house, Charlie. I've noticed again and again, the very ones keenest to put down concrete and build bungalows get up on their hind legs when it comes to an old building. With what you got from Aunt Mary and what I can scrape together, you should be all right."

The kettle boiled. Charlie made tea and carried the tray to the fireside. Snape had had its good times. The teapot was genuine Queen Anne—and silver. Two of the three cups came from Woolworths; the third was Rockingham.

Mrs. Polstead poured half a cup, set down the pot and, taking a spoon, stirred vigorously. Then she resumed pouring—the liquid slightly, not much, deeper in colour. "Tea like this," she said, "always reminds me of the woman who said, 'When I make tea, I make tea; and when I make water, I make water.'"

Not a particularly coarse thing to say. You could hear far worse any evening on TV, and Charlie, who was a representative of an agricultural machinery firm and often consorted with other commercial travellers, was hardened to really vile language. But there was a difference. One's own mother! Across a tea tray. And in front of Sonja. But of course she was doing it deliberately. Trying to put Sonja off. Not, Charlie thought, that anything would. He was reasonably sure that Sonja was as much in love with him as he was with her.

Still, he cast a half apologetic look in Sonja's direction and as usual took pleasure in her appearance: up to date without being aggressively modern—at forty he was old enough to deplore ragged hair-styles, faces that looked as though they had been oiled, and rag-bag clothes. Sonja wore a pretty, pleated dress, the colour of milky coffee. Her hair was only a shade darker, short and curly, her eyes large and dark. It was a face which could be called kitten-like or pansylike, if one wished to be fanciful. It was rather triangular, sloping down to a small mouth—the under lip thicker than the upper, and an inconspicuous chin. She looked younger than her age, which was twenty-six. She had been engaged twice before.

". . . old, as I was saying," Mrs. Polstead said, resuming the speech which the arrival of tea had interrupted. "I had a coupla busybodies here not long ago, poking about. Pre-Tudor, they said, whatever that may been. I could have told them that!" She was happily unaware of anything contradictory in the two statements.

"Saxbys—that's my family name—been here a long time. The Snape land once ran clear down to the river."

Sonja said, "How interesting" in a voice that belied the statement. And as though to emphasize the depths to which The Snape had fallen, Mrs. Polstead stood up. "Pigs gotta be seen to. They don't observe the Sabbath."

Charlie said his mother was seventy, but the years had not yet undermined her. She was thin, but in no delicate way, rather stringy, hard looking, and her movements were brisk and assured. She went to the far end of the kitchen where pegs on the inside of the door held some clothes. Over the good plum coloured silk dress of antiquated fashion, she pulled a kind of coat overall, dirty and stained. She opened the door, said, "Raining again!" and reached for a kind of sou'wester hat.

This, like the remark about weak tea was quite unnecessary. A demonstration of something. Pigs were perfectly capable of going from midday on Sunday until seven o'clock in the morning.

Not that Charlie knew much about pigs or any other aspects of life on a smallholding. Ma had been dead against his carrying on the business. "It'll see me out, Charlie, and that'll be about all. Times are against people like us. We've been the backbone of the country since time began, but they don't like folks with backbones these days. And it's a hard life, I doubt if you'd stand it. . . ." A perfectly normal succession of childish complaints had left Ma with the conviction that Charlie was delicate. He was six feet tall, weighed twelve stone, ate like a horse, and had never ailed with more than a head cold since he was twelve, but Ma's ideas did not change easily.

"Stick to your schooling, Boy, and get a nice snug office job to tide you over. Then, when I'm gone, sell the land for beastly bungalows. They'll let you keep the house." She had it all planned: her dear one, her darling, living the life of leisure, with, of course, some comfortable body to keep house and cook and coddle him when he had a cold.

Eventually Charlie had attained a comfortable, snug job in a local government office, and since Ma would never charge him a penny for his keep, he was well-to-do, able to run a car and buy good clothes. But sometimes he felt stifled.

Then his Aunt Mary, his father's sister, died, and Ma was much enraged, for Aunt Mary had willed her substance in three parts—two to nephews on the other side of the family, far away in Cheshire.

"And when," Ma demanded furiously, "did one of *them* send her a Christmas turkey?"

"Well, come to that, when did I?" Charlie asked.

One great thing about Ma, she laughed easily. She laughed then, and said, "Well, I suppose ten thousand pounds isn't to be sneezed at."

With a certain unearned income behind him, Charlie felt justified in abandoning the office job and taking service with a firm—its name a household word—selling agricultural machinery. It dealt in things that cost many thousands of pounds—combine harvesters, beet lifters, down, through tractors, to mere tools like spades and rakes. Charlie's official salary was modest, but the commission was generous. The firm supplied a car, and he was out in the country all day. And, curiously, because he was not, like so many of his kind, anxious to make a sale, he often succeeded where another man would have failed. Ease and optimism were fully as contagious as anxiety and tension. Charlie did very well.

And then he fell in love, the affliction hitting him, like mumps, far harder than it would have done twenty years earlier. Into the matter of being in love and getting married he threw himself wholeheartedly. It never occurred to him that he was a spoilt boy, to whom everything he wanted had, since his wants were limited, come to him easily; nor did he think that his feeling for Sonja had a large element of possessiveness. He wanted to own her, and in order to do that, he must please her.

To please her he bought—or appeared to buy—a house that he would never have chosen, Number 8, Mulberry Close. It was in the same area as Beechwood Avenue but far newer. It was one of eight bijou residences squeezed into a cul-de-sac, and as Sonja said, it had everything. Even in his pre-marital euphoria, Charlie was capable of thinking, Everything except living space! But perhaps that was because he was such a great hulking brute and took up so much room. The place suited Sonja perfectly, because she was a doll, and this was a doll's house.

Expensive, though. Such houses, having everything if on a tiny scale, were much in demand, and Charlie had to find £30,000.

Aunt Mary's legacy gone in a flash, and £20,000 more to find. His savings were small, considering how cheaply he lived, but he had always been notoriously open-handed, the first to say, "This round's on me," the first to subscribe to any worthy cause. Also, though his courtship had been brief, it had cost him money. Mr. Armstrong did want, in fact needed, a motor mower, and if Charlie gave him that, then he must give Mrs. Armstrong something commensurate—a fridge with a freezer. He'd given Sonja a silver grey squirrel coat in which she looked wonderful, and the ring upon which she had set her heart had cost £850, sapphires nowadays being rather more costly than diamonds.

So now his savings were down to £2,000—and he'd need that for furniture.

"Nothing for it, Ma, but a mortgage."

"No," Ma said. "I can't have you starting off with a millstone round your neck. I'll find the money, and I won't charge. When you pay a bit back, we'll knock it off the loan."

"That's mighty nice of you, Ma."

"It'll save a bit in tax. What I've saved by hard work and thrift, they have the bloody nerve to call unearned interest—what the Building Society pays me, I mean."

She did a bit of reckoning with her perpetually blunt pencil on a pad that lay by the telephone. On it she wrote down orders which people telephoned, certain telephone numbers which she wished to remember, and other bits of information which might slip her mind. It was a jumble, quite unintelligible to anyone else, but it provided blank space enough for a simple sum to which the answer was that she was the one who would need a mortgage, £6,000 worth.

Charlie insisted upon having the whole thing put on a legal footing. Ma was not exactly the person to rouse protective feelings in the male breast, but Charlie had a flash of thought: Suppose anything happened to me before I'd paid back? In that event Sonja would have a widow's pension, quite possibly something from the firm and from the insurance which Charlie fully intended to take out as soon as he was married; Sonja would also have the house—and poor old Ma would have nothing.

"All right," Ma said, "we'll go to Secker and get it all tied up with red tape."

They were married in December, a quiet wedding which every-body agreed was best. Sonja wanted a honeymoon somewhere a little different and somewhere in the sun, so with staggering origi-nality they went to the Canaries, where Sonja ate something that disagreed with her and Charlie, most perversely, developed the worst head cold he had ever had.

They then spent a year in discovering that they hardly had a thing in common, but they never quarrelled because Charlie al-most invariably conceded a point. Sonja, so very dainty in every way, could always make him feel loutish. The most derogatory word in her vocabulary was "sordid" and this even applied to the news and anything of a political nature on the television. Despite her limited intellectual equipment, she could play bridge and so well that she was much in demand. Charlie tried to learn and failed. That was balanced by the fact that he was a useful if not spectacular performer at golf. Sonja had no eye at all. Charlie enjoyed a read now and then—indeed the habit was growing upon him. One day, reading, he gave a quiet but audible laugh, and Sonja said, "What's so funny?" He read the amusing paragraph, and she said, "Well, I think that rather vulgar." Which it was, no argument about that.

Sonja could not cook—she'd never had to, having gone straight from school to serve in a shop. To give her her due, she did try; she bought a number of cookbooks, all very pretty, well illustrated with pictures of delectable dishes and all promising expertise in no time at all. Sonja mastered the trimmings and could actually make a dish of salad, laid out on a flat plate, look too pretty to touch. But Charlie was, he admitted, a coarse feeder, and his work took him into the open air, often to remote places where only a midday snack and a pint were available. Then he'd come home and be daintily served with a sample of what was known as convenience food. All very good, no question of that, but in the quantities provided by Sonja not enough. In the first year of his marriage he lost a stone in weight. This fact delighted him, but distressed Ma.

It puzzled her, too, for she was faithful in supplying the little house with eggs and garden stuff, now and then a fowl, a game bird, a rabbit, a piece of fresh pork after a pig killing, a piece of ham when the curing process was complete. Sometimes, looking at Charlie—and seeing him wolf anything she could find to offer when he visited her—she felt inclined to ask, but so long as Charlie did not complain, she would not criticize. Marriage was tricky enough without any mother-in-law trouble. For the same reason she never commented when Charlie arrived alone. She'd say, "Sonja all right?" "Yes, playing bridge." And who could deny that it was a happy arrangement?

Ma had paid one visit of inspection to the bijou house. Her immediate reaction was, I'd hate to live in it. Her next thought: You don't have to! She went into the house on one occasion after that. Sonja asked her in to have a cup of coffee. On that occasion Ma had brought some eggs, a cauliflower, and a greenhouse grown lettuce which in February would have cost anybody else thirty-five new pence. These Ma put down on the nearest empty space, a flat, glittering white working surface. A little soil escaped from the lower leaves of the cauliflower. Sonja lifted it and the lettuce on to the draining board and reached for a cloth. . . . At the same time she said, "Do go through." The kitchen was so remarkably tiny— Or am I so cumbersome?—that passing Sonja was quite difficult.

In the Mulberry Close house the staircase went up from the sitting room, a great saving of space, but it meant that anybody of Ma's size, or Charlie's, must duck when coming through from the kitchen. Ma failed to duck and received a sharp blow on the head. She thought, I wonder how often poor Charlie . . . Well, presumably he was used to it now, and he hadn't knocked himself silly in any noticeable way.

Ma sat down in the likeliest chair, a pretty thing—in fact everything in the room was pretty. The chair was upholstered in pink velvet and had a buttoned back, a pseudo-Victorian "grandmother's chair." Victorian things were back, after a long lapse. Even the despised aspidistra now cost a pound a leaf.

Sonja brought in a tray and set it on the TV set while she dismantled a nest of tables. Each component part was probably strong enough for any burden it was likely to bear, but they did look frail.

Poor coffee. Granted, instant coffee was a blessing and good if made properly, which to her meant the necessary amount of hot milk—or, forced to it, milk and water—and then a good heaped spoonful, well stirred in. This, made with water and a little cold milk added, was horrible. But horrible or otherwise, coffee to her meant the accompaniment of a cigarette. Ma groped into the pocket of her dirty old duffle coat and took out a battered packet and the latest thing in lighters. A gift from Charlie.

"If I remember rightly, you don't."

Sonja said, "No—but don't mind me."

No ashtray in sight, and here one could hardly use the saucer.

"Sonja, I need an ashtray."

"So sorry. You see, Charlie's trying to stop, and I think it helps not to be reminded."

She went to a small corner cupboard and was so long disinterring an ashtray that Mrs. Polstead's ash had lengthened and dropped, luckily on to her own hunched up knee. She did not brush it off as she would have done elsewhere, but rubbed it well in, adding one more dirty mark to her old slacks.

They talked of this and that, perfectly amiably, but with no intimacy, strangers thrown together by some chance.

"Well," Mrs. Polstead said, "as they say, back to the salt mines." She stood up. O God! Horror of horrors. On that new, that dainty, that rose pink carpet, two distinct muddy marks where her feet had been.

That put her in the wrong, and that was a position which her mind occupied as uneasily as her body had done the silly little chair. She'd usually been right. Often over quite major decisions and now two mud marks . . .

"I am sorry about that, Sonja, but it is clean dirt, if you know what I mean. Not muck. It'll dry off and brush up, like dust."

Sonja said, "Not to worry!" in itself a silly phrase and spoken without any heart. So Ma was provoked and said, moving to the kitchen, "Funny thing, only the other day I was reading about Oriental carpets. When they're newly woven, they're put down in the road for donkeys and all sorts to tramp over. That ripens them off or gives—what do they call it—patina?"

Having said that, Ma felt better; she had re-established herself. She'd always been a voracious reader, and she had a vast vocabulary, many words laid away unused, like best clothes—like the plum coloured silk she had donned for Sonja's first visit and brought out again for the wedding.

After that, invited in, Ma always refused, being careful to vary her excuses: she had an appointment; she'd promised somebody a lift; she must go to the library, pick up a bag of pig meal.

A year passed very quickly. Business was bad. Charlie's area had been South Suffolk and half the East, but when the man who had half the East and all the North had a stroke and retired early, he was not replaced. His beat was added to Charlie's and in the ordinary way would have been a good thing. But not now. It simply meant longer journeys, longer hours, and precious little to show for it.

Sonja was not so much unsympathetic as obtuse. She related everything to something so narrow and personal that Charlie was astounded. "Oh. Does that mean we can't afford a holiday again this year?" she'd say, looking hurt, looking ill done by, looking pathetic.

And at the same time a more robust part of Charlie's mind asked, A holiday from what? What the hell does she do? And the answer—if you looked at it with an unloving eye—was, Nothing much. She now hardly cooked at all and most of what Ma brought ended up at 12 Beechwood Avenue, which was all right in a way, since Mrs. Armstrong was a good cook, but it did mean that a plump fowl or a good hunk of ham made one hot meal for seven people and left nothing over for a sandwich to take with him or a snack to come home to.

More and more often Charlie found himself planning his route so that he could drop in at The Snape. Ma not only had something to offer him to eat—and to drink—but an understanding ear. "I know," she said. "I know. I could use a new Rota Tiller, but I shan't buy one this year."

She spoke without reproach, just a general statement, but Charlie instantly remembered his debt, which so far he had managed to reduce by only £100. He had given up smoking—and the funny thing was that, though cigarettes were ferociously expensive, giving them up had not enriched him in the way it should. He now ordered half pints of beer instead of whole ones, but a half pint now cost rather more than a pint had done when he'd first started to drink. He treated people a little less readily, but he had a kindly streak and was aware that there were men worse off than he was. He now very seldom touched whisky at all, except at The Snape.

Ma might not be able to afford a new Rota Tiller, but she could always produce a bottle—usually a full one.

She now cut short Charlie's apologies for being so slow in repaying and his promises to try harder.

"Let that be the least of your worries, Boy. In times like these people like me do better than most; we can charge more for our stuff."

Sometimes, when Charlie thought about his marriage, he decided that by comparison with some men he knew, he was lucky. Some women, once married, let themselves go. Sonja had not done that. In fact, whenever Charlie went out with her, he felt proud; she was so pretty, so trim and well dressed. And, unlike many attractive women, she could be trusted absolutely. Men took to her on sight, and she liked men to some extent but in a strictly non-sexual way. As Charlie had quickly discovered, she was sexually cold. In the first flush of his infatuation, he had found this rather hurtful and once or twice wondered about those two broken engagements; had two less scrupulous fellows gone a bit far and discovered the truth? But now at forty-three, worried and overworked, Charlie saw the advantage of being married to a woman who was not demanding in that way.

She had other virtues, too. She was self-sufficient and, once he had made clear that he hated what the suburbanites called cocktail parties, was quite willing to attend them alone. And she was not, like many woman, nervous of being alone at night. With his area expanded again and now including the rich fenlands around Ely and the cornland of Norfolk near King's Lynn, it was often a saving of time, energy, and petrol to stay overnight. If you knew your way about, it was still possible to get bed and breakfast for £6 —chargeable to expenses and damned good breakfasts, too!

Above all, Sonja never seemed to resent the increasing frequency of his visits to Ma.

Yet it was about Ma that trouble began.

Began with a well meant gift.

It was June, and The Snape was in full production. On to the draining board—Ma was capable of learning—she unloaded peas, lettuces, radishes, a bunch of asparagus, an early cucumber, greenhouse grown, some eggs, and a punnet of strawberries. Then, diving deeper into her cornucopia bag, she produced a loaf of bread.

"These light mornings the birds start at four, and I can't sleep. It's too early for outside work, so this morning I thought I'd make bread. It turned out all right."

"It looks lovely," Sonja said. "Thank you very much."

The loaf, well risen and golden brown, still looked lovely when she set it, together with a picturebook salad, on the Pembroke table from which they ate—the kitchen being standing room only. Between meals the table folded down very small and stood in the window, supporting a house plant.

Charlie studied the salad. Pretty as a picture but not substantial. He recognized The Snape asparagus, which should be served hot, dripping with butter and accompanied with bread and butter; here it lay cold and flaccid, part of the pattern.

"Your mother also brought this loaf," Sonja said, lifting the bread knife.

"Oh, did she? If you don't want it, I'll have the crust."

She cut it for him, then took the next slice for herself and was about to butter it when suddenly she recoiled with such a look of disgust that Charlie said, "What is it? A slug on your lettuce?"

"Her hands!"

"Whose hands?"

"Your mother's . . . I suddenly saw them—kneading that dough."

Charlie appeared to go mad. He dropped his knife and fork.

"Let me tell you my mother's hands are as clean as anybody's. She's always at them with a nailbrush and carbolic soap."

Sonja had got herself into a position where no recantation was possible; she couldn't say that she had misunderstood or been misinformed. All she could do was to back up that statement which she had, by implication, made.

She said, "Well, they don't look like it."

"She works with her hands. . . ." God alone knew how hard Ma had worked. "Ingrained dirt," Charlie said, "a very different thing."

"I can't see the difference."

"You wouldn't. You never did see Ma straight. Too busy looking down your nose!"

They were quarrelling, and they'd both lived for two and a half years in such a cool, sterile atmosphere that a genuine emotion, even anger, even hatred, was not unwelcome.

But they had chosen the wrong thing to quarrel about. Had Charlie come home raving drunk and been violent, had Sonja been unfaithful, apologies, promises of better behaviour in future would have been possible. As it was, no amount of contrition could wipe out the fact that Sonja thought Charlie's mother a dirty old woman, and certainly Sonja had no intention of withdrawing what she felt to be true.

And once the screen of defence was withdrawn, each saw the truth—they didn't even like each other.

Charlie suffered more, partly because he had been infatuated, partly because he could speak to no one about the business, and partly because his job entailed long hours of driving when his mind was free to brood.

Sonja had never idolized Charlie, she had plenty of friends in whom she could confide, and she had the comfort of knowing that she was right.

Only her own mother seemed perturbed rather than sympathetic. "Really, dear, that was a thoughtless thing to say. Charlie's very fond of his mother."

And Mrs. Armstrong was quite fond of Charlie; he was quiet and generous and good-natured. Since Sonja's marriage Mrs. Armstrong had acquired another son-in-law, a very different character. If Margot had come complaining and crying . . . Not that Sonja was crying. Mrs. Armstrong remembered that even as a little girl her first-born had been a very stubborn child. Still, she spoke forcefully: "You must make it up."

"How can I? I can't very well say I'd made a mistake, can I? I mean if somebody's hands are dirty, they are."

"You could apologize . . ." But even she could see that it would be a difficult thing to put into words without inflicting more hurt. "Or be extra nice to him . . ." said Mrs. Armstrong who had weathered almost thirty years of marriage by doling out her favours sparingly.

"He's the one to apologize," Sonja said. "He lost his temper and stood up and pushed the table over. My very best dish—you know, the one Evie brought me from Portugal—smashed to smithereens. And mayonnaise all over the carpet."

Apart from her mother, everybody sympathized with Sonja, though some were cynical: "Well, dear, sooner or later. You've had a good run. If you knew what I have to bear from Terry . . ." In fact they were suddenly all revealed as martyrs, all wed to terrible characters who did much worse things than push over tables and break dishes. In fact they only stayed, snug in their little houses, locked up with such brutes, because of the children, or, to be frank, because they didn't fancy going out into the workaday world again. Not as things are just now, they said, meaning a market flooded with school leavers, all lustrous-eyed. Oh, well, we're all in the same boat. No use moaning. And how about a cup of coffee?

Charlie was really being abominable. She had no idea he could be so horrid. When he stood up that night and stalked out in fury, the table had suffered as well. It now had a lurch to the right.

Charlie said, "I told you at the time it was held together with varnish," and he did not offer to repair it.

Then he developed a really infuriating habit. Whatever she provided in the way of food, he'd look at and say, "I wonder who had a hand in this."

To Evie, happily and profitably divorced, Sonja said, "He does harp on so. Like a parrot," and Evie, who had done very well out of being firm, said, "Just be firm, darling. Say you don't want to hear another word about it."

That evening Charlie surveyed a really good slice of veal and ham pie and said, "Now how many people had a finger in this."

Sonja said, "I don't want to hear another word about that!"

"Maybe you'd better look," Charlie said. He took from his pocket his wallet and from the wallet a piece of paper, folded. He unfolded it and smoothed it and handed it over. It was a carica-ture. A factory entrance at closing time. A large hoarding an-nounced "Bestbik. Untouched by human hand." And all those scrambling on to bicycles and into cars were chimpanzees!

Sonja said, "I don't think that at all funny."

"I didn't think you would. You never did have much sense of humour."

The little house was not designed for dignified exits. Sonja could go into the kitchen and stand, or go up the steep, spirally stairway with a display of leg out of keeping with her mood. So she sat still, looking affronted.

"Ma'll see the joke, anyway," Charlie said.

"And that would mean telling her what it was all about."

"Well, you did say it, didn't you? And she might make the mistake of bringing another loaf."

Actually he showed Ma the cartoon without comment, and she laughed and said she only wished she could hire a trained monkey to pick raspberries.

For the next week or two Sonja and Charlie saw very little of each other, it being the season of outings. And even when he was in Baildon, Sonja was often out, leaving him something to eat on the working surface in the kitchen. He had not mended the table, and it had to be propped at one end to make it stand level. It hardly seemed worth the trouble just for one. Charlie did not in the least mind eating in the kitchen, but he hated standing up to his food. Like a bloody horse, he thought. Sometimes he didn't even bother to eat what she'd left; he'd work for an hour in the garden and then drive out to The Snape, where Ma always had supper when it was too dark for outside work. He did not notice how often the food provided was one of his favourites. And if Ma noticed the increased frequency of his visits, she said nothing.

So July passed, and one late evening as Charlie heaved himself from the settle and said, "Well, I must get back," something inside him asked, Why? And, Back to what? It then struck him that his marriage had failed, had probably been a mistake from the first. *Had better be ended.*

It was a staggering thought at first, but after a few days it grew familiar and ordinary. Divorce was quite a common thing these days, and there was no nastiness involved. No scandal, no guilt. A bit of talk, maybe, but he knew two men who had been divorced in quite scandalous circumstances some years ago, and they'd survived all right.

He thought about it a great deal, and the more he thought the better he liked it; but he said nothing to anybody until, as he phrased it to himself, he knew where he stood.

In order to reach such understanding, he must seek a lawyer, and he made the obvious choice, a pleasant young man called

Thacker of the firm Kennedy, Son, and Wayne. Mr. Thacker had done the conveyancing work when Charlie bought the doll's house. But unfortunately Mr. Thacker did not deal with divorce; that was Mr. Kennedy's speciality. Passed on to Mr. Kennedy, Charlie found himself liking him, too. His clothes were informal, his manner hearty, and although he had listened to many more pitiable tales—some indeed horrifying—he managed to convey understanding and sympathy as Charlie tried to explain that his marriage had irretrievably broken down.

Unperceived by anyone except Ma, Charlie had aged more than he should have done. The weight loss, which often rejuvenated men who managed it, had made him look older, and his thick thatch of fair hair was greying a bit.

"How long have you been married, Mr. Polstead?"

"It'll be three years come December."

"No application can be considered until a marriage has lasted three years." That was the law, and Mr. Kennedy was here to apply it whether he approved or not.

"That'll be another four months. Well, I can stick it till then."

"And this decision is mutual? I mean, your wife agrees that the marriage has broken down? And that there is no chance of a reconciliation?"

"I never thought about that. I mean about her agreeing. In fact I've only just made up my mind. Reconciliation? Not a chance. I wouldn't want it." In fact the mere prospect of being free again had gone to his head like whisky. "Nothing," he said, "will ever make me live with her again."

It was too early yet for Mr. Kennedy to bother about going thoroughly into Charlie's reasons for wanting a divorce, but not too early for some sound and informed advice.

"Mr. Polstead, you must not cease to cohabit. To leave your wife at this stage would be desertion and give her a distinct advantage."

"In what way?"

"Your wife would then appear as the injured person. Also by leaving home you would leave her in possession."

"I don't want that. But nothing's going to make me—er—sleep with her again. No law could make me."

Actually there was some moss-grown provision about the restoration of conjugal rights, Mr. Kennedy remembered. But no such case had figured in his experience.

"It would both ease and speed matters," he said, "if your wife also desired a divorce. But, as I said, nothing can be done before three years have expired."

It was still early in the morning, but for once Charlie was unmindful of business and drove back to Mulberry Close. Sonja, her hair protected by a gauzy scarf twisted into a turban, was Hoovering the living room. She hardly looked up. He'd probably forgotten some silly old paper. But he sat down on the chair he was always grumbling about and said, "Turn that thing off. I want to talk to you." And then she thought he looked odd. And back here at this time in the morning. He'd got the sack! This fear was confirmed when he said, "You'd better sit down." She was glad to do so for her legs had gone weak.

"It's like this. I'm putting in for a divorce."

Life and vigour flowed back. Sonja said, "Don't be so ridiculous! You can't. I've never misbehaved myself." Her resolute avoidance of the sordid, her reading restricted to magazines, her TV viewing embracing only light entertainment, and her devotion to films with happy endings, had left her stranded, her ideas as outdated as East Lynne.

Charlie said coarsely, "Adultery is no longer needed. Nowadays all we have to say is that we don't hit it off, don't like the same things or the same people, and both want a divorce."

"But I don't. I admit you went awkward and went to sleep in the spare room, and with this hot weather it is better. You didn't like what I said about that loaf. . . . But *divorce!* Divorce! You must be dotty. And what do you mean by putting in for one as though it was a dog licence or something?"

"I went to see a solicitor."

"Telling lies about me?"

"Of course not. Just the truth, Sonja. That the whole thing had broken down, and I wanted out. No blame attached to anybody."

"Except you. Losing your temper over nothing. Smashing dishes. Breaking up furniture."

"That was an accident. . . . But all right, put it that way if you like. Say mental cruelty. Or otherwise. Say I beat you black and blue. Say anything, just so long as we get free."

"I'm not having anything to do with it," Sonja said. To emphasize her attitude she switched on the Hoover again.

All that Charlie had felt, the disillusionment, the discontent, the feeling of having made a mistake, the feeling of not belonging and the wish to be rid of it all, suddenly crystallized into hatred. He was quite shocked by the vehemence of it.

Evie, Sonja's best friend, was sympathetic but practical. She heard Sonja out and said, "Frankly, what do you stand to lose? I always thought he was a dead loss so far as you were concerned. He wouldn't mix, would he? The only time we dragged him to a dance —my God, what a fiasco! And all the time sort of superior, in a sly way. Just because his mother has a place in the country!"

It was Sonja at the time of her engagement who had upgraded The Snape in this way.

"The fact remains, Evie, he is my meal ticket. I'd hate to go back to the shop."

"Don't be so silly! He can't leave you destitute. A friend of mine, Rosa Graves, got divorced and says she's much better off now. She had a smart lawyer."

"All so terribly sordid." Sonja sounded so mournful that Evie pointed out that it hadn't happened yet, might never happen. And how about a nibble of gin?

Charlie said nothing even to Ma until well on into November when he woke one morning knowing that he had caught a cold. Gargling had never yet done anything for him, but he did it conscientiously, sprinkled Vapex on his handkerchief, and took several spares. By the end of the day he felt ill and low spirited. Almost without thinking about it he turned towards The Snape, and Ma went into action immediately. First of all a good hot toddy, whisky and fresh lemon juice and hot water, well sweetened with honey.

"That should warm the cockles," she said. She had mislaid the thermometer, having had no use for it lately, but she felt his forehead with her fingers and his neck with her knuckles and decided that his temperature was slightly above normal. She had always obeyed the old axiom, Feed a cold and starve a fever, but her notion of starvation was lenient, and presently she gave him three moderate sized onions, boiled in good chicken broth. Later on he would have a bowl of bread and milk and a couple of aspirins.

"You must stay here tonight. Your bed is aired. Cousin Bertie was here only two nights ago. I'll just slip in a nice hot water bottle."

"No," Charlie said, "don't bother. I can't stay."

His cold was developing nicely, and his voice was already rather hoarse.

"Of course you can. If you think I'm going to let you out into the raw night air in the state you are now, you're daft. You'll go to bed here and stay in bed all day tomorrow. I'll ring Sonja and explain. And if you've got anything important tomorrow, I'll ring and excuse you."

To a man in his present state—already beginning to sweat a bit and his head feeling the size of a pumpkin—Ma's programme sounded like Heaven. And Sonja, even on their honeymoon, had been unable to disguise the fact that she considered a man with a heavy head cold faintly disgusting. As he undoubtedly was, Charlie had thought then.

"No," he said, "I can't. The lawyer said . . ."

Ma gave him a sharp look. Once or twice in the past, with a rather worse than usual cold upon him, Charlie had wandered a bit in his mind. She said, using the soft voice suitable for addressing temporary lunatics, "What lawyer, Charlie? What do you mean?"

He told her everything—at least everything that mattered. He did not mention the fatal loaf, and he was very careful not to criticize Sonja—much. He just said what Ma privately had known from the beginning. It never had been a suitable match, and the sooner the marriage ended the better. She was surprised that Charlie had actually made a move towards a divorce. Something must have triggered him off.

But her mind was more intent upon immediate things. "Do see sense, Boy. If you'd broken your leg instead of having a cold, you couldn't cohabit as you call it."

It often seemed to Ma that she was the one last reasonable person left alive in an unreasonable world.

Charlie, being unreasonable, insisted that he must get back to Mulberry Close.

Ma said, "All right, if you must. I'll go and bring your car right up to the door so you don't get chilled crossing the yard."

"That would be kind," he said. And for a moment or two he allowed himself to drift, a cosy, comfortable back-to-the-womb condition from which he was roused by Ma saying, "I can't start her. I've tried everything—even a jump lead from the Land-Rover."

And if Ma couldn't start the thing, Charlie certainly could not. She was far the better mechanic of the two. She drove an ancient, battered Land-Rover, heavily encrusted with mud. All she asked, she said, of any vehicle was that it should start when she pressed the starter and stop when she jammed on the brake. But lift the hood of this disreputable looking vehicle, and you saw an engine superlatively well maintained.

"You could lend me the Land-Rover, Ma."

"I could, but I'm not going to. Too draughty. You be off to bed. No. Ring your wife first."

She had realized that she could never speak to that girl again. Not because of anything she had done—Charlie had been far from specific—but because she had failed in what was her bounden duty, which was to make Charlie happy.

While Charlie croaked into the phone, Ma hid the rotor arm of his car behind the tea caddy on the dresser. And there it would stay until he was fully recovered.

Formerly there had been gallant attempts at correct get-togetherness at Christmas. Sonja and Charlie had gone to 12 Beechwood Avenue and eaten goose with her family on Christmas Day itself. Ma was always invited but always excused herself because the stock must be fed. On Boxing Day Sonja and Charlie, Mr. and Mrs. Armstrong, and those of Sonja's sisters who had nothing better to do, went out to The Snape and ate turkey. Then on the third day of Christmas the little house in Mulberry Close offered the only form of hospitality available to it—a cocktail party. Charlie never much enjoyed these occasions; even with everything except the little settee removed, the room seemed crowded. Sonja always invited a few friends as well, and as host he had to keep moving about, offering to refill glasses. He seemed to jog everybody's elbow, tread on everybody's toes. Still, their parties went well because Charlie had from the first taken a firm stand over the drinks.

Sonja's favourite magazine always celebrated the season by printing so-called new ways of using up left-overs, and how to make a bottle of gin serve twenty people. The mixture had pretty names. "Look at this, Charlie, Rosy Christmas. Isn't that pretty?" You needed one bottle of gin, one of cheap white wine, one of lemonade, and one of pink vermouth, "and one of those jugs people used to have on washstands." Charlie had said good humouredly, "No, darling, when I can't afford a decent dry martini, I won't have a party at all."

This year there would be no family gatherings for Sonja and Charlie. Evie had neatly solved that. She knew of a hotel down at Bywater, unbelievably cheap, putting on a good show for Christmas. "Trixie and Maud are coming. If we got bored, we could always play bridge. Look, I'll treat you."

Charlie bought a large box of Mrs. Armstrong's favourite chocolates and a bottle of whisky for Mr. Armstrong. He wasn't sure of his ground. He didn't know, or greatly care, how much Sonja had told anybody, but he was trying to behave decently. It wasn't their fault things had gone wrong.

Mrs. Armstrong said, "Really, Charlie, you are too kind." Her eyes, blue like Sonja's but slightly faded, suddenly filled with tears. "I can't tell you how sorry . . ." She never finished that sentence because her husband came into the room. The tears vanished— where did they go? ". . . about our happy Christmas arrangements being upset. But, of course, Evie being ordered sea air at such an odd time of the year, too, I suppose Sonja felt under an obligation."

Charlie, far less imperceptive than he looked, gathered that Mrs. Armstrong knew something and that her husband did not. He eyed the bottle and said, "Thanks, old boy. Very kind of you. And I do hope your mother will soon be better."

What on earth had Sonja been saying?

They then gave him their gift, a little pocket calculator. He owned one already, but he couldn't work it or it had something wrong with it. It came up with some most extraordinary answers. But he thanked the donors and went home to The Snape and had a thoroughly enjoyable Christmas. He and Ma took up their old

Canasta game, played for stakes high enough to make winning important; they worked on crossword puzzles and all the other mind stretchers thoughtfully provided by the papers Ma favoured. They ate and drank prodigiously, went to the meet of the South Suffolk Hunt at Clevely on Boxing Day, and sat up till midnight watching a real thriller. On the third day, Sunday, Ma cooked another hearty meal, and Charlie worked up a worthy appetite for it by doing a bit of digging in the morning.

The fourth day, Monday, found him in Mr. Kennedy's office again at the early hour of nine-thirty. He'd made the appointment before the holiday, on the very day when the three years expired.

Mr. Kennedy was a practical man, not much given to speculating about people's motives or even their characters. He liked people to be truthful because it simplified things, and he flattered himself that he needed no lie detector to help him sniff out an untruth. Charlie Polstead was obviously almost painfully honest, but there was something wrong with his tale. He was either concealing something, or he had been grossly misinformed about the process of the law. For, really, he had nothing to complain of in his marriage that couldn't have been outmatched by any one of the first ten men you might meet in the street. There'd been no quarrel, no misconduct, no nagging bone of contention such as differing views about religion, politics, or the bringing up of children. "It just didn't work. We've nothing in common. I just want to be done with it." There were many ways of saying the same things, and Charlie tried them all.

Mr. Kennedy moved on to discuss Sonja.

"And is your wife in agreement?"

"I don't think so."

"Don't you know?"

"Well, when I told her I'd been to see you about a divorce, she said I couldn't because she'd done nothing wrong. Since then we haven't discussed it. In fact we haven't said much since then."

"I'm afraid that your chances of a divorce are very slight. It would help, of course, if your wife did agree."

One could not use the word "bribe," one could say "generous settlement." "The matter of finance is bound to arise, sooner or later, Mr. Polstead. How are you placed? All this in confidence, of course."

Again that painstaking honesty.

"Well, I own the house. That is, half a house. I mean I bought it, but I put it in both our names. A sort of wedding present . . ." Just for a second the candid blue of his eyes clouded as he remembered those besotted days when he'd wanted to give Sonja the earth. "I gave thirty thousand pounds for it."

"Any mortgage?"

"Oh, no." He had no intention of lying; a free loan from one's mother couldn't be regarded . . .

"What other assets? Property? Income? Salary?"

"I had a bit of income once—but that went towards the house. No other assets, now. Oh, I have a job. I get a basic three thousand a year and commission. So it varies. This has been a bad year, prices up but orders down. I might clear six thousand."

Very low! School caretakers and nightwatchmen earned far more. Mr. Kennedy's glance rested for a moment on Charlie's clothes—all bought, presumably, in the days when he had an income.

"You have a car?"

"No. It belongs to the firm."

"I see. Well, as the law stands, your wife will be entitled to half of what you own. And possibly an allowance—the court enjoys considerable latitude in such cases."

"Just to be done with it, I'd give her the lot."

"Oh, no. Generosity, up to a point, would be advisable, but we must not be rash." He added almost as an afterthought, "If your wife consents to the divorce, it make take two years. If she contests it, five."

"Good God!" Charlie was truly startled. "I know a fellow who got one in six weeks!"

"On more substantial grounds, I have no doubt."

"Well, yes. I suppose he had. But I'm sure I understood that not wanting to go on with a marriage—which I don't—was proof of breakdown."

Mr. Kennedy allowed himself a smile, "Were that so, Mr. Polstead, how many marriages do you imagine would stay in being?"

"I suppose everybody feels now and again . . . But I've felt it for years. And nobody can say that I didn't try to make it work. I tried to like the things she liked, and the people . . . Or to get her interested in things I liked. I gave way to her. And now you say I've got to go on in this creeping misery for two years."

"Two, with her consent. There is one question which might have some bearing. Was your marriage sexually satisfactory?"

Interesting to see a man, no longer young, in fact growing bald, blush like a girl.

"If you want the truth, no. I don't say she ever refused outright, but that sort of thing never appealed to her much. I'm not complaining about that, though; I'm no Don Juan, and I know it. Still . . ." He left that in the air, remembering wistfully other more exciting if casual encounters with women whom he did not love at all. "And of course, since June . . ."

What a slip. And trust a lawyer to pounce on it.

"What happened in June?"

"Nothing. Nothing happened. I just realized I'd got to get out."

Mr. Kennedy would have been mildly surprised could he have heard the man he considered rather simple talking that evening to his wife.

He was a few minutes earlier than usual and just caught Sonja on her way out. She looked very pretty in the grey squirrel coat and a blue headscarf. A sight to melt the heart, but it left him unmoved. He could see his supper in the usual place, three thin slices of some anonymous pink meat and a flaccid looking tomato.

"I'd like to speak to you, if you can spare a minute."

"I'm just on my way to Evie's."

"This is important."

She gave a small, resigned shrug and led the way into the sitting room which offered its usual cheerless welcome. He stooped and switched on the electric fire, sat down on the uncomfortable chair, and deliberately lit a cigarette. He had resumed the filthy habit.

"I went to see Kennedy this morning, and I've more or less got it straight now. We talked about how you'd be placed *if* you agree to a divorce."

"Oh, not that again! I told you. I'm not having anything to do with it."

"You can't take that attitude about such a thing. You are con-

cerned, whether you like it or not. Because I tell you straight,
Sonja, I mean to go through with this. I'm offering you a chance of
making it easy for yourself."

"You mean for you."

"All right, for us both. We own this house between us. I don't see
why it shouldn't fetch what it cost, maybe even a bit more. I've
done quite a bit of painting and got the garden round. Still, say
thirty thousand. I'll buy your half. And give you two thousand as
well."

"And where would you get the money from?"

"From selling the house of course. I'd give you your half and two
thousand out of mine."

"But I don't want to sell the house. I like the house. And what
should I get half as nice, even with seventeen thousand pounds?"

"There're places going for fifteen. After all, you don't want two
bedrooms. You don't want a garage. . . . You could rent a flat
perhaps. Something like Evie's."

"Twenty pounds a week."

"I'd give you what I do now—thirty pounds a week. And you
wouldn't have me to keep."

"But I don't want to sell the house. And I don't want to be
divorced. I've told you that before."

"You'd better think," Charlie said. The malice in his voice surprised him. "Stay obstinate, and you'll be a lot worse off."

"I don't see how."

"If I just took off and left. Chucked in my job and disappeared."

"I should sue you for maintenance."

"That's my girl! You'd sue me for maintenance. But you'd have
to find me first. And that might take some time. The police don't
hurry much if a man just disappears, no crime committed, no foul
play suspected. Meanwhile, what do you live on? Not to mention
the rates, the bills for electricity and the telephone."

"I should think there's some provision made for women whose
husbands desert them."

"Some. But not much. Not if capable of working, have no children. *And own half a house*. And then, think—and I mean *think*.
Say I'm tracked down, and you sue me for maintenance. I owe you
X pounds and have no money, but I own half a house. They'd sell it
before you could blink."

Now and again one of Sonja's magazines did dip a fastidious toe into the turbid waters of real life problems. And there was a thing, not largely recognized, called the male menopause. Nothing like so bothersome as that which afflicted women, but tiresome none-theless, showing itself more in personality changes than in physical symptoms. Hitherto sober men might take to the bottle, faithful husbands fall victim to what the article archly called the Secretary Syndrome. But, as with most other such deplorable things, pa-tience and tact and understanding always won in the end.

Charlie was a bit young for it. And he'd never had a secretary or, to be truthful, shown the slightest flicker of interest in any other woman, but that was evidently what ailed him. And she did not feel tactful or patient, merely disgusted, and since so many things were disgusting, Sonja had developed her own protective tech-nique. Ignore it.

She said, "Really, Charlie, you could talk all night and not change anything. I don't want a divorce. And I do intend to stay in my dear little house."

With blinding clarity Charlie understood why men killed their wives in peculiarly brutal ways and buried their remains in coal cellars.

Well, if she wouldn't agree, wouldn't even listen—five years. He might as well be hanged for a sheep as for a goat. He had no intention of deserting in the way he had described, no intention of giving up his job. But he wouldn't live here any longer. Mr. Ken-nedy, the Lord Chancellor, the House of Lords in full panoply could say what they liked. Enough was enough—and he'd had it. In a furious temper he drove out to The Snape where Ma said, "You're just in time. I was about to have a bit of a fry up." Charlie said words alarming to the maternal ear, "I'm not hungry."

"Don't be so daft. Anybody in good health can always eat." And so presently it proved.

Unknown to himself Charlie had an ally, a sort of Devil's Advocate, in of all people Evie.

"I could understand it, darling, if you were still keen on him. I mean . . . You know what I mean. But you aren't. So why not get out while the going's good? He sounds pretty crazy, and then he always was a bit odd. And you are in a strong position now. You can raise the ante."

"The what?"

"O God, give me patience. Can't you see? Half the house is yours. Right? Then he's giving you nothing so far as that is concerned. And two thousand out of his fifteen is just peanuts. Ask for ten and then settle for five. With that, and the thirty pounds a week, you'd be comfortable."

"But I shouldn't have my dear little house."

Evie said with marked lack of elegance, "Oh, bugger the house! It's silly to get attached to places. If you'd moved as often as I have, you'd know that. Which reminds me. Ask for *all* the furniture. You're entitled to half, but ask for the lot."

Sonja tried, and failed, to visualize all her pretty things against some other background. But she dared not repeat her words about not wanting to move. To do so might provoke Evie to even worse language.

"Sonja, you must face up to the alternative. Suppose Charlie did just scarper. What would you live on while you found him and sued him? Of course," she said loyally, "you could always count on me for a meal but . . ."

"I think he was just trying to scare me. It's a phase. That's what it is. Just a phase. But nasty. And I can't see why I should be uprooted and have to leave my dear . . . D'you know, Evie, perhaps I'm the one who needs a lawyer."

"Maybe you do. But they cost."

"How much?"

"Rosa reckoned about a pound a minute. They even time a telephone call. Still, it might be a good idea. Now how about a drink?"

It was still the post-Christmas lull, and Sonja was able to make an appointment for the next afternoon and, moreover, with Mr. Bridges himself—a stately figure with an excellent bedside manner which cost nothing and invited confidence.

"Just tell me everything," he said.

It did not amount to much. Her husband had got cross with her away back in June and had stayed cross. Now he wanted a divorce. And she did not.

Like Mr. Kennedy, Mr. Bridges felt that something was missing. So he probed gently, and Sonja told the story of the loaf. Mr. Bridges remembered the proverb about the last straw. Only a very unsound marriage could have been wrecked by so small a thing.

"Prior to this unhappy episode, your marriage was happy?"

"Absolutely," Sonja said. "In fact we'd never had a cross word. I really can't think what's got into Charlie."

Mr. Bridges easily could. Granted, she was as pretty as a picture, but as near a moron as made no matter. He'd had ten minutes of her company, and he could imagine how long three years must have seemed to that unfortunate man.

It was also evident that she was completely insensitive. She kept saying, "I just took no notice," and "I thought Charlie would get over it." Mr. Bridges saw that the loss of her husband's affection meant far less to her than the prospect of losing her home. He eventually felt that if she said "my dear little house" just one more time he would lose his professional calm.

Yet, for all that, she had such a helpless, harmless kind of appeal that if he could possibly have seen a way of ensuring that she held on to the one thing for which she had any feeling, he would have seized upon it.

The law had lately shifted in favour of women. A woman in Mrs. Polstead's position was entitled to half of the couple's joint property. But half was already hers. And until the dear little house could be offered with vacant possession, it was virtually worthless.

"If your husband persists in his determination to get a divorce—even, as he threatens, by desertion—it will come about, and the property will be divided. But to be worth anything, the house must be sold. With vacant possession. You follow me? There is a solution. If you could raise fifteen thousand pounds, you could buy his share of the house and remain in it."

"With a mortgage?" He was rather surprised that she even knew the word.

"Yes."

"Then I'd have to pay interest. Fourteen per cent at least. And the rates and the telephone and the electricity. I don't think I could do it. Not on the thirty pounds a week Charlie more or less promised. But, you see, that was more or less a condition that I agreed to be divorced. I mean, if he turned nasty, and I think he would, he might say he couldn't pay. Or wouldn't. I know now. He can be very awkward."

Mr. Bridges knew just how awkward people—not only men—could be.

"I have no wish and no right to dictate to you, Mrs. Polstead. The decision must be yours. But I seriously think that in the circumstances it might be better to agree and make the best possible financial arrangement. Who is acting for your husband, by the way?"

"I think he said . . . Mr. Kennedy."

"Ah, yes. I will get in touch with him."

Mr. Kennedy and Mr. Bridges were related both by blood and by marriage. The four big law firms operated under different names, occupied different buildings, carefully preserved professional etiquette, but in the previous generation and the one before that, intermarriage had been forced upon their members since they couldn't marry into the county families and wouldn't marry into the town—meaning shopkeeping—circles. So Mr. Kennedy was Mr. Bridges' nephew, by a second marriage, and also his father-in-law. But where business was concerned, they might have been strangers or even enemies.

Now, each with his client's good in mind, they began something much resembling the courtship dances of certain birds, a small advance, a tiny withdrawal, a concession, a demand. Mr. Kennedy, sometimes hampered by Charlie's impetuosity, was fighting to get his client let off as lightly as possible; Mr. Bridges, his hand strengthened by Sonja's vacillation, was bent upon extracting the last possible penny. His feeling that she was witless increased. She'd listen and say, yes, she understood but she needed time to think things over. She would seem on the point of accepting the terms offered and then stiffen up again and suggest something which even to Mr. Bridges sounded extortionate. And she so often mentioned the dear little house that finally he lost patience and said quite sharply, "There are many equally desirable properties, Mrs. Polstead." Then he softened and said, "I am sure that it is your capacity for home-making which has made the Mulberry Close house so attractive. You could do the same anywhere." But he had discovered what it had taken Charlie rather longer to learn, that Sonja was obtuse in a peculiar way. She only took in what she wanted to.

She was, most surprisingly, good at mental arithmetic, but when talking about money, she missed the main point—that the argument centred about money which could only be divided after it existed, brought into being by the sale of the house. Even when Charlie said, "All right, then, seven. Beyond that I just can't go."

Charlie was beginning to wonder now whether the thirty pounds a week he had promised would be possible. Business was very bad. It was now late January, the time of year when farms stirred with the earth from winter's sleep, but he had not made a single substantial sale. His nerves were fraying, but his determination held, and one day his temper gave way.

"Look, I've had about enough of this. Tell her man to tell her that if she won't accept what I've offered—and damned quick, too —I'll withdraw it. I always knew she was stupid. Now I know she's greedy. I won't be reconciled; I won't live in the lousy little rabbit's hutch, and it'll take a court order to make me pay a penny."

"Morning, Tom," Mr. Kennedy said. "Nice day. Spring in the air."

"Crocuses in full flower. A bit early. Not a good omen." Mr. Bridges was not only a nature lover but an observer of bits of weather lore, ages old. Something about if the crocus opened its cup before Christmas day, it was to receive snow.

"Polstead," said Mr. Kennedy. "My client says that unless your client agrees to our latest offer, he'll withdraw it. Technically he has already deserted her. Now he threatens to refuse to support."

"There he would be in default."

"Agreed. But before any action could be taken about that, your client would be, shall we say, severely inconvenienced."

"I'm very busy at the moment. But I'll try to see her tomorrow morning."

It was, of course, by now generally known that Sonja and Charlie had split up. Mrs. Armstrong had made a piteous appeal—there really were tear blotches on the paper—urging Charlie to forgive whatever there was to forgive, to go back, to honour his marriage vows, to remember that he had taken three years of Sonja's youth.

Mr. Armstrong had behaved rather badly, coming up to Charlie in the bar at the golf club and saying, "What a rotter you turned out to be!" His terms of abuse were curiously out-of-date, he said scoundrel and cad, and as Charlie stared, he spat out, "May you rot in Hell."

Charlie felt misjudged and ill done by. Only Ma, taking it all as a matter of course, and perhaps Mr. Kennedy, seemed to be on his side, and the reservation "perhaps" was applicable because sometimes Mr. Kennedy seemed to be making the thing hang on and on. For example, when Charlie said, "Oh, let her have the lot. I don't care." Mr. Kennedy had said, "We must not be rash."

For Charlie time seemed to drag. To Sonja it seemed to run by with dizzying speed. Partly because Evie was being so very kind and helpful, but somehow in the wrong way. Finding places where Sonja could live, a really decent little house in a run-down area, on offer for only £15,000, and all it needed was a lick or two of paint. A brand new flat in a converted house almost next door to Evie. "Thirty pounds a week, darling, but constant hot water and central heating. Think of the saving." Somebody with the tag end of a lease to sell. Only £20,000 and really quite spacious. "You could find somebody to share." Kind, indefatigable, but a million miles from understanding.

And now here was Mr. Bridges delivering an ultimatum. He used the deadly word.

"I'm afraid, Mrs. Polstead, that your husband has delivered an ultimatum. The last offer was as far as he would go, and if you refuse, he will withdraw it. You recall the terms. Not, on the whole, ungenerous."

£8,000, all the furniture, and £32 a week.

She said ungraciously, "Well, if that's the best you can do. I still think it's cruel of Charlie. Making me give up my dear little house."

Any sympathy Mr. Bridges had felt for her on that score had been eroded by the mechanical repetition of that term and also by the reception she had given to a suggestion he had made just after he'd screwed Charlie from £30 to £32 a week; this was that the house should not be sold, so Sonja would get no lump sum, but would remain there and augment the allowance by seeking employment of some kind. She had recoiled, as from something most improper. "Oh, no, I don't think I could do that. Being divorced for no reason at all is bad enough."

Now laying before her what Mr. Kennedy had said was the most that his client would yield and actually rather more than he could afford, Mr. Bridges explained once again that the only money to be shared was what would come from the sale of the dear little house, that Sonja must face facts, unpleasant as they were, and make preparations to vacate the property.

"And suppose I say 'No' to everything, I don't agree to a divorce, and I don't want to move."

"Mrs. Polstead, the immediate consequences would be unpleasant. Your husband is legally bound to contribute to your support, but delay would be inevitable. Also, we must bear in mind that every offer he has made so far has been on condition that you agree to the divorce. And another thing . . . whatever any court would award you as maintenance would be in relationship with your husband's resources. With the house unsold, he would have no capital, and his salary would certainly not warrant a payment to you of thirty-two pounds a week."

"There is that, I suppose," Sonja said slowly. "All right, if I must, I must. I agree. He can divorce me, and I'll move. On the terms you just said. Oh, and one other thing. I think Charlie ought to pay all the expenses—what I owe you, Mr. Bridges, and what selling the house costs. And," she added with positive inspiration, "what it costs me to move."

"I'm sure that Mr. Polstead will agree to that."

He saw her to the door and, coming back to his desk, switched off the tape recorder which he used for any crucial interview. It saved him from taking notes and was an aid to memory which was not quite what it had been. It was also very useful when clients thought they'd be clever and said, But I never said any such thing.

Just before five o'clock, when all business stopped, he rang Tom Kennedy and could now speak with the frivolity hitherto unthinkable. And he could say *we*, meaning himself and Tom Kennedy.

"We've won! I've had Mrs. Polstead here. She has agreed to everything, with one trivial condition." He described Sonja's latest stipulation.

Mr. Kennedy said, "A true daughter of the horse-leech if ever there was one! My poor old chap will be relieved."

Curiously, as Mr. Bridges' sympathy for his client had waned, Mr. Kennedy's for Charlie had waxed. He still thought him stupid and pigheaded, and he still thought that he was concealing something, probably from a chivalrous motive.

Sonja said, "I feel now that I can't get out soon enough. It isn't mine any more. And I should absolutely hate anybody who came to look at it. Some lucky bitch in my—home."

She had decided upon the house that needed only a lick or two of paint, partly because it had now been reduced to £14,000, partly because it was immediately available and also because, looking at it again, she could see that given those licks it could be as nice as the house in Mulberry Close, if not rather better in that the stairs did not go up from the living room. And being in a less desirable area, it was much more moderately rated.

When Charlie received a command to present himself at the company's head office in Luton, he was not at all alarmed. The worst thing he visualized—and the most probable—was a further extension of his beat. He was enough of a countryman to know that when gleanings were sparse, gleaners had to cover more ground. He didn't mind that. The days were perceptibly lighter, and he would not have a garden to keep in order. He didn't mind long hours.

He was rather surprised to find four other representatives, similarly summoned, in the waiting room. All known to him by sight and by name. One, always a lugubrious fellow, said, "This means the sack." Charlie said, "Never! We'd have been asked to bring our cards." Another man said, "Yes, so they would. I guess it's a pep talk about greater productivity, which is daft where we're concerned. How can you sell when nobody'll buy?"

There was some general talk about this. Maybe a coal miner could work a bit harder, but a train driver couldn't drive more than one train at a time, could he? Well, maybe not. He could work longer hours. Yes, and put some other poor sod on the unemployed.

Half an hour later, they were all unemployed. And the sacking was done in the shabbiest possible manner.

Quite incredible, but it happened. When the door opened and

they all straightened up, expecting Old Andrews, head of sales, to emerge, instead there came a boy with a few papers in his hand. Operating alphabetically, beginning, "Mr. Archer?" and ending with Mr. Smithers, he gave each his paper. End of engagement, from today. Firm in liquidation. Redundancy payments, five months' salary—salary exclusive of commission. All cars to be called in. Cards to be surrendered.

There was a stunned silence, then an angry hum.

The lugubrious man said, "What did I tell you? Ruin, plain ruin."

A less resigned man, very red in the face, said "They can't do this to us!" He went and smote upon the door. The boy who had distributed the papers opened it. "I want to see Mr. Andrews." The boy said, "He is not here. I am employed by the receivers." He shut the door smartly.

Charlie, neither the oldest nor the youngest, recovered first. It was a shattering blow, and the way it had been dealt was despicable—he'd always been rather proud of his firm, English to the core and renowned for their fair dealing. But he realized in that dreadful moment that he was a very fortunate, indeed a privileged man. No wife, no children. He remembered that he had agreed to pay Sonja £32 a week. Well, she could damn well whistle for it!

"Come on, boys. What we all want is a good stiff drink. On me!" It would probably seem indecent to celebrate the dissolution of a marriage. "It happens to be my birthday."

"And what a nice present you've had," said the melancholy man. He went with them to the little pub just round the corner, but was prevented from sharing the heartening effects of one stiff drink, and then another. "Stomach ulcer," he said, and confined himself to tonic water. Later on it occurred to Charlie that it wasn't an ulcer in his stomach; it was a ravening wolf. He downed three thick cheese sandwiches and two slices of the veal and ham pie of which in three years of marriage Charlie had had a surfeit.

Even after the drinks and the food, the mood was gloomy. Without exception they had obligations and commitments all incurred when the firm seemed sound and their jobs reasonably safe. The man who had hit on the door and demanded to see Mr. Andrews remained truculent. The redundancy pay offered was ridiculous. And they weren't going to get away with it. There were tribunals that dealt with such things. Five months basic. Criminal! Ren-

dered even gloomier by the food—easily understandable—that
gloomy man said that he had read of cases where the tribunals had
reduced what employers had offered.

Charlie, who had had three drinks and no pie—he had taken a
cheese sandwich and bitten into it once, then incautiously put it
down and somebody in greater need must have snatched it up and
consumed it—was about half-way home before depression struck
him. He then realized that he liked his job, liked most of the
people he encountered. And he was now forty-three in a commu-
nity where a man was too old at forty to be taken on except as a
night watchman. And he would miss his car. It was not a showy
vehicle, but it was sturdy and reliable. He thought, The brutes!
Sacking us like that and cheating on the redundancy, they might
have let us keep the cars. If they're broke, what good will five
second-hand Fords do them?

In this sour mood he reached home and broke the news to Ma as
abruptly as it had been broken to him. Ma made one unusual
gesture; she pressed his shoulder, said nothing for a moment, and
then, "Never mind, Boy. We'll weather through. Fretting never
helped anything yet." She dished up the supper, one of Charlie's
favourites, steak and kidney pudding, and pretended not to notice
that he lacked appetite. Not usually a talkative woman, this evening she exerted herself so that the silences never became actually
painful. Charlie wondered how the other chaps had got on and
how their wives had reacted. He could imagine how Sonja would
have carried on even in the early, supposedly fond, days. Finally
he said, "I'm luckier than most."

"Of course you are. Sure of a roof and three square meals a day."
An ancient grudge surfaced. "And if your Aunt Mary hadn't
turned bloody senile, you'd have been even luckier."

As though from habit—which it was not—she placed the whisky
bottle and two glasses on the table. It was at low ebb, and presently
she picked it up and eyed it sternly.

"We can't have this hanging about looking like low tide off the
coast of Lincolnshire. Put it out of its misery, Charlie. And then off
to bed. You've had a hard day."

Mr. Stockman, the house agent, kept his finger on the pulse of
the market as assiduously as a nurse with a patient in intensive
care. He had sold 8 Mulberry Close for £30,000, but he knew he

wouldn't get it now. The market had sagged. Also, and he had spies everywhere, he knew that Number 6, almost identical except that it had a small greenhouse, was about to be for sale for £27,000. So when a likely young couple came and fell in love with the dear little house, but said, almost tearfully, that £28,000 was the very utmost they could afford, he said that he was practically certain that the vendor would give this offer serious consideration, not because the house wasn't worth the asking price but because a quick sale saved expenses. . . . Hanging boards out, taking them in again, pictures and details in the window, running about with keys and the tiresome delays while a would-be purchaser raised the money or sold the house he already possessed. This young couple, head over heels in love with each other and both in love with the house, could produce £28,000 down.

Mr. Stockman took his well earned percentage; Mr. Kennedy estimated that he had given service worth £300; Mr. Bridges claimed only £200. The difference arose from the fact that Mr. Bridges still reckoned in dignified guineas and then had some difficulty in converting to decimal coinage. In addition there was the fee for conveyancing. At the final reckoning there was the sum of £26,000 to be divided between Sonja and Charlie, and in addition Sonja would have the £8,000 which Charlie had promised.

But they were all reckoning without Ma. Incredible as it now seemed to everybody, even Charlie had practically forgotten that loan. He was so accustomed to Ma's doing all the providing, and on the rare occasions when he did think of it, the accompanying thought was reassuring: Some day—pray God it would be far distant—all that Ma owned would be his, so in a sense he was borrowing from himself.

Only once, right in the middle of the bargaining, had he and Ma spoken on the subject. Charlie said, "I suppose I should tell Kennedy that you loaned me twenty thousand."

"Oh, I wouldn't do that. At that rate you'd never be free." She spoke as though she'd loaned her son a stamp.

Now, however, she spoke in a different voice. Not to Charlie, poor boy, depressed over the loss of his job. She went direct to Mr. Kennedy who, hearing that Mrs. Polstead wished to see him for a moment, imagined that the daughter of the horse-leech had dreamed up some further exaction. The sight of Ma, her corduroy slacks tucked into the tops of her muddy Wellingtons and her sheepskin coat scruffed and dirty gave him quite a shock. Beautiful hair, though, dead white and shining, and a face from which age seemed to have stripped all superfluous flesh, no jowls or sags or deep folds. She had a profile as clear-cut as a cameo, and her manner was so unconsciously dignified as to be regal.

She said, "Good morning. This won't take a minute. It's just something I think should be brought to your attention."

Mr. Kennedy said, "Good morning, Mrs. Polstead," and reached out to shake hands. Her hand, thin and narrow, was as hard as horn.

Once the contest had ended Mr. Kennedy and Mr. Bridges had felt free to speak freely, and as example of how very odd people could be, Mr. Bridges had told the story of the loaf which had triggered off the whole thing. So now Mr. Kennedy looked with special attention at Mrs. Polstead's hands. Knuckles and finger joints roughened and, yes, grimy.

But his attention was soon diverted, for Mrs. Polstead was offering him a paper. The first word to catch his eye was—not surprising since it was at the top—Secker.

Mr. Secker was in no way related to any of the members of the Big Four. He'd popped up from nowhere and set up a practice in a couple of shabby rooms. He had never expanded and still ran his business with the help of a now ancient man whom Mr. Bridges had sacked for getting drunk every market day. So low had this one-time clerk fallen that he occasionally swept the front and even more rarely cleaned the window.

Mr. Secker was patronized mainly by people who were intimidated by mahogany and glass and receptionists. They made the mistake of thinking that he was cheap. He merely looked cheap. Even his paper heading! Printed not embossed.

But nobody had ever denied that Mr. Secker was a sound man of law. Mr. Kennedy found himself reading a properly drawn up agreement between Katharine Ethel Polstead (widow) and Charles Saxby Polstead by which, in return for a loan of £20,000 which enabled Charles Saxby Polstead to purchase the property known as 8 Mulberry Close, Baildon in the County of Suffolk, the said Katharine Ethel Polstead was granted a lien upon the said property in the event of its being sold. There were the signatures, properly witnessed.

It was incontestable. If Charlie had gone bankrupt for some fantastic sum and had been obliged to sell the house, Katharine Ethel Polstead's claim would have been given priority.

Mr. Kennedy said very gravely, "Mrs. Polstead, had this been disclosed earlier, events would have shaped themselves differently."

"So I thought," Ma said. She looked at Mr. Kennedy with the same apparent, blue eyed candour that he had noticed in Charlie, but in her voice there was such a cold, implacable malice that he felt chilled.

Evie said to Trixie and Maud and anyone else who would listen, "You must give Sonja her due. She never cried. No, not even when she knew the worst—that great lout had lost his job, and even when he got Unemployment, it'd only be about twenty-eight pounds. She never cried, she just said, 'Well, it looks as if I shall have to go back to the shop—if they'll have me.' You must give her full marks for guts."

And Mr. Bridges, who had enjoyed an advantage unknown to Mr. Kennedy, indeed to few of the younger—a sound grounding in the Bible, once known as the Good Book—recalled that the proverb ran, "The horse-leech hath *two* daughters, crying, Give, give . . . ."

8

Debt of gratitude

It happens so often that there might almost be a rule about it—when girls go in pairs, one is always pretty, the other plain.

Both benefit by this arrangement. The pretty one has company without competition, and the plain one enjoys many fringe benefits.

Gloria Hanbury's parents had shown presentiment when they chose her name, for she was no more beautiful than the average baby, but she grew to be lovely with thick almost truly golden hair, periwinkle blue eyes, and a perfect complexion. Valerie Cobb was simply plain, in no way disfigured but plain and, at a critical age, sadly given to acne. But they were best friends and had been for years, for they were so nearly of an age that they had started out for Infant School together, escorted by Mrs. Hanbury in the morning and fetched home by Mrs. Cobb in the afternoon. The crime wave at the time had barely begun and had not yet reached Baildon, and Mrs. Hanbury and Mrs. Cobb were not haunted as parents thirty years later were to be by the thought of lurking sex maniacs. Their concern was for the two roads to be crossed and of Gloria and Valerie lingering about and getting into undesirable

company. There was an element known as rough. And both the
Hanburys and the Cobbs held identical views about roughness.

They lived in the same street, in almost identical houses, relatively modern but built in traditional style; each had a parlour, a
living room, and kitchen with upstairs one fair sized bedroom, two
small, and a bathroom. As time passed and the links between the
two families strengthened, even the interiors of the houses came
to bear a strong resemblance to each other. Mrs. Hanbury admitted that Mrs. Cobb had taste and copied her shamelessly, and Mrs.
Cobb, so far from resenting this, was flattered. When Mrs. Hanbury said, "Oh, Ella, what lovely new curtains! I should like some
just like them." Mrs. Cobb replied, "Why not?" told her where she
had bought the material and the price, the amount of stuff needed,
and as a final gesture, offered to run the things up on her new
sewing machine.

Mr. Hanbury and Mr. Cobb enjoyed much the same relationship, conferring together over their gardens, lending and borrowing tools, often regretting that they were not actually next door
neighbours instead of being separated by the suburban road. They
were in almost exactly the same income group, enjoyed the same
social status, played bowls together on Saturday afternoons, and
enjoyed a modest pint now and then at the Magpie, their local.

Into this humdrum but happy circle there came a slight disrup-
tion when, seven years after Valerie's birth, Mrs. Cobb had another baby—a Mongol. Really an extreme case, obvious at first
glance. Sympathy abounded but of understanding there was a
shortage; both Mr. and Mrs. Hanbury thought that the best, the
only thing, to do was to put the poor creature in a home at once.

"It would be far the kindest thing to do, Ella. Think of the
future. He'd be much happier in a place where everybody was the
same."

"He'll be happy here, so far as I can manage it. After all, he is my
baby."

Mr. Hanbury's well meant advice, over a pint, met with the
same reception from Mr. Cobb.

So after that Gloria could not come to play with Valerie any
more. The Hanburys couldn't risk her seeing anything so awful.
When the little girls played together, it must be at Gloria's home,
and gradually all Valerie's favourite toys and some of her clothes

went across the street to the Hanburys' house. "Your mummy has enough to do, dear, without busying herself about parties," Mrs. Hanbury said kindly, "so bring your frock across and change here." Mrs. Hanbury even tried to do something to improve Valerie's appearance; she tried to wave her hair, but it was intractable; she cut a fringe, hoping that it might detract from the length of the poor child's face. Nothing availed.

It was a situation calculated to foster complexes and resentments, but Valerie showed an unchildlike fortitude. She did not mind spending more time across the road, for she now preferred Gloria's home to her own, where her mother was so much occupied with that ugly baby. She was not envious of Gloria's looks, in fact she admired them and was proud to be Gloria's best friend. She also had the consolation of knowing that she was by far the cleverer of the two. When they both moved into the Senior School, where streaming was in vogue, they were separated for the first time, Valerie being judged "A" and Gloria "C." This however made little difference to their basic friendship.

They both left school at sixteen. Various people urged Valerie to continue with her education, to become, perhaps, a teacher, but since Gloria was leaving, then Valerie must leave too. Their choice of career seemed almost destined; Gloria was just right behind the cosmetic counter of the largest chemist's shop, Valerie slipped just as naturally into the obscurity of a solicitors' office. They remained best friends.

The time had now come for the preliminaries of the mating process. Mr. and Mrs. Hanbury were lenient, if a trifle old fashioned. They liked to know where Gloria was and with whom; they liked a boy-and-girl relationship to remain just that until the time for more serious affairs arrived. They liked Gloria to bring her boy friends home for that comprehensive meal, a hybrid between tea and supper but always called tea. And of course there was always dear Valerie, so sensible and such a good influence on Gloria, who was—let's face it—inclined to be flighty.

Dear Valerie, poor Valerie, had no boy friends of her own, and had she had, she could hardly have taken them home where the idiotic—and often violent—brother was so much in evidence. And both Mr. and Mrs. Cobb had lost all zest. Someone had once told them, and they had believed it, that Mongoloid children seldom lived beyond the age of seven. And surely anybody could, in the name of love, serve so short a sentence. But that general rule had not worked for them; at seven their afflicted boy was as healthy as a horse, growing fast, and becoming, it sometimes seemed, deliberately destructive. He needed, and received, constant attention from parents who were now looking towards the next critical age, fourteen. Beyond that they dared hardly look.

Gloria liked to arrange foursomes and did it with superlative ease. "Of course, Tom, I'd love to come to the Cooperative Dance —but only if you can rustle up a partner for Valerie." Given such incentive, any boy worth his salt could rustle up half a dozen, the more easily because now, for almost the first time in history, there were surplus boys about. And neither the rustled up boys nor Valerie had too bad a time, because she could dance and could be quite witty.

The chemist in whose shop Gloria worked had a son, very handsome and intelligent. He was up at Cambridge, not with a view to qualifying for any profession—he would inherit the shop and other properties which his industrious father had acquired. He was at Cambridge to obtain polish and standing and to enjoy himself. In his second long vacation he came home, saw Gloria Hanbury, and fell in love. He retained just sufficient sense to realize that such an attachment would be unlikely to meet with his father's approval, so the affair was kept secret. But Gloria was so sure of herself and of him that she talked to Valerie about her wedding—timing it for the next June. And of course Valerie must be a bridesmaid, with Hazel and Sandy and Maureen. "I will," Valerie said, "if you promise not to make us wear blue. It's not my colour."

"Why, Valerie," Gloria exclaimed, startled, "I never knew you were so vain."

"I'm not. I've got nothing to be vain about. But I do know about clothes. God! If I could once get my hands on some *real money* . . ."

Mr. and Mrs. Hanbury were not told about Gloria's secret engagement. Gloria was shrewd enough to know what their reaction would be. Why secret? What has Mr. Agnew got against you, against us? They thought well of themselves and so highly of their lovely daughter that they wouldn't see the social gap. So they would be offended, and Mr. Hanbury, despite his mild appearance and blameless way of life, had a pugnacious streak. He was quite capable of confronting Mr. Agnew and saying, "Here, what's all this?"

Unthinkable!

The secret engagement was not allowed to inhibit Gloria's social life; the foursomes continued, their component parts varying, and, shortly before Christmas—wonder of wonders—there appeared upon the scene a young man who seemed to be attracted to Valerie, actually to prefer her to Gloria. And he was quite something: tall, good looking in a rugged kind of way, the owner of a car. He was local, being the son of a farmer at Muchanger, but he had not been "one of the boys" because he'd been away to school and then to an agricultural college. His name was Ian Ferguson.

It was late in November when he first asked Valerie, alone, to visit Four Elms farm and meet his parents. Valerie's joy at this undoubted sign of favour was mitigated by the need to explain to Gloria. It was a unique situation and therefore difficult to handle, for, love and admire Gloria as one might, there was no blinking away the fact that she always took it for granted that in any group she was the main attraction. Also the invitation emphasized rather sharply the difference between their situations, for Ian Ferguson was just as much of a catch as Godfrey Agnew.

However, after an unflattering display of surprise, Gloria was kind, even helpful.

"What will you wear? Tell you what, I'll lend you my new coat."

"That is sweet of you! But, darling, it's blue. Not my colour."

She knew exactly what she was going to do. She had a little money saved—her parents, aware of the deficiency in the home, barely charged for her keep. She went to the best shop in the town and spent her all, excited beyond caution at finding a frock and matching coat of the warm tan colour in which she looked her very best. There was some fur on the collar, just a shade darker and at a glance almost mink. She had long since abandoned all attempts to wear her hair short; it too easily resembled a sweep's brush, so she'd grown it and now had a coil high on the back of her head. A little rouge mitigated the sallowness of her skin. She did not look pretty, nothing but a miracle could make her that, but she looked her best: neat, smart, and eminently respectable.

So Ian's parents saw her and were relieved. You heard such things, saw such sights these days.

Christmas brought the usual round of parties, enhanced this year by a super one at Four Elms, and Ian gave Valerie a combined Christmas present and engagement ring, a huge golden topaz beautifully set in silver filigree. There was talk of an Easter wedding.

Every now and then a small voice in Valerie's mind would remark, "Too good to be true!" She was now very deeply in love, what had begun as a kind of astonished gratitude deepening and warming into an all embracing emotion.

At four o'clock in the morning of the second Sunday of the New Year, Valerie woke suddenly with a pain in her stomach and a feeling of nausea. She was sleeping at Gloria's, because there had been a party the evening before and coming in late to her own home, she might wake poor Tom.

She reached the bathroom in time to be sick tidily, but the pain in her stomach persisted, growing worse rather than better and keeping her awake until morning when Mrs. Hanbury, sympathetic enough, was inclined to blame something she had eaten at the party.

It had been a grand party, because it was to celebrate Hazel's twenty-first birthday, and eight of them had clubbed together to give her a treat, dinner at a newly opened eating place, Nettleton Grange, where there was also a disco. Mrs. Hanbury, always suspicious of any food she had not cooked herself, asked, "What exactly did you eat?" Prawn cocktail, roast turkey with trimmings, and ice cream. Seeking goodwill, the Grange was for the moment charging moderately. Mrs. Hanbury would have suspected the turkey, frozen and insufficiently thawed out, but Gloria had eaten the same food and was perfectly well. So it could be one bad prawn.

Gloria filled a hot water bottle to apply to the seat of the pain and then rang round to enquire if anyone else of the party had suffered at all. Nobody had. Valerie grew worse, was sick again, started a temperature, and at six o'clock in the evening, diffident as she felt at doing such a thing at such an hour on a Sunday, Mrs.

Hanbury rang up Dr. Orwell, mentioning her fear that the girl might be suffering from appendicitis. Dr. Orwell came, prodded gently, and said he would have been inclined to agree except that the pain was in the wrong place. But he did not seriously consider food poisoning since this had another unpleasant symptom, absent in this case. And while he spoke and meditated what best to do, Valerie's appendix burst with a soft but audible pop.

She was in the hospital and operated upon in less than two hours, but peritonitis had already set in. She had never been an outstandingly healthy girl, and now she was very ill indeed. Too ill for the open ward, she lay in a little single room called an amenity ward, with the "NO VISITORS" plaque exhibited on the door and more flowers than there really was room for.

Her father was the first person allowed to see her. Her mother couldn't leave Tom; she was the only person who could handle him now, and she was far too much ashamed of him to be seen with him. They took the very vital daily exercise after dark, he wearing a toddler-type harness and reins, made to his size by his mother and of very strong nylon thread.

"Mum sends her love," Mr. Cobb said, "and these are from us all." He handed a bunch of freesias to the collection. But it was not a successful visit because, upset at seeing his daughter look so wretchedly ill, he was incautious and said, "You know, your Mum says that if you'd been home that Sunday, she'd have got the doctor sooner, and you'd have been spared all this." Years of rancour lurked behind this opinion.

"I don't see that," Valerie said. "Even the doctor was deceived. They say now there's such a thing as a transferred pain. But never mind that. Dad, could you give Gloria a message for me?"

"Of course I could."

"Tell her to look after Ian for me and thank him for the . . . the flowers." She was obliged to speak vaguely because she'd never got the floral offerings sorted out.

"I'll do that right away, on my way home," Mr. Cobb said, getting up a trifle too eagerly from one of the chairs designed to deter visitors and understanding what they meant by a transferred pain.

And at the next testing Valerie's temperature was up and the "NO VISITORS" sign was exposed again. And after it was again removed, Mrs. Hanbury came with a bunch of grapes and a book and a bit of breast beating about the delay.

"But how could I know? Even Dr. Orwell didn't know until . . . Oh, my dear, I am so very sorry."

"Really, you have no reason to be. I'm all right . . . Tell me, did my dad give my message to Gloria?"

"About taking care of Ian? Yes, he came specially. And Gloria said of course she would."

After that, visitors, one at a time, were allowed in, and eventually Ian himself came. She was so glad that on that day, for the first time, she had mustered strength enough to do her face and her hair.

That wasn't a very happy visit either. The truth was that men couldn't be comfortable in such places; he was as ill at ease as her dad had been.

She said, "You are allowed to smoke in here. One of the privileges." She said, "I'm now making rapid progress. Today I sat out for two hours." She said, "Tell me what *you* have been doing." She had served a long apprenticeship in the art of pleasing males who would have preferred to be elsewhere, with somebody else, and an invitation to talk about themselves and their doings had never before failed to bring at least a temporary response. This evening it did though. Ian said, "Oh, nothing very much. Working. Hoeing beet mostly."

"With the new machine?"

"Yes. It's very good."

"Have you seen anything of Gloria?"

"Yes. I've seen Gloria."

"And Hazel?"

"Oh, yes, Hazel."

Valerie thought, But of course he wouldn't—none of them would—want to come into this prison cell and tell me what a good time people outside were having. So she changed the subject and said, "My ring has been much admired. They're very scrupulous here. I came in wearing it. They took it off and then gave it back to me. In a little envelope." She was well aware that, although her face was not pretty, her hands were well shaped, very slim with long fingers. Too slim at the moment, for she had lost a good deal of weight. As she waved her hand, the heavy ring seemed to fly off,

describing an arc in the air and falling with a little clatter under
the wash bowl. Ian retrieved it and stood up, rather red in the face,
and put the ring back on her finger, awkwardly. Quite unlike the
first time.

"I think I'd better go. They said not to tire you," he said. "So
good night. Get well soon." Then he did kiss her but in a perfunc-
tory manner. Well, let's face it; men don't like sickrooms or sick
people.

Sitting out for more hours, taking a walk in the corridor. Better
every day. The stitches out. Allowed two visitors at a time. Hazel
and Sandy; Maureen and Bobbie; Ruth and Ken. But Gloria did not
come. She had a bad cold and was nervous about passing it on.

Then the surgeon—very pleased with her—and two of his un-
derlings discussing her immediate future. All things considered
would not a spell in the convalescent home at Bywater be a good
idea? It was February now, not the ideal month for the seaside, but
there was a glassed-in verandah that caught all the sun there was.
And there she could have a special building-up diet.

The surgeon who prided himself on taking a personal interest in
his patients said, "You're doing very well, but you still need a bit of
looking after, and I understand that your mother has enough on
her hands."

Valerie agreed to go to Bywater. She would much have preferred to go to the Hanburys, but no invitation had been forthcom-
ing, and one could not very well suggest . . .

Then a thought struck her, a morbid one because having been so
ill herself and cooped up in a place of suffering, she was more than
usually aware of physical ills. Gloria's cold surely was long lasting.
Did something more serious ail her? And did everybody hesitate
to tell her because of upsetting her in her frail state?

Somewhat agitated, she got herself to the telephone in the corridor and rang the Hanburys' number. Mrs. Hanbury answered.

"Mrs. Hanbury, I've just been inspected and judged fit enough
to go to Bywater. To convalesce."

"Oh, good. I'm sure that is just what you need."

She sounded a bit odd, unlike herself. Did she feel a little embar-
rassed about the unproffered invitation? Or was Gloria . . .

"How is Gloria?"

"Oh, Gloria? Well, she's better. But you know how a cold can hang about at this time of the year."

"But it *is* just a cold? I mean, nothing serious?"

"Just a cold, dear. When do you go?"

"Tomorrow. My bed is needed."

"Then I'm afraid I shan't see you. We're going out this evening. But you'll want your clothes." Mrs. Hanbury had undertaken Valerie's laundry. And of course she would need her outdoor clothes as well. "I tell you what I'll do, dear. I'll pack a case and take it across. Then perhaps your dad, this evening . . ."

"That would be kind. And you could explain. It'd save me ringing Dad at the office. Well, give my love to Gloria. Tell her to write. Everybody might write. I shall feel a bit cut off down there."

The convalescent home was very comfortable and almost nice. Valerie was the only patient under sixty, and many of the older people treated her as though she were a child, always offering her chocolates or some other little delicacy. What was not nice, what was downright depressing, was the fact that no matter where a conversation started, it invariably ended with a detailed description of an illness or an operation. Valerie decided that a week of this was as much as she could stand. No matter what everybody said, she'd go home on Saturday and back to work, back to life, on Monday.

She received a number of Get Well cards, but only one letter—and that from Hazel. Ian sent a card, one of the would-be comic ones. A boxer who'd taken a bad beating, bandaged and plastered, and inside the words, "Hoping you'll soon be fighting fit again." Perhaps the operation had removed her sense of humour as well as the offending appendix; she did not find it amusing. Rather touching, in fact.

Then, on Friday, there was a letter from Gloria who still wrote an unformed, childish hand—curious medium for so lethal a communication.

"better to let you know before you came home. Ian and I . . .

"hate doing this to you of all people but Ian and I . . .

"not to feel too badly about it. You see, Ian and I . . .

The words danced, swam together, blurred. An old, quavering voice said, "Nurse!"

A little set-back, they said. A slight relapse. She must stay here another week. And that gave her time to make plans. When she left Bywater, she did not go back to Baildon, she went to London where she had one contact, a slightly older girl called Liz, with whom she had, most fortunately, kept in touch.

Perhaps there was something in the superstition about Mongoloids and the seven year cycle; poor Tom died a few days after his twenty-first birthday, and in response to her parents' urgings, Valerie went home for a funeral. Their argument ran that, as poor Tom had never had anything proper in his life, at least they must give him a proper funeral.

Over the years Valerie had kept in touch, writing regularly, remembering Christmas and birthdays, and once she became prosperous, sending considerable sums of money. Hers had been a success story as dazzling as Dick Whittington's. She had arrived in London with one suitcase of bed wear, one outfit of ordinary clothing, and about £8 in cash—a waif, not yet fully restored to health and with her heart broken. She had been very glad to accept the hospitality of a sleeping bag on the floor of Liz's bed-sitter in Notting Hill Gate. Then, nothing augured well. In fact, said Liz very gravely, Valerie must be flexible and not expect immediately to find a job with a firm resembling Turnbull's; she might even have to take, *pro tempore,* a job as a waitress or *au pair* for a family with children. However, she added, "We'll ask Mike. He's coming to supper."

It just so happened that Mike knew of a vacancy in his own firm, Cawley and Stead, Foreign and Money Brokers. Valerie went in as the lowest form of life, but her star was in the ascendant—or perhaps a genuine talent for figures and complete concentration on the job in hand were rare. In no time at all she was on her way to the top. Even the mental climate of the day was in her favour; in many walks of life it had become almost necessary to show that there was no prejudice against women. Cawley and Stead were favourably regarded when they made Miss Valerie Cobb, aged twenty-seven, a director.

And before that, Miss Cobb had discovered that she had another talent. An almost supernatural ability to guess how markets would move. Making cautious little investments on her own account, she did well. So well that when Liz and Mike, married and expecting their second child, needed to move from the flat they had taken when they were married, she could lend—a simple, friendly loan, no interest required—the money needed to buy a pleasant little house within spitting distance of Richmond Park. She was not one to forget a favour, or a grudge.

After the funeral which had been as correct and proper as Mrs. Cobb could have wished, many wreaths from neighbours, one from the Bowls Club, one from the customers at the Magpie—just as though poor Tom had been a normal young man struck down in his prime—Valerie went across to see Mrs. Hanbury.

Over the years her gifts to the Hanburys, beginning modestly, had soared into lavishness, and Mrs. Hanbury had sometimes felt uneasy, wondering how the girl could afford them. Now she saw, with considerable relief, that Valerie's coat was of mink. And the car parked across the road hadn't been bought for peanuts! Reassuring as the sight was, it made her heart sore for Gloria. Who would have thought? Who could have believed? Admittedly Gloria had seemed to play a dirty trick on Valerie, and Mrs. Hanbury had been almost ashamed at the time, but who could help falling in love?

When Valerie asked—lightly, casually—"And how is Gloria?" the tears welled up and had to be blinked away.

"She's all right—in health, I mean. She's got two dear little boys." Utterly untrue, they were ill behaved, roughly spoken, destructive, and quarrelsome. Little thugs. After a visit from them, however brief, there was always something to be mended, and Mrs. Hanbury had to go to bed for the rest of the day. And now Gloria was pregnant again. With no help in that big inconvenient old farmhouse. Gloria's looks had gone, and her figure and her spirit. And what had happened to Ian was a puzzle over which Mr. and Mrs. Hanbury often brooded. Was the general depression to blame? Had Four Elms ceased to prosper since the death of Ian's father? Or had Ian become plain mean?

Valerie was by this time well skilled at detecting nuances; there were unwritten things to be read between the lines of the dullest page of figures or the most accurate findings of a computer. It would have been possible to think that kind-hearted Mrs. Hanbury had been on the brink of tears because she remembered what had happened ten years ago. But there could be another explanation.

Taking her time, Valerie opened her cigarette case—gold, and not bought with *her* money—and extended it to Mrs. Hanbury who said, "No, thank you, dear. I gave up. Some time back." There was a message there, too.

Valerie said, "Mrs. Hanbury, for a long time now I've been wanting to give Gloria a present."

"*You* give *Gloria* a present! But why? I mean after what she did to you! We all felt so badly about that. Really, Valerie, we did." The tears threatened again. But nobody ever made the progress that Valerie Cobb had made in a harsh world by sparing attention to non-essentials.

"Can you think of anything that Gloria would particularly like?"

In her confusion Mrs. Hanbury reached out and took a cigarette from the case which Valerie had left open. It was wise to leave every option open!

Valerie flicked her lighter—that also was of gold.

"I can tell you what she really *needs,*" Mrs. Hanbury said, misery breaking through. "A washing machine with a tumble drier. Two boys and Ian's shirts—and a new baby coming. The thing is . . . her dad and I do try. I gave up smoking, and he hasn't had a drink for ages, but you can't catch up. The sort of thing she needs is about five hundred pounds now."

Five hundred pounds. A negligible sum in sterling, even more negligible in dollars, Deutsche marks, Swiss francs, or yen. Yen!

"Mrs. Hanbury, I should really love to give Gloria the thing. But she might find it more acceptable coming from you. Could you possibly pretend?"

Mrs. Hanbury hesitated, balancing between downright common decency and motherly love. Gloria really needed the washing machine and the tumble drier. And Valerie could well afford . . . Mr. Hanbury had actually crossed the road to have a closer look at that car and reported that it was a Porsche. A continental make and expensive.

And there was poor Gloria with a husband who couldn't or wouldn't afford a washing machine to do his and his children's laundry.

"I could try," Mrs. Hanbury said.

Valerie took out a cheque book and a pen—also gold—and wrote a cheque with the swift confidence of one to whom £500 meant little.

"The machine is from you," Valerie said, capping the pen.

Mrs. Hanbury's mind spun. Five hundred pounds! It might just be possible to find a cheaper machine, take advantage of a sale, get a rebate for cash, and then Gloria could also have a much needed new frock.

"It is most terribly kind of you, dear. And I really can't think why . . ."

"I owe Gloria *such* a debt of gratitude," Valerie said.

And as Mrs. Hanbury told her husband that evening, it wasn't said sarcastically. She sounded as though she really meant it.

9

A late flowering

Once upon a time, Margaret Ambrose and John Turnbull had achieved the well nigh impossible by conducting a love affair about which nobody ever had the slightest suspicion. They were both eminently sensible, level-headed people and set about the business of sharing a bed and enjoying each other's company with almost military precision.

"A cottage at the end of a lane may sound ideal," said Miss Ambrose, "but it would be conspicuous. Gossip is nowhere more rife than in a village. . . . I'll go and do a bit of house hunting. And for that, alas, my car is all wrong."

It was quite a wrench to part with it, for it was a recent acquisition and suited her well. An MG convertible, built for speed.

She had bought it when the aunt with whom she had lived since she was orphaned at the age of two died and, still angry because Margaret chose to go out and earn a living, instead of staying at home and providing constant attention, had left her only a token legacy—£500 and the choice of some furniture. The rest of a sizeable fortune she had left to various charities. Miss Ambrose had chosen her pieces of furniture and put them into store. One day she hoped to have a home of her own. Meanwhile, the year being 1946, £500 was not negligible. It had bought the MG and a few articles of clothing. She was vain as well as good looking.

Chugging along in the Morris Minor—the sturdy willing donkey which had replaced the race horse—she drove about and eventually found exactly what she wanted, a spoiled village, all new houses, full of new people, almost a dormitory town. There, in quite pleasant surroundings, an enterprising builder had erected rows of bungalows to let. Miss Ambrose hired one, called Briarwood, had the telephone installed, and moved in. A weekender, not a commuter.

With those with whom she was forced to make contact, the Miss Ambrose at Briarwood, in the ruined village of Slipwell, was not the Miss Ambrose who worked at Turnbull and Son's. She wore a hat, a deplorable affair of navy blue felt, and a brown rainproof, far too long even for the New Look. Her face was innocent of all make-up, her shoes low heeled. Dark glasses, she had decided, would be rather obvious, but hers were tinted enough to dim the positive green of her eyes. Had Mr. Turnbull Senior encountered her in one of the Slipwell shops, he would not have recognized her.

In these shops she was a well liked customer, for she paid cash and bought only the best—not in great quantities, except when she was expecting her brother. It was the butcher, a native of Slipwell and a member of a large family, who found her a woman willing to go in once a week and clean the bungalow. No weekend work, for Miss Ambrose had an exacting job in London and needed quiet when in the country. So did her brother, a schoolmaster in Norwich.

To her employer, Miss Ambrose explained that, having done her duty by Aunt Flora, now dead, she felt bound to give attention to another aunt who lived at Slipwell; but she could be reached by telephone, and should an emergency occur outside office hours and her services as confidential secretary be required, she could be in Baildon in just under an hour. Mr. Turnbull felt some relief at the prospect of Miss Ambrose's leisure being thus occupied, for John had an eye for a pretty girl, and it would never, never do for the son and heir to become entangled with a girl from the office. Mr. Turnbull's ideas were as old fashioned as the furniture in his office; John must marry within the professional clan. He would have wide enough choice there, for the war had culled the herd. Mr. Turnbull's own choice was Verity Bridges, but he had enough sense to keep that to himself.

John, or J.E. as he was known in the office, had no need of alibis. He had gone straight from Oxford into the army; the world owed him some gaiety, and naturally he had friends everywhere.

Life at Briarwood, if not exactly gay, was very happy. Bed was entirely satisfactory, which as J.E. knew but Margaret did not, was not always the case. Margaret, declaring that she cooked like the devil, donned a pretty apron and proceeded to cook like an angel, and J.E. saw to it that the apertifs and wines were always good. Both enjoyed talking and could be amusing, though her wit was the more acidulous. The sense of masquerade lent a special zest.

Never once did they succumb to the temptation of being seen together in any public place. The lights had gone up in London with a vengeance, and he would have liked to take her to dine and dance at the Savoy. The continent beckoned, too. How pleasant it would be to get into his car—a car never seen in Slipwell since schoolmasters did not drive Jaguars—and just wander. But more and more people were going abroad now, and Mrs. Grundy, also well disguised, might be lurking anywhere. And amongst the things tacitly understood was Mr. Turnbull's blood pressure. The slightest upset was a threat, a real fit of rage might carry him off.

A softer, more feminine woman than Margaret Ambrose might have felt slighted, humiliated, resentful of this assumption that she was not good enough. She never once had any such feeling. She was that rare thing, a truly emancipated woman, not seeing Mrs. as preferable to Miss. Moreover she had never felt inferior to anyone in her life and was unlikely to start now. She was not jealous when J.E., to please his father, took Verity Bridges to dances. She herself never lacked an escort and indeed, during the first winter of the liaison, derived a mischievous pleasure in attending one of Baildon's holy rituals—the Hunt Ball—in the company of a handsome young man in the privileged red coat. She could, indeed, with the minimum of effort have married him and in due time have become Lady Fennel, but since one evening of his company bored her almost to tears, marriage would have been a life sentence.

J.E. had his faults, and she was not unaware of them, but he had not bored her—yet. And when, as was bound to happen, tedium crept in, it was largely because he could always be counted upon to say, as nearly as possible, the right thing, and to do as nearly as possible what was correct. On the night of that Hunt Ball, for instance, cantering round in the final "John Peel," she knew that when she and Johnny were alone he would say . . .

And he said it: "Darling, sometimes I feel so guilty. I feel I am wasting the best years of your life."

"What an unwarrantable assumption! It is my life. Nobody wastes it but me. And if you imagine that you stand between me and a title, you flatter yourself. Tom Fennel does that most effectively."

It occurred to him, and not for the first time, that there was a hard streak in her. Admirable up to a point, but to live with . . . To feel that always, whenever he did or said the right thing, that imp of mockery would be ready with a barb, was not exactly comfortable.

Old Mr. Turnbull had been warned, time and again. But on an unusually hot August day he went to his club and ate a good portion of beefsteak pudding, helped down by half a bottle of Burgundy; then, feeling what he called sluggish, he drank a large cup of black coffee and a brandy, and strolled back to the office.

By this time Miss Ambrose had attained the unique, the hitherto unthought of privilege of a room of her own, and on his way to his own, he paused there and said, "Miss Ambrose, will you see that I am not disturbed for the next hour?"

She ran a glance over the duplicate appointment book and said, "You have only one appointment this afternoon, Mr. Turnbull. Four-thirty. After tea."

He looked her over. She looked cool in a short sleeved open necked shirt blouse of pale green which emphasized the colour of her eyes and went well with the almost amber coloured hair, curly and cropped close.

"You women," he said, "don't know how lucky you are. Well, I'll go now and cast loose my buffcoat, each holster let fall . . ." He was much given to quotations, which it pleased her to match. She said, "I'll see you in aix. With a cup of tea." And if Robert Browning turned in his grave at this irreverent bandying of his immortal words, nobody noticed, for Mr. Turnbull sat down in his chair and died as any man would wish to do. A massive stroke, which, had he survived, would have left him paralysed and probably speechless.

He had been an orderly man, there was no confusion, just a period of mourning and readjustment. There was a month during which Miss Ambrose rightly gauged what would happen and what she would do when it did.

The so-called garden at Briarwood was too small to contain a tree, but over the fence in another and older garden stood two lime trees. The hot summer had yellowed their leaves prematurely, and the equinoctial gales brought them down, fluttering, wounded, against a grey sky. For some reason the somewhat dismal scene took a permanent place in her memory.

It was Saturday evening, and Johnny had only just arrived. In the past he had always used the train, but today he had driven in the unschoolmasterish car. They'd greeted each other effusively and were now sitting down to dry martinis made with just that dash of brandy which made all the difference. He took two sips, set down the glass, and said, "Darling, will you marry me?"

"Kind sir, I am conscious of the honour you do me. But the answer is no."

She knew him too well. The look of relief on his face was unmistakable.

"But you haven't even thought about it."

"I have. And not only since your father died." She lit a cigarette with care. "Probably, had you asked me when I first became your mistress, I should have said 'Yes.' A certain recipe for disaster."

"Why?"

"I'm just not the marrying kind. Not pliant enough. Far too self-centred. Your father was right—though for the wrong reason. Utterly unsuitable. Quite apart from everything else, you must beget a Turnbull son, and you know how neurotic I am on that subject." He knew and had appreciated her carefulness, but had attributed it to the wrong reasons and even now, when a fraction of his mind was saying, Free! Free! he felt bound to expostulate.

"Once you were safely married, you'd feel differently."

"You think a wedding ring would blind me to the bulging, the bloating, and the ultimate horror? No, Johnny, you must marry some nice sensible suitable girl, and I hope you'll be happy ever after."

Something, he felt, was lacking, so he supplied it.

"All this," he said, glancing about the impersonal, furnished-to-let room, "has been something I shall not easily forget."

Outside the sky was darker now, the leaves a more lurid yellow. Miss Ambrose rose and drew the curtains. Mr. Turnbull refilled the glasses while he pondered the problem of the correct thing to do in the circumstances. A has just proposed honourable marriage to his mistress; she has refused him. Should A leave at once? Stay for supper which she had doubtless made ready? Stay the night?

"I shall always remember it too. A very happy interlude," Miss Ambrose said.

"There is one other thing, Margaret. If this is the end, I should like to give you something. I mean something substantial . . ."

Present giving had always been a bit tricky; she'd been so over-anxious to avoid the slightest hint of being "a kept woman" that anything he gave her she had matched—sometimes outdone. Lately they'd compromised with token presents.

"Will you allow me to buy you a house?"

"Oh," she said, "what a kind thought! I do appreciate it. But, my dear, just too late. I never had time to tell you. I did have another *genuine* aunt. She lived in Cornwall, and I last saw her when I was about twelve. But she died just two days after your father and left me her all. So I bought that place they call Tudor Cottage—actually it is much older—in Whiting Street."

"God!" he said, jerked out of decorum. "They were asking twenty thousand for that!"

"I haggled a bit," Miss Ambrose said. "I actually beat them down to fifteen. But I always liked the look of it, even before the restoration started. . . . It has all been done most imaginatively."

It occurred to him that her legacy must have been sizeable. And immediately a question arose.

"Are you planning to retire?"

"Not unless you wish me to. I mean that very seriously, Johnny. I'll go if you don't like the idea of having me around. But only to

another job. What should I do with myself? I play no games—
except bridge, and once a week of that suffices."

He said, "Please stay."

"That suits me well," she said, and went into the kitchen where
a casserole bubbled gently and potatoes were baking in their jack-
ets. Goodbye to all this pretence at being domesticated. Never
again will I do more than toast a slice of bread and make a cup of
tea or instant coffee.

The only thing which she found disconcerting was waking at the
deadly hour of three o'clock in the morning and finding herself
weeping, her pillow soaked. There was some connection with a
dream, less vivid than many, a dream in which John Everard
Turnbull did not emerge with any clarity. He was always hidden,
yet she was acutely aware of him and of the fact that he alone was
not hostile to her. Everyone else was. That, she would reason with
herself, soon after waking, was no explanation for the tears. In real
life, hostility would neither cow nor depress her. The dream and
the crying fit became less frequent as time went on, but she was
never absolutely free of them.

Perhaps the very smoothness of life, after she parted from Johnny,
made the years seem to pass unnoticed. She woke up one morning
and realized that she was fifty. There had, of course, been small
signs of age catching up on her; the amber tones in her hair had
vanished, giving way to a shade which her hairdresser called ash
blonde. She now needed glasses, but only for the villainous small
print which was becoming more and more prevalent. She
weighed exactly four pounds *less* than she had at twenty-two. She
enjoyed uniformly good health, suffering only one bout of influenza.

She was—and being honest, she admitted it—a singularly fortu-
nate woman. In the office her position had never been challenged.
She had a steel trap memory, she read a great deal, she had expe-
rience. Mr. Turnbull often said, "Have a word with with Miss
Ambrose." Lesser men said, "I'd better have a word with Miss
Ambrose."

Her domestic life was equally satisfactory. Part luck and part a
willingness to overlook foibles and shortcomings had ensured that

she had never been completely without help and had long ago
acquired the services of an old sailor, once cook aboard a cargo
vessel. An accident had robbed him of one leg, but he managed his
artificial one nimbly. He cooked surprisingly well, was versatile
and resourceful. He had drunken spells during which Miss Ambrose, keeping her promise to herself, lived on tea and toast.

It was ironic that she, able to establish a working relationship
with so many diverse people, should fail to get along with the new
Young Mr. Turnbull. She thought him pompous, conceited, and
aggressive; he refused to recognize her status, considered her
conceited and arrogant and a bad influence on his father. She also
committed the capital error of having on two or three occasions
been right, for, unqualified as she was, her experience of practical,
country-town law could sometimes outweigh his four years at Oxford and two years in London with a very smart, very sophisticated
firm.

At first she was disposed in his favour, for he strongly resembled
his father as a young man, and naturally Mr. Turnbull adored him,
his one and only, his clever son. Motherless, too, for Mr. Turnbull's
wife—who was not, after all, Verity Bridges—had died young.

There were two young men in the firm, both qualified. Red
brick, of course. Mr. Kelly was by far the cleverer, but inclined to
be self-opinionated and, alas, in moments of excitement, a little
unsure of his aitches.

One afternoon, when Mr. Jonathan, as Young Mr. Turnbull was
known in the office, had been installed for about three months, Mr.
Kelly came down to Miss Ambrose's dingily comfortable little
room, seeking to have a word with her. It did not concern business,
except perhaps indirectly; it was about his own future.

"Nobody can say I 'aven't tried, Miss Ambrose. I 'ave. I just can't
get along with Mr. Jonathan, and I know now that I never shall. 'E
wants me out. 'E's done nothing but criticize. I always did things to
Mr. Turnbull's liking. Anyway, I've got an offer." His haggard face
brightened. "That is what I want to consult you about. Bridges and
Lomax," he said, naming the firm next door but one. "Specializing
in tax, which is my strongest line. Miss Ambrose, what do you
think?"

"What a leading question! You know I'm always willing to help
in any way I can, but I couldn't possibly advise on such a personal

matter. I should feel so responsible. Do you think perhaps you should speak to Mr. Turnbull before deciding? I know he thinks highly of you, Mr. Kelly."

"You mean he *did!* Actually I did once speak about Mr. Jonathan's interfering. 'E laughed it off, said new brooms always raised dust. And it's the sort of dust I'd be 'appy to shake off my shoes. Still, I'll give 'im one more chance."

"I heard his client leave a few moments ago, and Mr. Turnbull has no other appointment today."

She had been carefully non-committal, but he felt that she had not been unsympathetic. Therefore he paused in the doorway and said darkly, "Once they start pruning, you never know who's next for the chop." And that was as clear a hint as he thought wise to drop.

The interview did not take long. She heard Mr. Kelly leave Mr. Turnbull's room, walk swiftly past her door, and go upstairs, two at a time. She then gathered some papers tidily and went along to Mr. Turnbull's room herself. In his old fashioned way he still liked her to do most of his typing, saying that the girls upstairs couldn't spell, a statement which was not altogether untrue.

Mr. Turnbull occupied the room that had been his father's, a pleasant, spacious room at the rear of the house, overlooking a space which she could remember as a pleasant small garden. Much of it had vanished under concrete to make way for cars, but a fragment was left, a narrow strip supporting a laburnum tree, already in bloom, a lilac which would follow, and an acacia now so aged that every summer threatened to be its last. On this afternoon Mr. Turnbull stood, staring out of the window—a sure sign that he had been upset. He was not the choleric type that his father had been; over the years he had grown slightly more solid, far from fat, and not in the least florid.

He turned and said, "I've just had young Kelly here. Giving notice! Like a goddam kitchen-maid in the old days! Better prospects, more money, and more elbow room. A crude expression if ever there was one."

"And you accepted his—resignation?"

"I did. And smartly. Why are you looking so solemn about it?"

"Do I? I was only thinking. . . . Some clients may go with him —wherever he goes. People who felt at home with him, because—

well, to be frank, he speaks their language. And knows every tax evasion trick in the book."

"I don't think anyone of importance will desert us. And there has been friction between Kelly and Jonathan." He sat down and signed his name several times. Then he shuffled papers, some handwritten, some typed, and a few newspaper cuttings into an untidy heap and pushed them towards her.

"I wish you'd cast your eye over these. They're in a terrible muddle, and the client—a Mr. Briscoe—was not exactly coherent. I'd be grateful for one of your masterly synopses."

"Is it urgent?"

"I would like it tomorrow—if that isn't too much of an imposition."

"I'll see what I can do. It looks pretty formidable."

"It sounded even worse. What with that and then young Kelly . . ."

She thought, I shall soon be fifty-five; he's almost six years older, and every year tells.

"I'll see what I can do," she said and went along to her own room, never bright because its one window looked out on to the blank wall of the next-door building. Now, going in, she switched on the light, meditated for a moment, weighing the choice between taking the untidy bundle home, and dealing with it here. She decided upon the latter course because at home she would need to use the dining-room table, and her man, known inevitably as Long John Silver, would by now be laying the table. Also, some typing might be needed, and at home she had only a portable.

She pushed her old, very shabby but comfortable chair a trifle nearer to her desk, switched on and adjusted her Anglepoise lamp, which she, not Turnbull and Son, had provided. And then looked at her watch. It was ten minutes past five. Edging past the edge of her desk, for the room was rather cramped, she opened a cupboard and took out two bottles and two glasses, one stemmed, elegant, and engraved, the other squat and plain. From one bottle she poured the sherry she favoured, very pale, very dry. Then, everything within easy reach, she sat down and put her feet up on the only other chair and her reading glasses on her nose. Then she began to read, lost herself and all count of time in the labyrinthine story of which she had been asked to make a synopsis.

When the door opened behind her, she said, "Hullo, Peter. Come in. Help yourself. I'll be with you in a minute . . ."

Jonathan Turnbull said, "Good evening, Miss Ambrose. I saw your light. You are working late. . . ."

She took off the glasses and saw him clearly. Rigid, disapproving —and for once with something to merit disapproval.

"I occasionally do," she said mildly.

"You are expecting someone?"

"No. Why? Oh, the bottles. When I work late and Peter looks in, I like to offer him a drink."

"You mean *Thompson?*"

"I mean Thompson."

"I must say that is a habit of which I cannot approve."

"Really? Why not?"

"Drinking with the caretaker! Indeed drinking at all, in the office . . . Think how it looks!"

"To whom? Peter has never registered shock. I, of course, long ago abandoned self-criticism as a futile exercise. So, who else? Unless you . . . Were you one of those unfortunate children who slept with 'THOU GOD SEEST ME' over his cot?"

"Miss Ambrose! I think you are being deliberately offensive."

"You are correct. It would irk me to think I had been offensive by accident."

This was their first head-on confrontation, but he had been warned that she had a waspish tongue.

And that was all that she had. No qualifications, no assured position. The Old Man liked her and depended upon her far too much, but in every contest with his father, Jonathan had come off best. Ousting her should be easy. With that comfortable thought he changed the focus of his attention.

"Is that, by any chance, the Briscoe case?"

"It is."

"Have you formed an opinion?"

"Yes, though I am only about two thirds through. Personally, I wouldn't touch it with a barge pole."

"Then how fortunate it is that you are not required to touch it in any way! Good night, Miss Ambrose."

"Good night."

She replaced her glasses, drank some sherry, and read on until
Peter arrived.

He was very old—he'd seemed old to her when she first joined
the firm—but he still got through an incredible amount of work,
making himself responsible for most of the cleaning and all but the
most technical maintenance.

"Hullo, Peter. Help yourself. I've just finished."

"Thanks. Cheers, Miss. Anything you want seeing to?"

One thing about keeping in his good books, she never had to
wait for the bulb in her overhead light to be replaced, a broken
window cord made good, an ineffective radiator spurred to fresh
action.

"Nice day," he said. "But it'll rain tomorrow. The forecast said
otherwise, but I go by my bones."

All this was completely in order. Her needs, the weather, a
glancing reference to his rheumatism, and in the season the Pools,
which she did not understand and never would, and his conversa-
tional resources were exhausted. He never toyed with his drink,
he applied a suction pipe, wiped his mouth with the back of his
hand, said, "Thanks again, Miss," and was gone. Drinking with the
caretaker was as dull as it was innocuous. But tonight he lingered,
engaged in some inward struggle, and the thought occurred to her
that Jonathan could have offended him, too. And if so, he was more
of a fool than even she had suspected.

Finally speech came.

"I bin here a long time, moren't sixty years. Did you ever know
me to gossip?"

"Never. I always thought you rather tighter than a clam."

"I've heard things in my time, but to all but a straight order,
properly expressed, I turn a deaf ear. But . . . Well, now I'm
asking you. You heard anything about a new carpet?"

"No."

Automatically she looked down at her own. A relic indeed. Its
pattern had long ago faded, its pile worn away. It was now quite
threadbare over most of its surface and the colour of sacking.

"I bin asked to measure up this room," Old Peter said.

She wanted to say, And not before it was needed! But the words
would not come. She knew that never, never would Jonathan
dream of providing her with a new carpet. So the inference was

obvious. And she knew better than anyone how fundamentally *weak* John Turnbull was. Unable, all those years ago, to stand up to his father.

Next morning she carried the Briscoe papers, now in chronological order and enclosed in a box file, into Mr. Turnbull's room and set it down on his desk.

"I managed a miracle of compression and got the gist of it into a page and a half," she said.

"Thank you. And what do you think?"

"Cold poison."

Then she said, "John." And that jolted him because for so long they had avoided their given names. In public, "Miss Ambrose" and "Mr. Turnbull," in private, nothing.

"I am not about to give notice, bearing in mind what you said about kitchen-maids. But I have decided to retire."

She recognized that look of relief. Long ago, in Slipwell.

"I am almost fifty-five, and I've worked here since I was eighteen. I want to go while I can still enjoy myself—and see something of the world."

"How wise. How indeed enviable . . . But, my dear, how I shall miss you!"

"I should hope so! Otherwise I have been wasting my time. Oh, and I particularly don't want a song and dance about it. No farewell dinner, no presentation. I shall simply not be here."

Even to herself, she would not admit that the next two and a half years had the stale flavour of boredom. She could be rational about it, saying, Not educated for leisure. It was now recognized as a problem; so many men, once they retired, dwindled and died that some big firms were actually educating men on how to enjoy retirement. Women seemed to adjust more easily, perhaps because they had led double lives, family and home really paramount.

She knew that she was lucky—retirement had affected her financial position hardly at all; she had her house, her garden, her books. Seeing something of the world had been disappointing on the whole. She was no sightseer and had little sense of history; one ancient ruin was much like another, and she lacked the "Queen

Elizabeth slept here" mentality. She was always glad to be back in Baildon, with her own things around her.

She played more bridge than formerly and liked it better as she grew more expert. About once a month she gave small but enjoyable dinner parties and was entertained in turn. She never went back to the office and had maintained no contact with anybody there.

She had begun to keep a dog as soon as she was sure that Long John would stay with her. Her choice of pet was unusual, not a pretty puppy, not a small, cuddlesome creature. She had a superannuated greyhound, saved from unwantedness and seeming to know and be grateful. Very affectionate, highly intelligent, not, alas, very long lived. The one which she took for the necessary morning run, on a snow threatening November morning of her third year of retirement, was her third. His kennel name, Handsome Moonlight, was too much of a mouthful for general purposes and had been pruned to Handy.

She was crossing Market Square—at Handy's pace—when a man halted and said, "Good morning, Miss Ambrose."

It was an only-just-recognizable Mr. Kelly, grown sleek, grown neat.

"You're up and about early," he said.

"Oh, I'm usually early. It's all right, Handy. All right! He's a friend! Usually we make for the common, but the wind is straight from the north this morning. And how are things with you? I need hardly ask—you're looking very well."

"A compliment I can return—wholeheartedly. Yes, clearing out of Turnbull's was the best move I ever made. And largely thanks to you!"

"Oh, come! I'm sure I never said anything."

"It was what you didn't say. . . . Tell me, do you ever go back?"

"No. When I retired, I retired. Do you?"

"I had occasion to look in last week. Purely business. I must say, I don't like the look of things at all. I always liked Mr. Turnbull."

"Is he ill?"

"No. Not ill." Mr. Kelly said those three words in a significant way. No further questions would be acceptable.

They said goodbye and parted.

It was impossible to think very connectedly when holding the leash of an impatient dog, but as soon as they were in the Abbey Grounds, in the part where dogs were allowed to run free, she began to consider what Mr. Kelly's restrained statement might mean. Could a recession in business be visible to a *look*, when most lawyers kept their premises deliberately shabby?

Mr. Kelly had said, I always liked Mr. Turnbull. And now Miss Ambrose thought, God help me, I *loved* him. So well that I was thoroughly inoculated and never gave another man a serious thought. There had been other men; Tom Fennel had been finally dismissed with difficulty. . . .

Handy exercised himself thoroughly, chasing imaginary hares, but always in a kind of oval, so that he could pivot about her. When she called, he came immediately and, as always after the briefest separation, went through a canine declaration of love. She said, "I love you, too, you old silly," and snapped on his leash. And something of, well, almost compunction stirred in her, for she would never let anybody or anything hurt Handy, whereas, the man, John Turnbull, she had abandoned.

Sentimental tosh! she told herself, as she and Handy walked home at a more sedate pace. I was the one abandoned. Not just once. Twice. That look of relief, of gratitude at having his way made easy for him . . . But then, he was a weak man.

At half past eleven she rang the office and asked for an appointment with Mr. Turnbull Senior and was told that he could see her at three-thirty.

She had made her will some years ago, leaving everything to Long John, but she could, if necessary, add a codicil, making the inheritance dependent upon his caring for Handy or any other dog of which she died possessed. Utterly unnecessary, but a valid excuse for a visit.

If Turnbull and Sons were in low water, it wore a brave face; its whole stucco front had been painted French grey, its massive front door stripped of all paint and oiled. The entry had been renovated, too, moss green carpet, white paint, and a cage of mahogany and glass for the receptionist, also new and very smart—but entirely lacking of old Miss Murray's pleasant manner. She began to offer a languid direction, and Miss Ambrose said, "Thank you. I know the way." She began walking towards the room overlooking the garden.

The receptionist said, "Second on the left!"

Her old room!

Mr. Turnbull sat behind what had been her desk, but now incredibly cluttered. Physically he had changed very little, was in fact still handsome for his years. Since her retirement she had seen him perhaps half a dozen times, always at a distance. And there were certain gestures and phrases which, learned enough and practised long enough, became automatic.

"Good afternoon, Madam," he said, getting to his feet. "Do sit down." He moved the chair—the very same one in which she had sat, drinking sherry—and when she was seated, noting that it had deteriorated, one spring gone, he moved back to his place, moved a few papers, and without difficulty disinterred his appointment book, one of the same kind as those she had kept so meticulously in order for so many years.

One glance seemed to satisfy him, and he said, "Ah, Mrs. Burgess. How tiresome for you! I think the whole thing hinges on the question—has your dog ever bitten anyone before?"

One must never jump to conclusions. A wrong entry perhaps, or a cancelled appointment. Perhaps she had changed more than she realized, and he had never seen her in a hat except that terrible old thing at Slipwell.

She said, "Don't you recognize me? Margaret Ambrose?"

"She is no longer with us. And what a pity! I trust you will not think me unduly superstitious, but when she left, luck went with her. At least, my luck. In her day I never made muddles. Now I seem to do nothing else. A most sorry situation. And this is no help. Look at it . . ."

He held out the appointment book; there were entries in his own distinctive, elegant hand and others in a childish half script, but another hand had been at work here, crossing out, altering. This afternoon's space said clearly enough: "Miss Ambrose. 3.30." But a line had been run through it and above it was written: "Mrs. Burgess. (Dangerous dog.)"

"I admit, I am forgetful, but not more so than most ageing men. Confused I am not, if I could be left alone. Contradictions and arguments. New faces, too. Spies, of course! Spies everywhere."

Mentally confused people often thought they were being spied upon, or robbed. He claimed not to be confused. Would he, in his right mind, talk like this to a stranger?

That at least could be put to the test. She said, "Look at me. Who am I?"

He reached for the book, which she had replaced on the desk and said, "Well, here it says Mrs. Burgess, but you look uncommonly like Margaret Ambrose to me! A typical trick!" His face reddened. "Well, you can go back to Grindal Bloom and say my answer is 'No.' And will always be no, so long as I am head of this firm."

The name alerted her and, taken in its context, was alarming. She pushed the edge of her fur coat aside, put her thumb under the lapel of her jacket and eased forward the ornament she wore there, a square of jade, framed in seed pearls and gold filigree. He had given it to her all those years ago.

"I am Margaret Ambrose," she said again. "How else would I be wearing this?"

"Margaret! It is! My dear, my dear . . ." He got up again, more clumsily this time, edged round the desk, and took both her hands. "I can't tell you how glad I am to see you. I can't tell you how sorely I have missed you."

Then the old rule—No betraying sign in the office—asserted itself, and he did not kiss her as he seemed about to do. Instead he dropped her hands and offered her a cigarette. And the lighter he produced was the one she had given him, flint motivated, petrol fuelled, practically a museum piece now. And never used to her knowledge, since the break between them.

"Now, sit down, and tell me everything."

But then he frightened her a little.

"First of all, this matter of the dog. There is an old tag: A dog is entitled to one bite. Roughly true. One little snap, a complaint, and the animal is deemed to be vicious and its owner ordered to keep it under control. If a dog known to be vicious attacks again, then the owner is culpable."

Miss Ambrose said, "I did not come here to talk about dogs. Just sit quietly and then try to tell me what is wrong here. And whether I can help in any way."

What he said after that was quite rational, if one believed him, as she did. Jonathan wanted to amalgamate with Grindal Bloom, the big, international firm of law givers with whom he had served what might be called his apprenticeship.

"How could I agree to that? Turnbulls have been here since the Restoration—and probably before that if all were known. Father to son, except in one instance where a nephew took over . . . Honest, respected, and, on the whole if I may say so, well liked. Of course, we never flew about in Concordes or laid the law down in Brussels because . . . well, because Concordes had not been invented, and Brussels, if I remember rightly, was renowned for an inferior brand of carpet—and, of course, sprouts. And I know what would happen if I allowed this to happen. Turnbull and Son would be gulped down, and Grindal Bloom would gain a superior errand boy. Jonathan is well qualified. Good manners. Good appearance. All the requisites of a successful commercial traveller! So, in his own interests as well as everything else, I refused. And then things began to go wrong. I'm getting on, you know."

"You're not yet sixty-four. How long since you moved into this room?"

"You noticed? Yes, you always were observant. It is a horrid little den. Yet it seemed different when Miss Ambrose occupied it. Plants. Yes, plants. There wasn't enough light for ordinary things but she found an astonishing collection of shade tolerant plants. 'A green thought in a green shade.' Not that she was at all green, in the vulgar sense of the word."

She said again, "I am Margaret Ambrose. You must try to concentrate."

"I am trying because there was something else I wished to consult you about. Most important. Just give me time."

He looked at her with the expression of a dog, willing to obey but unable to understand an order. Then he said, with triumph, "I know. Power of attorney. Jonathan demands that I give him power of attorney. And you know what that would mean. Imagine the letter heading: Turnbull and Sons, A Subsidiary of Grindal Bloom. I simply will not agree! I can stand a certain amount of persecution, and I never sign anything without reading it at least three times. The confusion, such as it is, comes and goes, but of course the strain, the pressure, the downright nastiness is no help."

"I should think not."

"You agree? What a change! Nobody else does. Jonathan surrounds himself with yes-men. And, of course, this room. It is a constant reproach to me. I should at least have given you a new carpet."

It was the one she had lived with, slightly more threadbare.

"Tell me," she said, "have you had a medical check-up lately?"

"Yes, and I went of my own accord. Sound as a bell. No hypertension, which was my father's trouble, reflexes absolutely normal. And even that neurologist fellow to whom I went at Jonathan's insistence couldn't fault me. It happened to be one of my better days, and he really asked the silliest questions. Did I know the name of the Prime Minister? Imagine how puerile! Not that Jonathan wants me certified—yet. Power of attorney granted by a lunatic is not, as you know, valid. Like wills . . . I remember you advised against taking on that Briscoe case. At least your summing up was right. Contested wills are always tricky and with the chief witness dead and two others exposed as congenital liars, we should have been well out of it. But there again Jonathan had his way and was soundly trounced. . . . I now need glasses for distance, but of course I have mislaid them, which makes things difficult. I am so afraid of ignoring somebody who should be recognized that I go about, tipping my hat to all and sundry. No wonder people think I am mad."

She sat quite still and considered his plight.

"I don't think you are mad," she said at last. "Everything you have said to me, so far, has been quite sensible. You do . . . now and then . . . tend to stray from the point."

"It's this room! It may sound absurd, and I should not like you to imagine that I'd gone over to all this psychological stuff, but the truth is that when you were here, you did the concentrating. Here we could relax, unwind. I often think . . . No, if I said that, you'd say I was straying again. But, no doubt about it, I did better in my own place. Untidy, of course—after you retired. But, as you know, it was superficial. I could always put my hand on what I wanted. . . . Here I cannot even find my spectacles. And the light. Very poor indeed. If I remember rightly, you had a lamp. I always felt guilty about that, too. Especially when you left it . . . Then it disappeared. And look at that radiator!"

She had no need to look; she knew it too well. Unlike most, it had two controls and could be half on, half off.

"Permanently at half strength now," Mr. Turnbull said. "Something about a knob, too antiquated to be replaced. Not that it matters. They shan't win. I will not be coerced."

"Do you think you would feel better, more coordinated in your old room?"

"What a silly question! Of course I should. There I had room to move, and I liked the trees, even in winter. And in summer . . . Did you know that acacia tree was one of the first to be introduced into England? My own room. But of course Jonathan would never consider it. Would you believe that even at the club I am allowed only two whiskies, very small ones and completely drowned. I dare not make a fuss. If I lose my temper, coherence goes with it." He sighed. "If only you'd come back! Not full time. That would be too much to ask. Just for an hour or so, say three days a week. I can remember your once saying that retirement would bore you. Have you found it boring?"

"Let's leave that for the moment. Now listen carefully. I could see you back in your own room. I would keep things tidy, see that your appointments were in order. But I can only do these things if you . . . grant *me* power of attorney."

"I'd do that most willingly. What a brilliant idea. There are forms, are there not? I wonder where . . ."

"I think it would carry more weight written in your own hand. Less as though I had hustled you."

He wrote a very distinctive hand, cultivated deliberately as a protest against what he called the illegible scribbles of most lawyers and doctors.

She went back to the entry hall and to the door which gave upon a few steps leading down to Peter's domain. Three of the four rooms were crammed with ancient files and black boxes bearing the names of clients long dead. The fourth housed the boiler, Peter's tools, his deck chair, and his library, as lurid a collection of "horror" paperbacks as could be found anywhere.

She called, "Peter! Peter!" and he came to the foot of the stairs, staring in disbelief.

"Miss Ambrose! What you doing here? Anything wrong?"

"Nothing much. I want you to bring your trolley." (Everything which Peter ever used became automatically "his.") The trolley was a wide shallow basket mounted on two wheels and was used for the transport of things too heavy or bulky to be carried.

"Where to, Miss?"

"The room that used to be Mr. Turnbull's."

"Mr. Jonathan ain't there."

"I know." She'd been told who was and who was not available when she'd phoned for her appointment.

She flung open the door, but, before switching on any light, she went to the big window. Dusk was thickening, but she could see that the trees had gone, and the ground on which they stood had been incorporated in the car park. Never mind, nowadays one could buy quite sizeable trees in tubs. Mr. Turnbull should have a little paved garden.

"I want everything that belongs to Mr. Jonathan removed," she said.

"Where to, Miss?"

"Upstairs. To the room he had before."

"Can't be done. There's three up there now. Mr. Saunders, Mr. Carey, and Mr. Pearson."

"Not Mr. Winter?"

"No. He went and joined Mr. Kelly, just along there."

"Start on the books," she said.

The room had been painted a delicate blue-green and given a new carpet, matching that in the entry. The old desk, a genuine antique, had been retained. It was very tidy. There were two comfortable looking new wing chairs, upholstered in green leather.

Reinstalled here, she thought, sheltered and not harassed, propped up instead of being downtrodden, John would recover. And that reminded her.

"Peter. Why had Mr. Turnbull had no tea this afternoon?"

"Because, as you know, he'll only drink Earl Grey. And Mr. Jonathan said it was waste to make two sorts. So then the old gentleman turned nasty one afternoon and chucked the lot—cup, tea, saucer, and all—straight in my face."

"Well, when this job is completed, perhaps you would just step along to Pilson's, buy some Earl Grey, and brew up."

"There'll be ructions, Miss."

"I don't doubt it." She went to the desk and pressed the telephone buttons which served as internal communications. She asked Mr. Saunders and Mr. Carey, please, to come down to the room at present occupied by Mr. Turnbull. "Just to witness a signature," she said. "It won't take a minute. In ten minutes' time."

The room was quickly stripped, and the trolley had no distance to trundle.

"Wait here, Peter," she said and went into the dismal little room where her mandate awaited her.

Mr. Turnbull had written the date and four words: "I, John Everard Turnbull."

The rest of the sheet was blank.

So was his expression. Blank, infantile, helpless.

"I forgot," he said. "I do so tend to forget. . . ."

She thought, with surprising ferocity, And this is the third time you have let me down! I will not take a third dismissal!

She said soothingly, "Never mind. It will do later," and slipped another sheet of paper, slantwise, so that at the top was the heading, the date, and four words, and at the bottom ample room for three signatures. To prevent any accidental shift of the papers, she set a paperweight in place. Then she called in the two young men and said, "It is something of a private nature. . . . Now, Mr. Turnbull, all that remains is your signature."

He wrote it with his usual flourish. The young men appended theirs.

"Thank you," she said. "And now, Mr. Turnbull is returning to his own room. It would speed the removal if each of you would bring as much as he can carry. Then put Mr. Jonathan's things which are in the trolley in here. Come along, Mr. Turnbull, we shall only be in the way here. I'll take care of this." She lifted the paper which would shortly bestow upon her unlimited power so far as business matters were involved. And beginning as she meant to go on, she halted by Peter. "Mr. Saunders and Mr. Carey are kindly going to complete the removal, Peter. You go and buy that tea."